HIS
SECRET
CHILD

BOOKS BY COLE BAXTER

The Anniversary
Her Secret Revenge

HIS SECRET CHILD

COLE BAXTER

bookouture

Published by Bookouture in 2024

An imprint of Storyfire Ltd.
Carmelite House
50 Victoria Embankment
London EC4Y 0DZ

www.bookouture.com

ISBN: 978-1-83525-239-0
eBook ISBN: 978-1-83525-238-3

PROLOGUE

This party is the most luxurious I've ever seen. As I raise my chilled champagne flute to my lips, I can't help but wonder how much all of this cost. My eyes flicker from the staff in their crisp white shirts, to the bejeweled guests, congregating and laughing under an eyesore of a chandelier. I suppose money can't buy taste.

The room is filled with warm bodies, and I'm happy to blend right in. He can't see me, but I can see him, looking jovial and playing the part of gregarious host. I find it sickening. The least he could have done was offer a better champagne. I toss the swill he has on hand into one of the plants. All this wealth and he doesn't make good use of it. I shake my head. My gaze travels the room, picking out members of the family among all the finely dressed guests. I spot *her* and smile, almost fondly. She's not really like the rest of them, but in the end it won't matter.

Tonight would be the mark of a new beginning. Fitting that it is New Year's Eve.

I make my way around the room, murmuring here and there

to various guests. No one in the family really notices me, which I'm glad for. I have a job to do. I have to set things in motion.

This would be the beginning of the end of them, and I am going to enjoy every last second of watching them fall.

One by one.

ONE

Next time, just say no, Rose, she chastised herself as she ducked into another room to avoid her awful aunt. It was the night of her mother's famous New Year's Eve party, and Rose was doing her best to hide from as many family members as possible.

She couldn't think of a worse way to start the year, yet here she was, simply because she didn't know how to say no to her family.

It had all started with a family dinner two weeks earlier...

It had been a dinner she was forced to attend like always. And it was especially hard considering her new fiancé was obliged to come with her as well. They had all been seated around her mother's grandmother's dining room table. Her mother was always proud to have the family gather around the antique table, seated in the heavy, cherry wood chairs. The table was, of course, set with the family heirloom china that was probably worth several thousand dollars. Her mother always preferred it when hosting any kind of family meal. And of course, everyone was required to dress as though they were attending dinner with the queen. Rose had worn a blue silk dress and heels, which her mother had claimed was barely passable.

There had been no turning down the invitation to dine with them.

Her mother didn't like hearing no for an answer, and Rose never actually learned how to do so in the first place. Her family could be pretty overbearing, to put it mildly, and she would love nothing more than to completely distance herself from them.

She was already on a great track to achieve that. She finished college, unlike her brother, and had a job of her own, unlike most of her family, who had never worked a day in their lives. To be fair, her mother had charities she occupied herself with, but her younger brother, who wasn't that young anymore, was still trying to 'find himself', which in reality meant he did nothing, spent all his time drinking, partying, traveling, spending family money. Despite her family looking down on her for working in a publishing house, with no six-figure salary to impress their society friends, Rose couldn't be prouder of her job. At least she wasn't wasting her life in front of a TV like him.

Her brother might call her bitter, but she simply felt different to them. She had always felt different. And yet, despite that feeling, she knew she could never fully break free from them. No matter how much she wanted to. No matter how much she needed to.

One of her ex-boyfriends had called her a doormat during one of their fights, and that really stuck with her over the years. She couldn't remember the exact color of his eyes anymore, or how his voice sounded when he was all playful and loving, but that line definitely stuck.

And the worst part was that there was a chance he was right. There were certain people in her life she couldn't turn down no matter what was asked of her. And they knew it, took advantage of it. Especially her mother.

That was precisely why she ended up at this dinner party with her parents and her new fiancé. That was how she ended up being expected to attend a New Year's Eve party when she really wanted to do something, anything, else. Because she couldn't say no to her family.

Luckily, Adrian, her fiancé—she really liked using that word —wasn't anything like the members of her family. She could spot him now, politely making small talk with one of her brattier cousins, his black hair falling into his gorgeous brown eyes. Her fiancé was a classically handsome man. He stood at about six foot two, and he had one of those golden brown tans all year around, and a strong chin that gave his boyish good looks a masculine edge. Rose thought she was the luckiest woman on the planet to have become engaged to him. And even if he knew her true nature, he never took advantage of her. He was loving, and caring, and he supported her no matter what. He loved her without judgment.

That truly made him stand out from all the rest. He was different, not simply from her family, but from all her previous boyfriends as well.

In her youth she'd dated a lot of Ivy League brats trying to please her parents, only feeling miserable in the process. Then Adrian came along, and her entire perspective changed. He managed to stick with her through all her family dinners without any complaints. No matter how uncomfortable they tended to get, because her brother had no filter, and her mother got overly dramatic after a few glasses of wine, not to mention how her father treated everyone as though they were his employees, Adrian stuck by her side like glue on paper.

It was refreshing, to say the least. She just hoped that the trend would continue no matter what. Especially while her father was eyeing him with open distrust.

Ever since she was a teenager, and tentatively dipped her toes in dating life, her father hated every boy she brought home.

He immediately distrusted them and wondered about their true motives. In other words, he was convinced all the boys who were dating her only did so because of the family name, because they were after her money.

"You might think these boys like you," he'd told a tearful fifteen-year-old Rose, after practically pushing a boy from her class outside of their house, "but they're vultures. They're only after the money. Make sure you check the silverware before you go to bed. There's sure to be a few pieces missing."

That screwed her up mentally. Which was why she built all these walls around her heart. He was the reason she learned to hide who she was, even from prospective lovers, so she could be sure they were with her because of her personality, not the number of zeroes in her bank account.

Rose wasn't proud of the fact she'd done the same with Adrian. It took her some time to share the truth with him, but luckily, he hadn't held that against her. He understood the necessity of her doing so, and even laughed with her on how well she'd hid it from him.

Unfortunately, her father remained adamant that Adrian wasn't for her. His animosity only intensified after Rose shared that the two of them were going to be married. And trying to point out to him how Adrian was a very successful lawyer with plenty of money of his own made no difference. Her father was convinced that everyone was obsessed with gaining the kind of wealth he'd spent his own life building. He couldn't comprehend that some people were fine just being comfortable, like she and Adrian were.

Eventually, Rose stopped trying to convince her family she made the right choice. Apart from those dinners, they didn't see each other much in their day-to-day lives, so their opinions didn't really matter.

With all that in mind, Rose still couldn't fathom why her mother insisted they gather and go through those extremely painful dinners at least once a month. Including everyone's birthdays, holidays, and anniversaries. Rose thought she was seeing too much of them. Part of her felt bad for thinking like that. She felt like a bad daughter, but it couldn't be helped. She simply didn't fit into their life, their lifestyle. Sadly, instead of letting her go to live her life the way she saw fit, they held onto her and wouldn't let her go.

Rose had been dragged in as usual when, at her mother's last get-together. Her mother had pulled her away from the conversation she'd been having with her father to ask whether Rose had heard what she was saying to Adrian.

"I asked, when will you be here on Sunday? I need your help with last-minute adjustments."

That was such an excuse. Her mother never needed her help with organizing one of her parties. Thelma Blaisdell's parties were legendary, and always the talk of the town. It was considered prestigious to be invited to one of them.

So, it was obvious she had a different agenda.

"Actually, I wasn't planning to attend this year. Adrian and I wanted something more private, maybe to travel instead."

Her mother had immediately stopped eating. The horrified look on her face spoke volumes. She looked at Rose as though she had suddenly grown three heads. As far as her mother was concerned, Rose had said the worst possible thing in the world.

"What do you mean you won't come?" she asked incredulously. "You've attended every party I've thrown since you were five years old."

And now, Rose was thirty. Perhaps it was time to break such a tradition. Besides, it wasn't like she particularly enjoyed them. On the contrary, she hated them. The New Year's Eve party meant the entire family—not just her immediate family, but all of the relatives—would gather under one roof for one night, and her cousins were never that kind toward her.

"We have other plans," Rose was adamant, looking at Adrian for help.

Her mother's gaze immediately swung to Adrian, her eyes filling with crocodile tears. Rose squeezed his hand to reassure him, but the sight of a crying relative would make anyone uncomfortable enough to give in. He didn't yet understand that her mother would break out the tears for any minor inconvenience or imagined slight.

"Perhaps we could swing by and stay at least for a little bit," Adrian offered, completely caving in.

"Thank you, Adrian," Rose's mother said taking a sip from her wine.

Rose groaned inwardly. *This is my fault.* She hadn't warned Adrian that her mother wouldn't play fair.

As her mum smiled and shuffled off to flag down one of the hired waiters to refill her glass, Rose whispered, "Why did you do that, Adrian? I really wanted to go someplace else with you."

"It looked like it mattered to your mother for you to be there."

It *had* looked like that. Her mother cared about appearances, but substance, not so much.

"Please don't be angry with me."

"I'm not."

"They're your family, and they love you. And besides, it's one night. We will have a lifetime to dodge all the family dinners or over-the-top parties," he reassured.

"Okay," she grumbled, kissing his cheek as he excused himself to the restroom.

So there she was now, on New Year's Eve, hiding in the cavernous kitchen of her parents' house, thinking about how she'd even ended up at this party she hadn't wanted to attend. She couldn't stand to have the same conversations with all her cousins over and over again. Everyone wanted to know if she and Adrian had set the date for the wedding yet. Why couldn't they just let her enjoy the engagement for a while?

Rose looked around the kitchen, noticing it was full of all the best quality stainless steel appliances, with marble counter-tops, and chic-looking cabinets. Not that her mother ever made use of anything in this room herself. She had a personal chef for that. Tonight, though, everything was provided by a top-notch catering services in the city. Nothing but the best would do for a Thelma Blaisdell event.

Even amongst the bustling activity of the catering staff in the kitchen, Rose's thoughts turned back to her nosy relatives. It wasn't that they were especially happy for her. To most of her cousins, a wedding meant free food and drinks. Although they were all rich, they were all extremely cheap. And her mother would be in charge of everything, of course. Rose couldn't stop her, even if she tried, and the day wouldn't even be her own. Her idea of a perfect wedding would be a quiet, small ceremony in a beautiful garden or maybe by a lake, but her mother would find that idea appalling. Instead, she'd be forced down the aisle in an overblown production that was more for her mother than for her.

Rose had the same answer for all of them. They hadn't set a date yet. And that was true. Ever since Adrian proposed to her a few weeks ago, on their six-month anniversary, they hadn't spoken about it.

To be honest, Rose didn't mind having a long engagement. She also wouldn't mind eloping, although she was aware her mother would never forgive her for something like that. Rose would marry Adrian anywhere. She didn't need all of the frills her mother would force upon them. They could get married in a swamp for all she cared as long as she got to marry him. Adrian was the man of her dreams, the man of most women's dreams she was sure, and despite her surprise when he proposed to her after a few short months of dating, her heart knew he was the one for her.

"So, did you and that boy set a date yet?" Rose's father asked, coming into the kitchen, his scotch glass empty in his hand.

Rose inwardly groaned. She'd been found. "Not yet," she replied, her eyes on one of the women filling a tray with finger foods to take out to her mother's guests. She was amazed at how skillfully she arranged the tray to resemble a flower. She glanced over at her father who was searching the counter for the harder liquor, she assumed. Rose knew he wasn't a fan of champagne.

She couldn't quite decipher his expression; however, Rose believed her father looked pleased at her words. Of course, he was. He didn't like Adrian. He had already informed her that he fully expected Adrian to sign an extensive prenuptial agreement if he wanted to marry her. Rose still had no idea how to broach that subject with Adrian. She didn't want it to appear as though she didn't trust him. It was just that she couldn't say no to her father.

Her father had always been a formidable man. He was very old school, upper-class elite, the kind of man other men generally looked up to and tried to model themselves after. He was strong and charming, always drawing people's attention with his charisma. He was smart as a whip too, and despite their differences, Rose had always strived to be more like him than her mother. Along with that, he had always been strict and very wary of any man who came calling on her. She doubted there was a man alive he would approve of as a partner to her; however, since she became an adult, he was always willing to let her make her own decisions, as long as she took precautions along the way.

Rose noted now how her father looked sallow and unhealthy. She felt a slight tug on her heart, wondering if it was because he was stressed and overworked. He had always been a workaholic and was rarely at home. And being seventy-seven barely slowed him down. Now, she had to wonder if something more was going on. Tonight, especially, seemed to have him fired up.

Did something happen? she wondered. *Should I even ask? He probably won't tell me if it's work-related though. Maybe I can find out after the party.* She decided to leave her thoughts about his health alone until later as she refocused on their conversation.

"You will be the first to know when we do set a date," Rose added, hoping to reassure him as she opened the door for one of the waitstaff who was trying not to spill a tray of champagne.

Her father snorted. "I know I'll be your first call since I'll be paying for the damn thing."

"Actually, Dad, I don't expect that. Adrian and I will pay for our own wedding."

A red flush crept up his neck, and he was about to reply when Mother appeared at the door, aghast to see them standing in the kitchen. Her abrupt entrance nearly caused the woman with the skillfully arranged tray of finger food to drop it. Rose quickly intervened and caught the edge of the tray before it all fell to the floor.

"Thanks," the woman murmured before escaping out to the other room.

"Why are you hiding in here?" her mother snapped. "I need you back out there, entertaining the guests. Do I really have to do everything around here on my own?" she added in exasperation.

"Relax, Thelma, we were just catching up."

"What were you talking about that couldn't be discussed in front of the rest of our guests?" she questioned.

"Your daughter informed me she wants to pay for her wedding on her own," he ratted her out.

Rose couldn't believe they were having this discussion in the middle of the kitchen with the waitstaff trying to work around them. It was humiliating.

Her mother looked appalled. "That is out of the question. I will take care of everything, and your father will pay for everything, and that is how it will be."

It was obvious her wishes for her own wedding weren't up for discussion, she thought as her mother grabbed her father's arm and drifted back out of the kitchen to the party.

Rose followed them and practically collided with Devon, her younger brother.

"Have you published any more biographies of the rich and famous?" he mocked.

She rolled her eyes. "You know we don't publish those kinds of books," she replied somewhat defensively.

She was an editor at a prestigious publishing house. She really loved her job, reading great books all day. Having a front-row seat watching so many amazing writers turn ideas into lavish worlds was a dream come true. It really got under her skin when her brother or anyone else from her family tried to diminish her work.

Of course, her brother hadn't picked up a book to read in years, well, at least not one that didn't pertain to some game he was playing. He read everything he could get his hands on for video games, but when it came to traditional books and to her job, he did nothing but criticize. She brushed past him now, trying to find Adrian in the crowd.

It was exhausting avoiding people all night while trying to rescue Adrian from all her prying relatives.

"I am so sorry for my family; I know they're insufferable," she muttered as she tracked him down and rescued him from yet another nosy relative.

He chuckled. "You know, you say that every time we're around them."

"That's because it's true, I'm sorry for their behavior."

Part of Rose still waited for that moment when Adrian would say he'd had enough, and run for the hills. So far, that hadn't happened.

"You have nothing to be sorry for, Rose. You're not your family. Besides, I'm marrying you, not them."

She wished that was true, and knew that reality would be something else entirely.

As soon as it was appropriate for them to leave, Rose and Adrian did so. She never did get to ask her dad about his health, but the party was still in full swing well after one a.m., and she was exhausted. It had felt like that night would never end, which was why it was that much sweeter snuggling in bed with Adrian, falling asleep in his arms.

She had no idea that once she woke up, nothing would be the same again.

TWO

The next morning, Rose was in the kitchen making breakfast when her phone started ringing. It was her mother, which was odd. Normally, her mother refused to speak with anyone before noon. Rose was tempted to let it go to voicemail, but something told her she needed to answer.

"Hello?"

"Rose. I need you to come home, right now," she said, her voice strange.

Rose was taken aback. Something was very wrong. "Why? What's happened?"

Her mother didn't reply. Rose's heart raced. She'd never heard her mother at a loss for words before, and the silence on the other end of the line was deafening.

"Mom?"

"Your father's dead."

All of a sudden, Rose couldn't feel her legs. The world turned topsy-turvy. "I'm on my way," she managed to choke out.

Driving erratically and running several red lights to get there, Rose arrived at her parents' house, but the coroner's office had already taken her father away. Rose begged her mother to tell her what happened, but her mother couldn't reply, simply staring into space and shaking her head.

Rose's mother, Devon, and Rose sat in the dining room, sharing breakfast as though it was a normal day. Her mother insisted that they all needed to eat.

Rose couldn't stomach anything but agreed to it because she knew her mother would be more talkative if things were just as she wanted them to be.

"Mom, what happened?" Rose asked.

"I wasn't there, dear." Her eyes welled up almost instantaneously. "One of the maids informed me they'd found your father unresponsive in bed. I had them call the paramedics and they called the coroner."

Rose knew her mother and father hadn't slept in the same room for decades, so she wasn't surprised someone else found him.

"Did they say anything? How did this happen?"

"They still don't know. I wondered if it was a heart attack, but we won't know anything until the autopsy."

Rose found that funny in a macabre way. Many people would swear Charles Blaisdell Junior never had a heart in the first place. So, for him to have a heart attack... well, it struck her as darkly humorous.

My father is dead.

Just thinking about him being gone made her stomach feel full of knots. She couldn't imagine the world without her father in it. He had always been such a formidable presence in her life that anything else felt completely unreal. And yet, here she was.

It was impossible to her that he could die so suddenly. She had seen him last night. And although he had looked sallow and unhealthy, clearly tired, perhaps sleep deprived, he hadn't looked deathly sick. She'd seen him looking much worse when burning the candle at both ends to meet deadlines. She'd always admired how much he pushed himself to achieve the things he went after, even to the point where he compromised his own well-being to get there. So it seemed unbearable to think that he was gone from some bizarre illness.

Would it have made a difference if she'd said something to him about his health last night? Rose stopped those thoughts. If she started thinking along those lines, blaming herself for what happened, she would completely lose her mind.

"He seemed okay last night when we left," Rose murmured, still trying to wrap her head around his death.

"He was fine," her mother replied. "Said he was really tired and was going to bed. That was the last thing he ever said to me."

Her mother began to cry as though she'd just realized again that her husband was gone. Devon soon followed, wrapping his arm around their mother. Rose felt tears sting her eyes as well.

As they sat around the dining table, Rose realized how much work was ahead of her: organizing the funeral, dealing with all her father's affairs, since she knew that her mother wouldn't be capable of handling anything important. Rose also knew she would have to manage everything on her own. Devon would be no help at all.

An image of her father came to mind. It was how he had looked last night, after their chat in the kitchen, and she felt a stab of anguish.

Why did you have to die?

I wish we'd had a more pleasant conversation.

I wish I'd told you I love you.

To him, that night had been business as usual. He was always a generous host, exchanging a few words with each of his guests, making sure the evening went smoothly. Rose recalled that around midnight he'd given one of his famous inspiring speeches. Rose had to admit it was a lovely speech. No doubt Mom had written it for him. She always had a hand in writing them.

And now, he was gone from their lives just like that, so suddenly, and Rose didn't know how to process it; her mind felt numb.

"Did you call Dr. Moss?" Rose asked, recalling the name of her father's doctor.

Her mother nodded and sniffled as she wiped her tears on the linen napkin. "Of course, he is the one who suspects Charles had a massive heart attack."

Rose hadn't seen the doctor here at the house, but she suspected he must have given her mother a tranquilizer before departing. Despite her tears, she was unnaturally calm. It was completely out of character for her often dramatic mother.

Devon still hadn't spoken a word. His tears had subsided, and he'd risen from the table only once to fix himself a drink. Now he sat, drinking whiskey, staring into his glass even though it was barely ten a.m.

"We need to discuss funeral arrangements. Do you think Father left us any instructions?" Rose asked, attempting to get things in motion for what needed to happen next.

Rose's mother looked annoyed for a moment, but whatever was on her mind didn't come out, as she was interrupted by the incessant ringing of the doorbell.

"Where are they?" a voice Rose knew all too well asked from the front hall.

Rose groaned. *They have arrived.* The relatives. Rose looked at her mother questioningly. *Who had called them?* she wondered.

Her mother ignored her look.

Melinda Blaisdell, her father's youngest sister, swept into the dining room with such confidence one would think she owned the place. Following close behind her was her only son, Joey Oldman, and his current wife, Nancy. Joey had been married five times before, or was it six? Rose had stopped keeping track after Michelle, the nineteen-year-old nursing student who had been as sweet as pie. She hadn't lasted more than a month. Last Rose heard she had moved to California just to get away from him. Secretly, Rose was glad someone had tipped her off to Joey's extra-curricular activities. She was too loveable to have to live with Melinda as a mother-in-law, let alone with Joey as a spouse.

Rose couldn't believe her mother had called *them*. And at the same time, she wasn't surprised they were the first to show up, not because they were compassionate and wanted to offer their support in such a trying time but because they were vultures, circling over the body of her father who hadn't gone completely cold yet, most likely looking for spoils.

Sadly, there was no love lost between Rose and her father's youngest sibling.

Aunt Melinda—not that Rose was allowed to call her that— had never liked her, and over time, that feeling grew mutual. Melinda was a short, sixty-year-old woman who'd had the same hairdo since Rose was little: a strawberry-blonde bob, small brown eyes, and very sharp features. Somehow, she was even more overbearing than Rose's mother, although that was hard to fathom.

In contrast to her, her son Joey looked like the thug he was. He and Rose were the same age, and it had been a pretty big scandal in the family when he was dishonorably discharged from the military. Rose was never exactly sure what it was he did, but from the whispered conversations between her parents, she was pretty sure he'd stolen weapons and sold them for cash. Of course, it might not have been weapons exactly, but it had been something along those lines. What else did the military have that would be worth stealing? Rose had no idea, but Melinda threw a bunch of money at the officers and hired big-name attorneys, and Joey was released from his service, but with the dishonorable discharge on his record instead of going to jail.

Rose figured he might have been better off if he had gone to prison for whatever he did back then, because after Joey got out of the military, he chose a life of crime for himself. Everyone knew how he made his money and chose to ignore it. Except for Rose's father, which was why he and Melinda had not been on good terms for years. They tolerated each other at family gatherings, but that was all.

Rose couldn't believe they had the audacity to show up here, pretending they grieved over her father. Then again, knowing what type of people they were, she should have expected as much.

Melinda kissed Rose's mother on the cheek, doing the same with Rose's brother, expressing her condolences before sitting down. She barely nodded in Rose's direction. Ever since Rose could remember, Melinda had acted in such a manner toward her. She had always wondered about the source of her aunt's animosity. It was a sore spot for her to think about.

Joey and his wife did the same as his mother, giving Rose a nod, but hugs and kisses to her brother and mother.

"Hello, Auntie Melinda," Rose greeted, feeling quite defiant all of a sudden.

Her aunt completely ignored her, looking at her mother instead. "Thelma, how are you holding up?"

Aunt Melinda had lost her husband pretty young in her marriage. She chose not to remarry because she did not have to, or so she'd claimed. Her late husband had left her plenty of money so she could live the rest of her life quite comfortably all by herself. Those were her precise words. The idea of marrying someone for love or companionship was clearly lost on a woman so miserable. She'd also chosen to take back her maiden name, which Rose had always thought was because she hadn't really cared for her husband in the first place.

"How I must," Rose's mother replied with a dramatic sigh.

The pills Dr. Moss gave her must have been wearing off, Rose concluded.

In the next half an hour the rest of the family showed up as well, and Rose didn't have a moment of peace to speak with her mother about their next course of action. That only proved what she thought before; it would be all up to her to deal with everything.

Unfortunately, the rest of the family thought so as well, but on their terms. They all had opinions. They all wanted to be in charge and steer Rose in the 'right' direction, so to speak, and help Rose's mother deal with this great loss.

Yeah, right.

It was hard to concentrate on anything, especially under those circumstances, thanks to all the noise coming from different sides.

Aunt Melinda tried to take charge, saying Charles was her brother after all, and she knew him best, but Rose was having none of it.

Eventually, she barricaded herself in her father's study, just to get some peace and quiet. Realizing where she was, and how strong the scent of her father still lingered in the air, she started sobbing.

She and her father had always had a very difficult, complicated relationship, but that didn't mean she hadn't loved him. That didn't mean she wouldn't miss him like crazy. He was the foundation of her family. He was the captain who steered the ship in the right direction, and Rose feared that without him, everything would go to hell.

Feeling absolutely miserable, Rose texted Adrian to let him know what happened. He'd called her immediately and told her he was on his way. She was grateful that he was so caring and attentive to her, especially at a time like this.

About an hour later Adrian arrived and found her rummaging through her father's desk. She hoped, if somewhat naively, that her father had left some kind of instruction for them in case this happened. He hadn't. At least not there in his study.

"The masses are getting restless," Adrian joked coming into the room and kissing her.

"How long have you been here?" she asked, furrowing her brow.

"About half an hour. I would have come to find you sooner, but your relatives were rather clingy." He shrugged.

Rose rolled her eyes. "I can't deal with them anymore. Clara wants to sing at the funeral, and three different cousins have demanded to give the eulogy, but only if the other two are refused," she complained. And those were the sanest requests she'd received during the day.

"Just say no to them, and do everything as you see fit," he advised.

"That's easier said than done," she grumbled. Rose wasn't good at confronting people.

"How are you?" he asked, before making a face. "That was such a stupid question. How else can you be?"

Rose shook her head. "I don't mind you asking, it's just that I honestly don't know how I am," she replied.

She supposed she was primarily in shock, but she was sure that wouldn't last long.

"Well, no matter what, I'm here for you."

She buried her head into the crook of his neck. "I know you are."

"I love you, Rose."

"I love you too."

THREE

"It looks as though there was release of inflammatory cytokines through mast cell activation, which led to a coronary artery vasospasm and atheromatous plaque rupture," Dr. Moss said later that evening, giving them the final diagnosis for her father's death.

Rose had no idea what that actually meant. She had never heard of something like that before, and she was still trying to process what he'd told her during the meeting with her father's lawyer the following morning. She was there to find out his funeral instructions, but she could barely take anything in, still hearing his diagnosis swirling around her head.

Dr. Moss's words didn't seem to do anything for her mother or brother either. Her dad was gone and there was nothing that would bring him back.

"I don't understand, Dr. Moss, what is all that?" Rose finally asked.

"It's called Kounis Syndrome. Basically, it means your father had a sizeable heart attack caused by an allergic reaction," he explained.

"An allergic reaction to what?" Rose asked, confused. As far as she knew he didn't have any allergies.

"According to his chart, your father had many allergies, so we're not sure which triggered this attack; however, whatever it was had to be in a large quantity to cause it to a coronary artery vasospasm."

Rose was numb, barely going through the motions as she sat and listened to Dr. Moss explain. She had never known her father was allergic to anything. She was very confused. "I don't understand. How did this happen?"

Dr. Moss shook his head, obviously he had no real answers. "A fluke, perhaps. He must have come across something that triggered the reaction. It could have happened anywhere."

None of it made sense to Rose. She couldn't believe her father had been taken out by an allergy of all things. Dr. Moss continued to speak with her mother, but Rose couldn't focus anymore. She was exhausted, and her mind was in a whirl over her father's death.

Rose had gone upstairs, determined to get some sleep. Adrian had followed behind her and stayed with her overnight in her old childhood bedroom. She was glad to have his comforting presence by her side.

"How are you feeling?" Adrian asked the next morning.

Rose was never the type of person to remember her dreams, but she remembered last night's perfectly. Rose had dreamed about her father giving the New Year's Eve toast, him beaming while looking around at his family. He looked so alive.

That brought tears to her eyes, but she suppressed them. She couldn't allow herself to fall apart, not now, not when there was so much work to be done.

Rose then realized she'd failed to answer Adrian. "Surreal," she replied. She couldn't believe she was back in her old room, sleeping in her old bed, in her parents' house.

She had worked so hard to run away from this place, yet

here she was, back again. It was something she couldn't avoid. She needed to be here for her mother and her brother as well.

Luckily, Adrian was there and more than happy to support her through all of this. God knew nobody else in the family was volunteering to help her or lend their support. He was her rock, her safe place to land, and she couldn't imagine going through all of this without him.

She had to admit there were times she still couldn't quite believe she and Adrian were engaged. Rose, like her mother, was a fairly short, extremely pale-skinned blonde with brown eyes. She knew she was okay looking, but had never thought of herself as pretty or beautiful by any means. Adrian was a huge contrast to her, with him being classically handsome, tall, and dark. And although he told Rose that she was the most beautiful woman in the world to him, there was no denying he was better looking than her, and he dressed better. She always wore whatever felt comfortable to her. She didn't care about designer labels or even if it was name-brand. Adrian, though, always dressed impeccably in tailored suits, or, if he was going to dress casually, in high-end Ralph Lauren shirts and name-brand jeans.

Rose was aware there were a lot of women out there in the world who were more attractive than her. Even at his office, there were some who would die to be with him. And yet he had chosen to be with her. And in her lowest points, she had to wonder why.

She tried to keep those thoughts at bay as often as possible because she really was happy in her relationship, and that was what mattered. She figured the doubtful thoughts were because their relationship had been such a whirlwind and she was still getting used to it all.

It was strange how life worked. Before she met Adrian, she had been devastated and heartbroken after ending another relationship with a selfish, rich man who didn't understand her need for her own career and thought she should stay home and play hostess for him. He'd been chosen by her mother, which was why she'd decided it was time to swear off men. Of course, that was when she met Adrian.

He had been representing a celebrity writer on a book deal, and Rose was brought in as the writer's editor, which is how they officially met. He was always very friendly, would make a point to smile and say hello. He would bring treats to their meetings, and after the first one, he always remembered to add Rose's favorite muffins. She hadn't been sure that he was singling her out though. He had just seemed like a nice guy. However, once the papers were signed, all the upfront bonus checks written, Rose realized she was still seeing him around her office quite often. He would pop in with a random question about something book-related, and always brought her coffee, or a muffin, even if he said it wasn't her he was there to speak to. It turned out he'd been making excuses to come to the publishing house while he worked up the courage to ask her out.

She had said yes and wasn't disappointed. He managed to change her mind and restore her faith in men. She was very lucky she had him in her life. She didn't know how she would get through all this without him beside her.

Rose had been quite surprised when he'd proposed since they hadn't been together that long, but she said yes. He made her happy, and that was what really mattered to her.

She was upset that her father had never approved of Adrian.

And now he never will.

Her father dying changed everything. She was aware of that; however, with Adrian by her side she felt confident she could overcome any obstacles life threw her way.

Was that overly naive, or optimistic? Perhaps. It was also something to hold onto during one of the worst weeks of her life.

"I'm here for you, you know that, right? Whatever you need," Adrian reassured, kissing her shoulder.

She loved it when he did that.

"I know, and I really appreciate it."

Adrian had cleared his schedule and took a few days off so he could really be there for her, lend a hand if she needed it, and take care of her.

That made her love him even more. That he was prepared to put his life on hold for her and help out. Help her family out when they weren't welcoming to him at all. Sure, they were all very polite, but no one would call them warm or accepting. And Rose was sure he was aware of that.

Still, he held no grudges and was there for them all, fielding questions, pouring drinks, and helping her deal with her crazy family. Her *entire* crazy family.

They were all gathered here like vultures. Even some distant relatives she hadn't seen in decades had decided to show up and act like they were completely torn up about her father's death.

They were a bunch of opportunists as far as Rose was concerned, but she kept her opinions to herself, knowing her mother wouldn't like it if she caused any kind of drama within the family. Her mother was the only person allowed to cause drama.

Rose had made sure to get them all hotel rooms—some at hotels far from each other because some branches of the family couldn't stand the others—but for some reason they all decided to hang around the house during the day as much as possible, which meant Rose didn't have a moment of peace. There was nowhere she could go to escape them, and it was slowly driving her insane.

Rose was terrified of being forced to handle everything her father had to deal with on a daily basis. And she wasn't neces-sarily speaking about the company he ran. She knew her father had good, competent people in place to run the company without too much of her input.

It was the family, who were another matter altogether. Dealing with all the petty squabbles, scams, and plots, all the while enduring their snide comments, wasn't how she pictured her life going forward.

Rose didn't get along with most of her cousins, and there were very few aunts and uncles that she truly liked who liked her in return. She knew it was because she and her brother were the heirs of her father's vast fortune, and now that her father was dead, she would definitely be the target for their sob stories or sucking up. Of course, there would be those who continued to bully her, probably in the hopes that she'd be intimidated and that she would give them a share of the money.

Aunt Melinda would absolutely come after her; she had no doubt about that. Melinda would try to make her life as miserable as possible.

With her father gone, it would be open season on her. Rose had no idea if she would be strong enough to endure it all, especially while grieving for her father.

"What are you thinking about so intently?" Adrian asked, his voice soft in her ear.

Rose remained silent as she stared out the window of the library into the back garden. She truly didn't want to share the mess that was happening inside her mind.

"You know you can tell me anything. We'll be married soon, and I want you to share everything with me, so I can help."

There was so much she wanted to say to him, but didn't know how. She didn't know where to start. "I don't know how to balance my life and my family now that he's gone. I don't know if I'm ready to deal with them all," she tried to explain.

"I know things look scary at the moment, but I'm sure you will manage just fine."

She knew he was trying to be reassuring, but it didn't help.

He still failed to grasp the severity, the potential craziness of the situation. Rose tried again.

"You don't know these people, Adrian. The people on my father's side of the family are ruthless, especially when seeing something they want. And my mother and brother are completely exposed now, vulnerable."

They had never had to deal with any difficulties in life. They didn't have to handle any kind of business or financial matters because her dad had done everything. Now he was gone, and everything would change. And Rose wasn't strong enough to defend them on her own. She just wasn't.

"What are you saying, Rose? Is someone going to try to harm them?" he asked, sounding worried.

"Not physically, I don't think," she replied. "However, I'm worried that things are going to turn pretty ugly when the will gets read," she explained.

Without saying anything, Adrian wrapped his arms around her. It was obvious he didn't have any kind of solution or suggestion for her problems. He was just letting her know he was there for her. That they would find a solution together. And that meant the world to her.

"I feel like I am losing my mind," she confessed.

"I know this is a lame thought, but you have to stop worrying so much. I'm here with you, and we'll get things done, together," he assured her.

Rose closed her eyes for a moment, letting Adrian simply hold her as she took a few deep breaths. Perhaps he was right. Perhaps she was worrying about nothing. Then again, what were the odds of that happening, especially with her family?

Slim to none, she thought.

When they parted, he placed his hands on her shoulders and looked deeply into her eyes. "We got this," he said with confidence.

Rose wasn't so sure, but she liked that "we" part very much.

Her face must have shown her true feelings because he continued speaking. "As you know, I lost my dad when I was young. And then Mom..." he faltered a little, and Rose took his hand, "Well, you remember. It destroyed me to lose them both. You're lucky to have so many relatives. I'm sure your father wouldn't want you to be scared of dealing with your family. If I've learned anything about your father, it's that he respected bold people who always pushed forward. So be bold, push forward."

Rose cracked a smile. "That was quite an inspirational speech."

"I have my moments," he replied in the same manner before giving her a quick kiss.

"Now let's go. We can't keep hiding in this room forever."

"Are you sure? We can try," she deadpanned.

He laughed, helping her up. It felt strange, wrong even to joke like this with her fiancé the day after her father died. And since she started feeling guilty, she stopped.

"Let's go," she agreed.

She knew Adrian was right. Especially the part about her father. He didn't like weak people, so she couldn't allow herself to be weak. And the rest would learn to respect her if she showed her teeth and refused to bend to their will. There was only one problem with that. She had no idea how to achieve it.

She had always struggled to see the best in her family. Her father, well, her entire family in one way or another, had taught her that people would try to take advantage of her, and so she'd always tried to hide her true self, and at times her physical self, from nearly everyone. It was a hard habit to break. How could she suddenly become bold now?

Adrian will help, she thought. *Won't he?*

She couldn't help the shiver of discontent that slid down her spine wondering if that was true or not.

FOUR

A week later, Rose stood by her mother's side at the graveyard. Her father's lawyer had all of her father's requests on hand for his funeral, and Rose had seen to it that everything was carried out to his specifications. Everything except for how her mother was behaving right at that very moment.

"Why did you leave me, Charles? How am I to continue living without you?" her mother cried out like an actress on a daytime soap opera, shedding crocodile tears as the casket was lowered into the ground.

She was making the biggest scene possible. Rose should have known this would happen; she always did this. Not at funerals per se, but in other social gatherings. Rose's sweet sixteen birthday party was a particularly memorable one, which added insult to injury when she considered that she hadn't wanted to have it in the first place, but her mother had insisted. They'd rented out the entire country club and invited nearly everyone on the planet, including the handsome Michael Conners, lead singer of Falling in Slow Motion, Rose's favorite band. When he'd actually shown up, Rose about died. Not because he'd shown but because her mother hounded him the entire time to sing, and when he finally did, she'd forced Rose up on the stage with him to stand awkwardly by his side while her mother proceeded to fawn all over him, acting as though she was the teenager in love with him. Rose had wanted to disappear on the spot.

Now, to make matters worse, she had walked closer toward the lowering casket, hitting herself in the chest as she spoke. "I will never forgive you for this, Charles. I will never forgive you for abandoning me, for leaving me all alone," she sobbed.

Her mother wasn't doing it to garner sympathy; this was just how she was. Dramatic with a capital D. It wasn't that she wasn't feeling this way; Rose knew her mom probably did feel as though her husband had abandoned her. Rose certainly felt that way, but her theatrics were a bit over the top, and to an outsider, it probably looked staged. Rose was very thankful that the paparazzi that had followed their funeral car, hoping for a scoop, had been stopped at the front gates. The press would have a field day with this visual.

Father Dominic started to raise an eyebrow in a disapproving manner, and he was not the only one. Rose could hear people behind them commenting in hushed, subdued voices about what her mother was doing.

Rose had no idea how to help her. She glanced at her brother and groaned. He could barely stand upright. It dawned on her that he was drunk. She should have expected that. She'd known he would be completely useless in this situation. Not only was he incapable of helping her, he wouldn't have even if he hadn't been drunk.

I have to stop her from making an even bigger fool of herself.

It was obvious to her that her mother was in deep pain, but she also knew her father wouldn't appreciate the spectacle she was creating. Rose neared her mother and put her arms around her in an embrace.

"It's okay, Mom, I'm here," she said softly, as she tried to pull her back, away from the casket.

Rose was afraid that in her craziness, her mother would try to do something even more foolish, like jump down on it to be buried with her husband. And Rose really didn't want to deal with that. The press was here, since her father had been such financial titan, and even though they were stopped at the front gate, they still had those long-range lenses where they could get photos, and she really didn't want to have her family's pain splashed across the front page.

She could already picture the headlines, and that made her shudder. Luckily, her mother allowed Rose to lead her back to their chairs, but she continued to sob uncontrollably on her shoulder.

"Everything is going to be all right," Rose continued to soothe her, or at least tried. Her words felt empty to her, probably because she didn't believe them herself.

"No, it's not," her mother sobbed, clearly feeling the same way. "Your father left me all alone."

"You still have Devon and me," Rose pointed out.

That didn't make her mother cry any less. Rose spotted Aunt Melinda standing to the side. Joey and his wife were right beside her, watching Rose with her mom.

It was obvious by Aunt Melinda's expression how much she disapproved of Rose's mother's behavior.

It went deeper than that, Rose knew. Melinda hated her mother with a deep, hot passion, and it showed. It colored everything she did and said toward her. That also meant that no matter what Rose did, or what her mother did, good or bad, Melinda would always act in the same manner, with utter and complete disgust.

When Rose was younger, she had been pretty bothered by it, and now she simply tried her best to ignore it.

"Mom, the service is over, we need to go," Rose said.

"Let me say one last goodbye," her mother replied, moving from her side as she returned to the hole her father's casket rested in. She kissed the red rose she was clutching, and then slowly dropped it into the hole, on top of the casket, before picking up a handful of dirt and tossing it in as well.

Rose sighed with relief. Maybe they were out of the woods.

While they were walking toward the limo, Rose got a strange feeling someone was watching her. Looking around, she noticed a very attractive woman dressed all in black, like the rest of them, staring at her. It was a strange look, and it caught Rose off guard. Something about her felt familiar, but as she craned to get a better look, her mother's stiletto heel sunk into the earth.

Since she couldn't deal with anything other than her mother at the moment, she brushed it to the side and got into the car.

One quick, silent car ride later and they were back at the house, where they held a gathering of family and close friends in her father's honor.

The whole ground floor was transformed to accommodate the hoard of family members that were descending on the house. Chairs were arranged at convenient points, and food and drinks were being served by her mother's household staff. Rose was sure they could feed a small European country with everything they had on hand. But her mother had insisted.

Rose stepped into the dining room to check on the food. She had just made it through the door when she overheard Joey and Melinda speaking near the buffet with their backs to her.

"So, who do you think will get what?" he asked, so blatantly it made Rose stop in her tracks.

"Thelma will get the most, of course," Aunt Melinda said with a frown. "Then Devon and that brat."

Rose knew that she was the brat Melinda referred to.

"You should get her share of the money, instead of her," Joey grumbled. "She's not even family."

Rose felt an arrow stab through her heart at his words. What did he mean she wasn't family? Of course, she was. Charles was her father.

"It's insufferable having to deal with how he claimed her, but Charles was cruel in that manner," Aunt Melinda complained.

Rose gasped. Her legs almost gave out from under her. Were they saying that her father, the man she had always known as her dad, the man she had admired and looked up to and loved, wasn't her real father?

They stopped speaking once they turned and saw Rose standing there. Melinda looked her up and down, almost daring her to say something. They didn't apologize or say anything else; they simply moved to a different side of the room. It was hard to decide who was the worst of the pair.

Joey was the blackest black sheep in the family. After his botched military career and dishonorable discharge, he'd gotten into more trouble and spent a couple of years in prison for running drugs. But even that didn't sober him up. He continued down that path. He went to prison for beating some guy to a pulp a few years ago, too, but Aunt Melinda managed to get him out early thanks to all the money she had, not only from her deceased husband but from her share of her own father's inheritance.

Joey was as ruthless as he was greedy. It was no secret he wanted the Blaisdell family wealth all to himself and tried to make deals with Rose's father many times in the past, but was always turned down.

The only thing Rose respected about him was that, since returning home from his time in prison, he didn't try to hide his true nature, unlike the rest of her family. Unlike his mother. While all the rest of the family pretended that they were nice and helpful, they were also trying to stab each other in the back in the most devious of ways. Joey did all that quite openly.

As Rose stood there reeling from what they'd said, she recalled the time Melinda tried to get her kicked out of college. Melinda was friends with the dean and spread so many lies that even a few professors started to turn on her. Rose's father had to intervene to put a stop to it all. Rose found out about that only a few years back. Her father had never said a word to her. Then again, that was how he operated. He kept things to himself a lot. Although he was pretty vocal when he didn't like certain things, when they didn't go his way, according to his plan, he always did his best to protect each and every member of his family, whether they deserved it or not.

Rose wondered if this rumor about her not being her father's child was simply another lie. She wouldn't put it past her. But something niggled at her. The snide comments from her relatives over the years were falling into place – had the entire family thought this the whole time?

"Hey, Rose, I am really sorry for your loss," her dad's cousin, Nick, said, approaching her.

She gathered herself enough to answer him. "Thank you."

He shifted awkwardly from foot to foot, clearly trying to be delicate. Which was hard work for a trust-fund loafer.

"So, do you know when the reading of the will is going to be held, my mom wants to know," he explained apologetically.

Rose wasn't buying the act. His mother was Rose's great-aunt Pamela who was nearly ninety. She didn't even know what year it was most days, so there was no way she was lucid enough to be worrying about the will.

"I'm not quite sure, in a few days probably," she replied. She wasn't sure why they were all so interested. She doubted her father had distributed his money to anyone beyond her mother, her, and Devon. Maybe a little for the staff, those who'd been with her parents for a long time, maybe something to her uncle who worked in the company with him, but beyond that, Rose didn't think there was much going to anyone else.

Unless Melinda and Joey were telling the truth, and she wasn't his daughter... Another stab of pain lanced through her chest at the thought. *Surely, they're lying. They have to be lying,* she prayed. She decided to ignore their words and continue on as if she hadn't heard them.

Still, as she predicted, all the vultures gathered. It was bound to happen with her greedy extended family.

Nick moved a step closer and whispered, "Do you know if your father left anything to my mom? I know they were really fond of one another."

Rose refrained from rolling her eyes. "I don't know, but I'm sure Dad was very generous to all the people he loved," she replied, considering he looked at her so expectantly. It was strange using past tense when speaking about her father.

It was obvious Nick was pretty disappointed with her reply. She excused herself, but not before she noticed Aunt Melinda watching her with a sneer.

"I better be in the will, or I'll raise hell," Aunt Melinda said in a huff to Joanne.

Joanne was the wife of one of Rose's cousins, but she couldn't recall which one. Her dad had six siblings. He had been the oldest, and Melinda the youngest. The others varied in age, but there were twin brothers who had gone on to each have their own sets of twins, one of which Joanne was married to.

Rose wasn't surprised Melinda was preparing for war if she was left out of the will. It was the kind of woman she was. The problem was that no matter how much money Rose's dad left her, if he left her anything, she would demand more. It was in her nature to never be satisfied with what was offered to her, what was given to her. Rose didn't like people like that, and she especially didn't like Aunt Melinda.

As far as Rose was concerned, they all had more than enough, far more than the regular folk, and they should all be grateful because of that. Of course, nobody thought like Rose in that regard. She herself had refused to allow her father to pay her way once she hit adulthood. She'd earned her way into college, and yes, he'd helped to pay for that and her room and board, but once she graduated, she went out, got a job, and started paying for herself. She'd very rarely touched the trust fund her parents had set up for her. Usually, she used that money to anonymously donate to charities her parents wouldn't, like the teen pregnancy center and the local homeless shelters, as well as a couple of food banks. What good was the money if she couldn't do something good with it?

"He used *my* daddy's money to create all this," Aunt Melinda continued to complain to anyone who was prepared to listen to her. There was always a crowd around her since her family was full of sycophants, unfortunately.

Rose suppressed an eye roll. Aunt Melinda never failed to mention that. How Rose's father took his inheritance of their father's money as a starting capital to create and grow his business. However, the way Aunt Melinda spoke about it, it was as though her brother stole all that money so he alone could advance in life.

That was furthest from the truth possible. Rose's father had inherited the same amount of money as Aunt Melinda, not to mention their other siblings, and their mother who had since passed on, leaving the same exact amount for each of them in her will.

With the money her father had gotten, he'd started his business, and the more successful it was, the more family members he'd brought in. Currently, three of his brothers, six of their kids, and a couple of their wives worked for the company. The other brothers and his other sister all had their own careers, or in the case of Aunt Sarah, her own family and charity that she oversaw.

However, Rose's father had been very business-savvy and more resourceful than all the rest of his siblings, which meant he managed to accumulate more wealth than them, which led to a lot of jealousy and envy.

"I need more champagne," Aunt Melinda yelled at Rose, pointing at her empty glass.

Then call for one of the staff, Rose wanted to snap, but held her tongue. Her mother wouldn't appreciate her speaking her mind. Instead, she nodded and fetched another glass. "Here you go, Auntie Melinda."

Of course, she didn't say thank you.

"Does it bother you they're all talking about Charles's will?" Aunt Melinda asked her, taking her by surprise. She rarely made an effort to make a conversation with Rose. Usually, she would make a snide comment and that was that.

Yes. Of course, it bothers me. He just died and all you people can speak about is his money.

Since Rose clearly took too long to reply, Aunt Melinda lost patience and continued. "I wouldn't expect much if I were you, Rose," she said snidely.

"And why is that?" she asked, genuinely curious as to why Melinda would think her father would leave her with little.

"You know why. Don't make me say it," her aunt replied, in a way that made it obvious she found this conversation vulgar, which was funny considering she started it.

"Please, do," Rose replied generously, praying she wasn't going to claim Rose wasn't his daughter again as she'd done earlier.

Melinda Blaisdell sighed theatrically. "We all know you're not really my brother's daughter. And he knew it too. He felt pity for you, took you in, raised you among us, but you were never one of us. You don't share our blood. I'm sure that my brother believed that everything should be kept *in the family*, so you will be left out," she replied condescendingly.

Rose's eyes filled with tears. How could this woman presume to know anything like that? Her father had never treated her like she was less than his. Was this just her jealousy speaking? Was she making stuff up to cause drama? Considering all the vipers in the family who talked trash over the years, she had to wonder if Melinda had been telling them all this from almost the beginning. She was nine when the bullying from her relatives had started to ramp up. She recalled that was when Joey had called her nothing but a peasant, no better than one of the staff, and she'd cried like never before because she'd been a sensitive girl and words hurt. It was shortly after that incident her father had stopped inviting Melinda and Joey to the house for anything other than official family gatherings. And even then, he'd barely given her the time of day. Now Rose wondered if Melinda had shared her theory about Rose not being his and that was why he'd stopped speaking to her.

Aunt Melinda looked victorious that she managed to rattle her. Rose couldn't stand the woman. She couldn't stand nearly any of them. Without saying anything she practically ran to her old room.

Adrian followed after her.

She couldn't stop tears from falling down her face. What if it was true? What if her father wasn't her father? Had her mom cheated? Was that why Melinda had bullied her all these years? Rose knew that her mom and Melinda had never really been close. All her life they'd sniped at each other. Rose had always thought Melinda bullying her was just an extension of her mother, but what if it was more than that? What if she really wasn't Charles's daughter?

What does that mean? she wondered.

Does that mean he didn't love me like I thought? Did he leave me out of the will? Have I been disowned?

Rose's tears fell harder, and she felt as though her whole world was collapsing.

Adrian wrapped his arms around her, pulling her into his embrace. He didn't say a word, and he didn't have to. He let her cry all over him until she was all sobbed out. He stroked her hair and murmured sweet little nothings in her ear telling her it would all be okay.

Eventually, she calmed and realized that no matter what Melinda said, she would always be Charles Blaisdell's daughter. She had his name, nobody else's, listed as father on her birth certificate. He'd always treated her as a beloved daughter. Surely, he wouldn't have abandoned her in his final wishes. It wasn't about the money, though. Rose didn't care about that. She just wanted reassurance that he'd loved her as she'd loved him.

Rose held tighter to Adrian. She was glad he was there with her. She would go mad without him. He was her rock. Her anchor in this episode of her life. She didn't know what she would do if he ever left her. Even the idea of that was heart-crushing, so she quickly shoved that kind of dark thought into a waste bin in her mind.

"They are so obnoxious," she complained, wiping her eyes. "I can't wait for all of this to be over, so I won't have to see any of them for the rest of my life."

Once all the legalities regarding her father's will were resolved, Rose planned on completely distancing herself from them all. She would still see her mother and brother, of course; however, she would definitely avoid everyone else. Life would be so much more pleasant that way.

"Dealing with family can be stressful," Adrian agreed, and she made a face.

"I can't believe they only care about his money, it's all they can talk about," she stressed, not wanting to mention Melinda's hurtful words toward her.

Her father had died, they'd lost a family member, and they only cared how much they would profit from it and nothing else.

"Being greedy is only natural when this much money is

involved," Adrian said. "Isn't there a small part of you, even the tiniest bit, that's excited about the prospect of becoming a billionaire?"

Rose pulled away so she could stare at him. She couldn't believe he said that to her. "What?" she choked out. Was she happy she might be receiving a boatload of money thanks to her father dying? Was he seriously asking her that?

"I know it's hard, but just think about it, Rose. You'll inherit all this money. You'll be able to do whatever you please for the rest of your life."

"Yeah, and to get it, my father had to die," she pointed out in disgust.

"I know, I'm sorry, I didn't mean it to sound the way it did…" He sighed. "I'm not very good at this. I just meant, well, that kind of money can be life changing."

She waved with her hand stopping him from saying anything else. He might mean well, but she was hurting. "My father is *dead*, Adrian," she stressed the words, "I loved him and would give anything to have him back, but it seems like everyone else in the family couldn't care less." *Even his sister is acting like an asshole.* "I don't care about the money, I never did. I just want my dad back." She looked at him trying to make him see her point.

Adrian nodded. "I don't know if I can relate exactly, I didn't have that kind of relationship with my father." He once again pulled her into his embrace. "I'm glad you did."

"But you understand what I'm saying, right?" she asked.

He smiled. "You're too selfless for your own good, Rose. It's one of the things I love most about you."

Rose wasn't sure what he meant by that, but something had her wondering if her father had been right about him. "Would you be interested in me if my family wasn't wealthy?" she asked. He hadn't known about her family and their wealth when they met; she'd kept it from him pretty easily, considering they'd met at her job. But now she wondered if he'd only proposed because of her family's wealth.

"Don't be ridiculous," he answered before kissing her on the lips. "I don't care about your family's money."

She was about to ask him if he was sure it didn't entice him to propose when he added, "Let's get back downstairs. You don't want them thinking they managed to rattle you."

She realized he was right. She shouldn't give them that satisfaction. Besides, she was sure the guests who hadn't attended the funeral would be arriving soon, and she shouldn't leave her mother unsupervised.

Rose ignored Aunt Melinda and a few others as she spoke with guests, made sure her mother wasn't drinking too much, and kept her gaze on Devon. And then, from the corner of her eye, she spotted that same woman she'd seen at the cemetery. And once again, the other woman was staring at her. Before Rose could ask someone who she was, the woman approached.

"I am so sorry for your loss," the woman said.

Despite her words, Rose had a distinct feeling the woman didn't actually mean it.

I must be tired, she thought.

"Thank you for coming," Rose replied politely.

The woman nodded.

Rose couldn't shake the feeling there was something very familiar about her, but she couldn't put a finger on what it was. Rose was sure she wasn't family. She would remember someone with such a look of old Hollywood beauty at family gatherings. That was the best description she had. The woman was tall, much taller than Rose, especially in heels, and statuesque. She had long, wavy brown hair and gray eyes. For some reason, Rose thought of her father looking into them.

And then she remembered she did, in fact, know who this was. Ava. She was a few years older than Rose, and she recognized her from college. They'd lived in the same dorms, on the same floor, but hadn't been friends. She had looked slightly different back then, always wearing glasses, however it was definitely her.

What is she doing here?

"I remember you from college, Ava Rothman, right? We were two years apart," Rose commented.

Ava nodded again, with a half-smile. "I remember you too."

"How did you know my father?" Rose asked next. She was politely trying to discover why she was there. There was a chance she was simply a plus one to one of her cousins. God knew she had plenty of those and they were all playboys, her brother included. Ava wasn't here with Devon though; Rose was sure of that.

Ava smiled again, and this time she showed her white teeth, but it wasn't a pleasant smile. "Actually, he was my father too," she replied.

Rose could feel her brain shutting down for a moment. "Excuse me?" she choked out the words.

"I'm your half-sister," Ava said. "And I came today because I want to inform you that I will be claiming my part of the inheritance, even if he left me out of the will."

She said all of that loud enough that quite a few people stopped their conversations, looking their way. *She did that on purpose*, Rose realized.

Rose could barely process what was happening. She scanned Ava's perfect features, wondering if her eyes were the same shade as her father's, or the shape of her jaw reminiscent of her brother's.

"That's not possible. The only children my father ever had are me and my brother Devon," Rose insisted.

"I beg to differ," Ava said producing a piece of paper from her bag and handing it to Rose.

"And what is this?"

"That is proof I am who I say I am. That is a DNA test proving I am Charles Blaisdell's daughter," Ava explained.

Rose felt lightheaded. *This can't be happening.*

"Charles's daughter?"

"Another daughter?"

"A secret daughter?"

"Is she his real daughter?"

Rose could hear various family members around her commenting. She also heard Aunt Melinda openly cheering this turn of events. Another daughter appearing seemed to be the best news for her. Of course, once she realized that meant less money for herself, she'd be back to her snide, petty self.

And then, to make matters worse, Rose's mother appeared. She had remained in her room resting for quite some time, but she was there now. *She always has perfect timing*, Rose grumbled.

Her mother simply glanced at the paper in Rose's hand.

"I'm telling the truth, as you can see," Ava insisted, although nobody was attacking her.

Rose noticed her mother take a sharp intake of breath, and her eyes narrowed with pain, but after a moment, her expression went blank, and she simply waved her hand in dismissal. "This is no time for such serious conversations. The lawyers will figure this out, but for now, welcome. The refreshments are in the dining room."

"Thank you. Nice meeting you," Ava said, before walking away. She didn't even glance in Rose's direction again.

A few of Rose's relatives followed her, probably hoping to hear all about Charles's infidelity.

Rose could only stare after her. Could this be real? *Do I have another sibling?* Her mind was reeling.

"Rose, what is the matter with you?"

Her mother's voice snapped her from her thoughts. She turned to look at her, her brow furrowed. "What do you mean?"

"Why were you making a scene with that woman at your father's repast?"

"A scene? I didn't say anything," she defended, still trying to get over the shock she had a sister. *Half-sister,* she corrected. A half-sister she knew nothing about.

"Exactly, mind your manners. This is a solemn occasion. I raised you better than that," her mother said heatedly before walking away to meet a few guests.

Rose stayed put. Her mind had exploded, and she needed a moment to catch her breath.

FIVE

Charles Blaisdell was Ava's father.

That would mean he cheated on Rose's mom.

That would mean he had another secret family, a family he visited, and spent time with instead of being with them. Rose stopped her thoughts there. Perhaps she was getting ahead of herself. Perhaps it was a one-time thing? A one-night stand? A one-night stand that resulted in a child.

Somehow, that didn't make it look any better.

Rose needed more than a moment to process what Ava had said. She recalled that Ava had been one of those popular but smart girls in college. Had she gone there because Rose was there? she wondered, but then remembered Ava was older by two years... wait... was she born before Rose's parents even married? *No,* Rose thought, remembering that her parents had been married for nearly three years when she'd been born. Still...

Rose dismissed those thoughts and forced herself to focus.

It took a moment or ten, but Rose managed to compose herself and continue to mingle and chat with people as though nothing had happened. Obviously, that wasn't completely possible since Ava remained in her peripheral vision.

Adrian had a strange expression on his face as the whole thing went down, Rose had noted at the time, and now she watched as he went over to Ava and introduced himself. Why would he do that? Then again, maybe she wasn't mentally or emotionally stable enough to recognize common courtesy. Perhaps her mother was right. She'd lost something ever since her father died.

All the same, since most of the guests had left and only their immediate family and her father's siblings remained, Rose decided it was time to speak with Ava and demand the truth from her. She had so many questions for the other woman and needed answers.

Rose wished she could do it privately, but as though sensing blood in the water they all, including Aunt Melinda, remained, waiting for the spectacle.

Very politely, Rose asked Ava if they could speak for a moment, and the other woman nodded. There was something pretty sultry about her mannerisms. Even when she was agreeing to something, she looked too proud.

The crowd gathered near them.

"You can probably guess what I want to know," Rose asked carefully. There was no way she was actually going to ask when her father managed to have an affair with Ava's mother.

Luckily, Ava had no problems sharing all the details with her.

"Charles got my mother pregnant during one of his work holidays in Cancun."

Cancun? Rose thought, confused. *Who goes to work in Cancun?* Then it became obvious Ava was mocking the situation. Of course, nobody went there to work but to have a good time.

And glancing at her mother, who was standing nearby,

listening but pretending not to listen, it was more than obvious she already knew about her late husband's holiday habits from the early part of their marriage, and Rose's heart dropped. Her mother raised her chin.

"He took a lover for his own amusement and then left her pregnant, alone, and unsupported when he grew tired of her," Ava continued, snapping Rose from her thoughts. "My mother wrote him letter after letter, but they all went unanswered. We had nothing, Mom worked herself to an early grave as a single mom trying to support me, while Charles just ignored us and my mother's pleas for help."

It was obvious there was no love lost between Ava and Charles, if she ever even knew him.

To Rose's utmost surprise, Aunt Melinda came and patted Ava on her back. "It's quite brave of you to come here and share your story with us, sweetheart," she complimented.

Rose had to make sure her jaw didn't hit the floor hearing that.

"Thank you," Ava replied.

"What is your name, dear?" Aunt Melinda asked.

"Dr. Ava Rothman."

"A doctor? How very impressive." For some reason, Aunt Melinda looked at Rose while saying that. As though saying, *look how much better Ava is than you.*

"Your story is very sad," Devon agreed. "I can't believe Dad was so heartless toward you and your mother."

Rose suppressed an eye roll. For some reason, she could not sympathize with Ava at all.

"Did your mother know he was already married?" Rose asked next.

Ava's eyes flashed with fury, but she composed herself quickly. That was all Rose needed to know about that. Her mother had known and decided to be with a married man all the same. She wasn't minimizing his culpability; however, it was obvious Ava's mother was to be held accountable as well. There was enough blame to go around.

"Rose, don't be so nosy," Aunt Melinda snapped.

"How do we know that you aren't some scammer looking for a way to get a quick buck," Joey asked Ava, eyeing her suspiciously.

Rose cheered inwardly. She could always count on her cousin to be as blunt as possible. To be honest, Rose was thinking the same thing; she just didn't know how to ask politely. Joey had no such holdups. Sure, Ava had that DNA test, but who knew if it was real or not?

Aunt Melinda looked at her son in a disapproving manner, although it was obvious that was exactly what she wanted to know as well. Although she was offering a welcoming hand, Rose realized that was all for show. Aunt Melinda would fight anyone who would try to take a cut of the inheritance. The inheritance she believed belonged to her.

"I have DNA proof that supports my claim," Ava replied raising her chin ever so slightly.

"To be honest, that's just a piece of paper. It doesn't prove anything," Joey replied instantly. "I can falsify almost anything, claiming to be the last king of Scotland if I want to, however, that doesn't make me royalty."

Rose almost smiled at that.

"I have no problems doing it again, at a laboratory of your choosing," Ava replied with such confidence as though to show she had nothing to hide.

Was that actually the case?

Rose had to admit this was all too convenient. Her father had just died, and on the day of his funeral, a secret daughter, with DNA proof at the ready, emerged. There was something about Ava; she couldn't put her finger on it, but she saw something shark-like in her eyes. *Perhaps you're just jealous*, a small, traitorous part of her said.

"And once you are all convinced that I'm Charles's daughter, I will claim my inheritance," Ava repeated her plans once again.

Maybe she is family. She is interested only in money, after all, Rose grumbled.

"Nothing can be done before the reading of the will. I doubt you will be in it, but should your words prove true, I am sure we can come to some agreement afterward," her mother decided to join in the conversation, much to Rose's surprise.

Was she truly prepared to give part of the inheritance to her husband's illegitimate child?

"That is very generous of you, Thelma," Aunt Melinda tried to jibe, clearly thinking along the same lines as Rose.

"If she is Charles's daughter, then she has every right to her part of the inheritance," her mother replied with dignity.

Aunt Melinda smiled. "Of course, you would think that, and be generous despite your husband's indiscretions. After all, your daughter is getting her share too," she jibed.

"Stop saying things like that, it's rude and disrespectful," Rose snapped, taking everyone by surprise. Usually, she was not so confrontational. *What has gotten into me?* she thought. She had no idea, but she liked it.

Aunt Melinda huffed as though thinking Rose was the unreasonable one in this situation, and before she could say anything else, her mother interjected.

"Thank you, dear, but I really don't need protecting from snide comments like that. Melinda is a bitter old hag; I wouldn't expect her to say anything nice. All the same, she is family, and now it seems Ava might be family as well. And we will all have to learn to live with one another, despite the person who brought us all together being gone."

That was very mature of her mother. Rose didn't know if she agreed, all the same, she would concede to her mother's wishes. Even Aunt Melinda nodded although Rose's mom had just insulted her.

I will never understand their relationship.

Ava continued to offer bits and pieces of information about her life while growing up, being fussed and fawned over by the cousins as she did.

Rose didn't like any of this one bit. Usually, she wasn't a distrustful person. However, all of this felt really strange to her. It was too conspicuous, and convenient.

Why did Ava choose this moment to reveal herself? Why did she wait for her father to die? Why not contact him while he was alive? Rose had too many unanswered questions swirling inside her head. And one thing was certain, she didn't completely trust Ava. Her gut feeling was telling her something was off.

"It's sad when parents don't support their children," Adrian replied to something Ava said.

Even he was enchanted by the possible new member of the Blaisdell family. How could he not be? She was a beautiful woman, and he was a man. They all behaved like hormonal boys in such situations. And unfortunately, Rose's fiancé was no different.

Rose resented that a bit. She couldn't believe how everyone around her was going out of their way to welcome this interloper into their family. *Maybe the problem is me,* she doubted for a moment.

Though it was quite selfish of her, Rose's stomach twisted in resentment at her relatives welcoming this stranger when they hadn't shown her the same courtesy all her life. Although she was recognized and legitimized by her father, who never claimed anything other than her being his daughter, the family hated her. Yet here they were, competing among themselves for who would offer more support to some secret child.

Rose wasn't saying she would prefer if they all started

hating Ava on the spot. She simply noted the hypocrisy, the injustice.

"Thank you all for your kind words," Ava said, looking touched, placing a hand over her heart. "To be honest, I dreaded this day, your reaction; however, I am deeply touched by how welcoming and understanding you all are."

Rose couldn't stand this charade a moment longer. "May I speak with you in private," Rose asked her.

"Of course."

They retreated to the library. It was obvious her mother wasn't pleased by that, and Aunt Melinda was clearly frustrated she wasn't invited as well. Rose ignored them all as she closed the door behind her and Ava.

"What can I do for you, Rose? I mean, I know this is all quite sudden—"

"What are you playing at?" Rose decided to interrupt her. "Why are you doing this?" she demanded, without bothering to beat around the bush. Perhaps the rest of her family were fooled by her act, Rose wasn't.

To her credit, Ava wasn't trying to fake ignorance. "I'm not playing at anything. I simply want what belongs to me. I want everything you have."

"Why now? On the day of his funeral?" Rose challenged. "Why not ten days ago, ten years ago? Why didn't you say anything to me in college?" she bombarded her with questions.

Though they hadn't been friends in college, they had a few mutual friends, and back then, if Ava had approached her and shared her story, Rose would have been more understanding, and helpful. Now she was full of doubts.

Ava sighed. "Look, I told you my mother wrote him letter after letter, but I wasn't aware of who he was until recently. I found several of the returned letters in her things after she passed away. All I knew was that he was a rich and powerful man with a lot of security around him. Mom told me she tried to contact him after she found herself pregnant, and his security team threw her out of his office building. A pregnant woman. So yeah, I was a little afraid he'd do the same to me, once I found out who he was."

"And?" Rose prompted.

"And despite my fear, I immediately went to CBJ Corporation to see him anyway."

"You met with him?" Rose asked in shock.

Ava nodded. "I was smart enough to make an appointment with him, so his security team didn't throw me out of the building. After sharing who I was, Charles demanded I do a DNA test, so I did. I just received the results. Unfortunately, it was already too late. He died without knowing the truth." She looked away.

Once again, Rose thought this was all too convincing to be the truth.

"I don't believe you," Rose decided to be completely honest with her.

"I really don't care either way," Ava replied raising her chin ever so slightly.

"Are you sure about that?"

Humor from Ava's face disappeared. She took a step toward Rose. "Please, don't get in my way, Rose, you won't like it," she threatened ever so slightly.

"Or what?" Rose demanded, agitated by this turn of events. What was this woman going to do if Rose got in her way?

She didn't know what she expected from this conversation, but being threatened in her own home certainly wasn't it.

"If you become a problem to me, I will reveal a secret about you to the entire family, to the whole world if I have to, that will completely ruin your reputation with your family, and jeopardize your inheritance," she replied in a deadly whisper.

Rose's heart started to beat a little bit faster. She started laughing, nervously. "My reputation in the family is already pretty shitty," she pointed out, wondering what on earth Ava would have on her that would make her look any worse to them.

People in her family were always vicious to her, not to mention how much they liked to gossip, so Rose was confident that what Ava said would make no difference at all. Nothing she could do would impact her life.

She said as much.

Ava smirked. "I wouldn't completely agree with you on that one."

"Oh?"

"Yes, because, you see, I have DNA test results proving you aren't Charles's daughter at all. I'm sure your aunts and uncles would find that very interesting. In fact, I think that will most definitely make you lose your current position in the family, no matter how low you think it already is."

Rose's mind stopped working for a moment.

How was that even possible?

SIX

Charles Blaisdell was Ava's real father and not Rose's. This was Rose's worst nightmare proven true. Rose had always felt out of place in the Blaisdell family, and here was this new daughter who fit in better than Rose ever had, and she felt like she was being replaced. And now, thanks to the real daughter of the family, who seemingly had conclusive proof that Rose didn't belong, Rose was devastated.

Sadly, that wasn't the most important thing at the moment, that Rose's whole life, her whole identity, had been shattered. It was that Ava was actually blackmailing her with that information. Ava has threatened her with exposure for the fraud she was if she didn't fall in line. If she didn't accept Ava into the family without a fuss.

Is it all just a bluff?

Looking into Ava's eyes, which had completely changed now, and become much colder since there were only the two of them, Rose knew her threats were no bluff. Ava was prepared to destroy her if she got in her way.

Why?

And how did this secret child of her father's know the dirty little secret of her family? Had her father told her himself? *No*, she instantly rejected that. There was no way he would. Rose was sure her dad would never do that to her.

Is Ava lying about the proof she has about me?

Her gut told her yes, but she was afraid to trust it. All these questions and so much more passed through her head as she contemplated her next course of action. Then again, what was there to do? If she didn't want everyone discovering the truth, or at least the proof that Ava said she had, Rose would have to play nice. She didn't like that option one bit. As she realized she was completely cornered by this stranger, a strange kind of uncertainty, even fear of the future ahead, washed over her.

This woman is dangerous, Rose thought with clarity. And there was nothing Rose could do about it.

Ava was there to get the inheritance, and nothing and no one was stopping her. She was obviously ready to make sure of that. She had come prepared, which was beyond suspicious. Terrifying too.

"I can see that we're done here," Ava commented nonchalantly, before leaving the room. Obviously satisfied that her message was received loud and clear, she didn't feel the need to say anything else.

Rose didn't say anything. She simply stood there in the middle of the room, trying to wrap her mind around what had just happened.

Ava was Charles Blaisdell's daughter. She was certainly as ruthless as he was.

I'm not his daughter.

Who am I?

Rose felt like weeping again. She felt like raging. She felt like storming back into the living room and screaming at her mother in front of everyone for lying to her for thirty years. She did none of those things.

Taking a deep breath, she returned to the guests.

Perhaps it was her imagination, however, it appeared to her that Ava looked pretty smug now, being able to defeat her so easily.

Rose sat down on the couch, watching her. Ava talked with distant relatives, aunts, uncles, and cousins with ease. It was as though she had known all of them for years.

Rose could never accomplish something like that. Probably because she always knew she didn't belong. It was a completely different story with Ava.

And then Ava neared Adrian. Rose gritted her teeth, watching the two of them interact, talking, smiling. *Does he really have to be so polite with her? Doesn't he know he should pick a side, my side?* She knew she was being completely irrational, but she couldn't help it. Ava had taken her father already – did she need to commandeer her fiancé too?

It was surreal how they all acted around Ava. How they all welcomed her immediately, as though it was the most natural thing in the world to have a bastard daughter crash her father's funeral and announce she would be taking part in the inheritance. *Perhaps in this family, that is normal,* she realized.

Why is she still talking with Adrian? Rose fumed, wondering if she should walk over there and crash that party. Ava could steal Rose's place in the family, but she certainly wasn't getting Adrian as well.

That thought made her pause. Was Ava trying to steal her life? The more she watched the woman, the more convinced she got that she was. Intentionally or not, she was definitely working the room, working the family. Even Rose's mother wasn't spared, and her mother seemed to undeniably be falling for all that charm – fake charm.

As more time passed, and Ava continued her shameless complaining around the room, Rose became convinced this was all an act. She was pretending to be all good and friendly because she had an agenda. It was clear she knew if everyone was infatuated with her, nobody would contest her claim on the inheritance, especially Rose's mother.

Ava was nothing but a snake. Her private chat with Rose had confirmed as much. That was why it was difficult to suppress an eye roll while Ava, with tears in her eyes, talked about her past, and shared how she always wanted to be part of a large family like this one but was denied that because her mother was just one of Charles's side pieces.

Rose didn't like one bit how Ava talked about her father in such a manner. Charles Blaisdell was many things, but he was never intentionally cruel. He wasn't a sleazebag. And this was his funeral, for goodness' sake.

Are you sure? She had a moment of doubt.

Thanks to all these revelations, Rose had to start questioning everything. Because people were complex beings. Just because Charles Blaisdell was a good father to her, or at least he tried, to the best of his abilities, didn't mean Ava shared her experiences. Not that she was defending her. That woman came here and threatened her. Despite her sad story, she was an enemy, Rose was adamant.

And even if Charles Blaisdell cheated on his wife left and right, and had illegitimate children all over the United States, it was still cruel to speak about him in such a manner, on the day of his funeral, in front of his widow and his other children.

Not that Devon looked like he cared about what was coming out of Ava's mouth. He just stared at her as though fascinated by her. Like she was the glamorous, interesting sister he'd always wanted instead of Rose.

Seeing how all of this was driving her mad, Rose decided to focus on her mother. None of this could be easy on her. And Rose was right. It was obvious how much having Ava around pained her. All the same, her mother tried her best to be kind and welcoming to a woman claiming to be the child of her husband's infidelity. Sadly, Ava didn't appreciate the gesture as she continued to slander Charles and speak about him in this cruel, bitter manner to anyone who would listen.

She was villainizing Charles while making a saint out of her own mother. But she was no saint in Rose's book. She intentionally slept with a married man, a man she definitely knew was rich, and clearly tried to exploit that.

That fact it backfired was the reason Ava was here in the first place. Not because she was trying to gain a family but because she was trying to get the money her mother failed to secure herself.

I need a drink, she realized, too tired of her own thoughts.

On her way to the table, she overhead Devon sucking up to Ava as though wanting his new big sister's approval. And he wasn't too subtle about it.

It broke her heart to see her brother act like such a fool. He was a complete disappointment, and looking at him, Rose didn't see that changing any time soon. He shared the fate of many kids with super-rich parents. He was utterly spoiled, entitled, and without proper direction in life. As much as Rose loved him, she knew he was a wastrel.

Sadly, his behavior today definitely overshadowed all the bad decisions he'd made in his life. Devon stared at Ava with open amazement. It was like she was the brightest, shiniest new sister he'd just custom-ordered off the internet. Devon hung on her every word, taking them all at face value. It was really disturbing to Rose to watch him like this. And then there was Ava, who seemed as though she was actually encouraging him to treat her as his real big sister. Devon's behavior was hurtful to Rose, and she felt like dragging him to his room so she could slap some sense into him and remind him that she was his real sister, not this fake woman.

"Let me get you another drink, sis," Devon offered to Ava, skipping off like an eager-to-please little brother before quickly returning to Ava's side, waiting to be praised for a job well done. And the worst part was that he got it.

Ava patted his cheek and gave him a disgustingly sweet smile.

I'm gonna be sick, Rose thought, looking away. Ava was stealing her family right out from under her, and there was nothing she could do about it. How could Devon not see she was playing this all up to garner his acceptance of her? Rose had to get away from there. Perhaps all of this, this entire day, was nothing but a nightmare, and if she returned to her room and lay down, she would be able to wake up.

Rose turned, only to see Aunt Melinda standing there, looking at her with a strange glint in her eyes. *Is that from the wine or all the delicious scandals flying around?* Knowing Aunt Melinda, it was probably both.

"You can't be too happy about this turn of events," Aunt Melinda commented.

Rose said nothing to that and simply walked away. She couldn't stand to be in her aunt's presence, especially not today when her emotions were all over the place.

Her father wasn't the man she thought he was, and that shook her more than anything else. All this drama also meant that Rose had no time for mourning at all. Fires were starting all over this family, and Rose was the only one who could extinguish them.

Lucky me, she thought as she started for the stairs, desperate to get away from them all.

"Where are you going?" Adrian asked her.

"I need some fresh air," she said with a frown. Rose felt like if she didn't leave that place, she was bound to make a scene, and that was something she needed to avoid, for her mother's sake.

Adrian was about to reply when they both heard Aunt

Melinda speaking to Ava. She was definitely speaking loud enough to make sure that would be the case.

"I suggest it's only fair Ava gets Rose's share, considering all the facts."

"And what facts are those?" Peter, one of the cousins, asked, obviously confused.

"The fact that Ava is Charles's real daughter and Rose is not," Aunt Melinda replied without a thought.

Rose instantly looked at her mother. As expected, her mother grew red in the face, eyes flashing with fury.

Perhaps this is good. This way Ava cannot blackmail me, Rose thought.

"Maybe you should get tested too, simply to make sure all the money is kept in the family," Joey said to Devon.

Devon threw his glass against the floor. It shattered into a million pieces. "What did you just say to me?" Devon shouted, advancing toward a laughing Joey.

Of course, he wasn't afraid of Devon. He was a violent criminal. He was tougher and more skilled than Rose's brother. Although he looked like the aggressor at the moment, Rose knew Devon was about to get hurt.

I need to stop this, she thought with exasperation, running toward the two men who looked like they were about to start throwing punches.

She looked behind her to see if Adrian was following her because she could definitely use his help to stop this possible bloodshed when she realized he wasn't there. He remained by the door, looking someplace else. She followed his gaze to see he was looking at Ava.

Rose gritted her teeth, "Adrian? Little help," she snapped at him.

He frowned. "With what?"

"This," she said, pointing at the two men who were in the process of pushing one another, talking trash.

"Oh right, sorry. What can I do?" he asked, rushing to her side.

Rose frowned at the fact he'd been distracted by Ava but was grateful he'd joined her all the same. "Grab Devon, please, get him away from Joey."

"On it," he murmured.

Rose moved forward and said, "Stop that, right this instance," as she came between them. She looked like a toddler, between her brother and Joey. "Have you forgotten where you are? Why we're here?" she challenged. "Have some respect for the dead."

"He started it," Devon said, his lower lip poking out like a petulant child as Adrian drew him backward.

Luckily, Joey decided to walk away, but his eyes promised this was far from over.

Devon sulked after Adrian let him go.

Shortly after that, everyone left, and Rose was rattled to the bones. Her mother was her usual self, ignoring everything, pretending all was well, while sporadically weeping for her husband. Devon simply continued to comment how great his new sister was.

Hearing that, their mother decided it was time to lock herself in her bedroom. Rose wished she could do the same, but had to deal with her moronic brother, who was always so drunk she wondered why she should bother in the first place. It wasn't like he would remember anything in the morning.

"Could you not do that?" Rose snapped at him.

"Do what?"

Treat Ava like she's your long-lost favorite sibling when you just barely met her, and she might not even be your real sister! Rose wanted to let loose with her thoughts, but in Devon's current inebriated state, it would all go over his head.

"Go to sleep," she snapped instead of stating what was on

her mind. She would definitely have this conversation with him when he was sober.

This whole day was a nightmare, and she couldn't decide which part was the worst. Was it Ava appearing and threatening Rose? Or Aunt Melinda and her son, constantly making snide comments, trying to rile them all up. Devon acting like he was an eager little brother to his new favorite sister. All of it was making her feel sick to her stomach.

Perhaps the biggest disappointment was watching her fiancé, the man she loved with all her heart, get distracted by Ava's pretty face. Maybe she was overreacting, considering he had come to her rescue when she'd asked for help, but it still bothered her that he'd seemed enthralled by Ava. Rose felt a pang of jealousy – if someone like Ava had been in the room when she and Adrian met, would he have even chosen her in the first place?

It was pretty hard not to have an anxiety attack about this whole situation. Ava blackmailed her, and yet all eyes, all sympathy, were on her. Rose had nobody on her side except maybe her mother, who seemed just as upset as she was about Melinda's comments. But then again, she didn't seem to be too upset, or even that surprised, to find that her husband had fathered another child with a different woman.

Life wasn't fair, and sadly, she was used to that. The question was, what she was going to do about it?

SEVEN

There was no doubt in Rose's mind Ava would become a problem. Threatening Rose on the day of her— *their*—father's funeral proved that.

And to make matters worse, Rose's mother invited a bunch of the relatives to stay at the house. Even though Rose had arranged hotels for all of them, her mother made her cancel everything. Her reasoning was that, in tragedy, family had to stick together.

Thankfully, neither Aunt Melinda, Joey and his wife, nor Ava accepted that offer; however, many others did. Rose didn't have to wonder why all of them decided to stay. It wasn't simply because they wanted to be there for the reading of the will. It was for all the spectacle that would follow, thanks to Ava appearing in their lives. There's nothing wealthy folk love more than free entertainment, she'd noticed.

Bearing all that in mind, Rose had a lot of work to do and not a moment of rest to stop and catch her breath. Being solely responsible for all her father's affairs because Devon couldn't be bothered and because her mother was in a fragile state wasn't easy. Rose felt exhausted mentally, emotionally, and physically.

Rose decided to forgive Adrian for his temporary lack of judgment on the day of her father's funeral, which was a stressful day for all of them, and things returned to normal between them. As much as they could, considering everything that was happening.

He was sympathetic when she told him she would be staying with her mother and brother for the time being. She was also given leave from work so she could fully focus on her family.

Her staying for the time being had another function as well. She felt like she had to protect her family from Ava. It didn't matter that nobody else saw what she saw, she felt like the woman was a threat, and she would do anything to stop her from hurting her family.

She knew that wouldn't be an easy task. Ava proved she would be a formidable adversary. Still, Rose was not going to back down.

She couldn't rest, she had to remain vigilant. She needed to watch Ava to make sure she wasn't trying to do anything dishonest to her family. Maybe if she could find proof Ava was a bad person, the rest of the family would believe her. Without it, she knew if it came to her word against Ava's, many, if not all, would side with the other woman. Actually, if it came down to Rose's word or anyone else on the planet's, most of them still wouldn't believe her.

It would be good if Rose had at least one ally, but who should she approach?

Seeing no other way, Rose decided to speak with her mother. She was an obvious choice. Her mother would side with her own daughter. *Right?*

Rose found her mother in her room, sitting at her vanity table, retouching her spotless makeup, making sure her hair was perfect. It was. Rose has never seen her mother with a hair out of place.

"I still can't believe what happened," Rose commented, sitting on the bed, looking at her mother.

Her mom glanced at her in the mirror. "All families have their problems, my dear, apparently this is ours," she replied calmly.

That was too calm of her. Rose wondered if she was on something, her eyes darting to find telltale signs of orange pill bottles.

"Mom, are you all right?"

"I'm fine, dear," she answered simply.

Rose gave her mother a look because she knew that was code for *I am most definitely not all right. I'm falling apart knowing my husband had a child with another woman.* It was a hefty under-exaggeration.

"Tell me the truth," Rose insisted.

Her mother sighed, putting the makeup brush down.

"To be honest, I'm not that surprised your father did something like this to me back then. I mean, I always knew he was unfaithful prior to your birth, but I admit it's difficult seeing the result of his infidelity." She looked away with a pained expression on her face.

If you knew he cheated, then why stay married to him? was on the tip of Rose's tongue. She tried to think of a way to word it, but before she could, her mother spoke.

"I loved him. He hurt me, so I went and hurt him back."

Rose sucked in a breath. "What do you mean you hurt him back?"

Her mother looked at her in the mirror instead of turning to meet Rose's gaze face to face. It was as though the mirror gave her some distance from the accusations Rose knew were showing in her own face. "When I found out he was cheating on me, I decided that I could do the same to him."

Rose had to agree with her mother's previous statement. All

families had problems. It was just difficult because Rose now wondered if she was one. She kept that to herself though.

"You cheated on him."

"Rose, this discussion is really not proper. It was between me and your father, and it's in the past. We resolved our issues and carried on. We had you and then Devon."

"In the light of recent events, I believe we need to be completely honest with one another. That's the only way we can beat Ava."

Her mother frowned, then turned to properly look at her. "What are you talking about?"

"Just tell me the truth, Mom. You cheated on Dad around the time I was conceived, didn't you? Am I his?"

Thelma sighed again. "I had a few short flings, Rose, a few indiscretions, if you will, but only because I was very angry with your father for cheating on me," she explained, defending herself.

"I know that part. He cheated on you, and you decided to cheat on him as well."

"Yes, yes," she replied impatiently.

"Am I the result of that?"

"Rose, what has gotten into you today? Why do I feel like I am being interrogated?" her mother said, getting flustered.

Was this an admission of guilt?

"Mom, were you with another man around the time I was conceived?"

"Rose," she snapped, clearly appalled. "That is none of your business."

"I need to know who my real father is," Rose argued, getting agitated herself.

She hated that she was forced to do this. She was angry at her mother because she was the one who put her in this position in the first place. If she'd only divorced her husband, or if she'd only stayed faithful to him, then none of this would have happened.

"You know who your real father is. Charles *is* your real father."

"But everyone is saying..."

"I don't care about all the petty gossip, and neither should you," her mother interrupted.

"That's not what I'm trying to say," Rose replied. She was trying to tell her about Ava's blackmail.

"This discussion is over, Rose. I don't want to hear another word about it, ever again," her mother was adamant. And to make her point even clearer, she resumed putting makeup on, completely ignoring Rose and the steam coming from her ears.

Her mother was so infuriating that Rose was at a loss for words.

Rose got up, ready to leave, and paused midway. "If you're telling me the truth then why are Aunt Melinda and Joey insisting that I'm a bastard?"

"I don't have the answer to that question," her mother said softly.

But something in her posture was definitely suggesting otherwise.

I'm not Charles's daughter, but why is it so hard for her to admit it? What else don't I know? Who is my real father? Is it someone I know?

"Mom, who did you sleep with?" Rose dared to ask.

For a split moment, she couldn't decide if her mother was about to start shouting at her or burst into tears. In the end, she didn't do any of those things. She flashed her trademark smile. "It doesn't matter who I was with all those years ago, Rose. They meant nothing then, and they certainly have no effect on our lives now." The smile was gone, and instead, she shook with revulsion.

Rose wasn't so sure about that. What if one of them were her biological father?

Her mother shook her head. "Please, Rose, stop with all the questions, I'm tired of them."

"I'll stop when you start being honest with me. I need real answers, especially now that this second daughter has appeared in our lives."

"Is that what all this is about? You feel threatened by Ava?" her mother asked.

Rose stayed silent. It was true she did feel threatened, but that wasn't the entire truth.

"Rose, I urge you to see yourself as a legitimate part of this family, no matter what other people try to say to you. Charles is your father. He raised you like a daughter, and he claimed you as his daughter. That should be enough to convince you that he is your father, and he would be heartbroken to think you don't believe that."

All Rose was hearing was that he wasn't her real father. And Ava claimed she had DNA proof that was the case. She knew she could easily find out if she went to a clinic and had a test done, but she wasn't sure she wanted proof that she wasn't his. It was bad enough her mom was basically confirming Ava's proof, she didn't need to see it for herself, not right now. Maybe one day when the thought wasn't so depressing.

"I'll start acting as a true member of this family, but you need to do something for me as well."

"What, dear?" her mother asked, in a much calmer manner now.

"Don't be so welcoming toward Ava. She's not family. She's not to be trusted," Rose insisted.

"Don't worry, dear. I don't plan on adopting the girl. As far as I'm concerned, she can have a small portion of the inheritance then go her way, out of our lives. You're so willful, Rose, in your own way, but you can't afford to be on your high horse here. Haven't you ever heard of keeping your friends close..."

"But your enemies closer." Rose had to admit her mother's words were reassuring.

Having that settled, Rose left. Although she didn't get the chance to share the whole truth with her mother, she realized she didn't have to. Her mother wouldn't be fooled by Ava, no matter how sweet-tongued the other woman was.

As Rose contemplated what to do next, she stumbled on Devon. Her brother was rummaging through their father's liquor cabinet, swaying slightly as he regained his balance.

Devon glanced at her over his shoulder before continuing with his search. "He always hid the good stuff in the study," he said, taking one of the bottles out, and then sniffing at the contents before putting it back.

Rose felt like snapping at her brother. Not just because he was disrupting her father's things when she wanted to preserve his study as it was, but because he'd clearly already had enough to drink.

It was time to admit her brother had a serious drinking problem.

"I need to speak with you about Ava." Rose decided to put everything to the side and focus on the main issue at the moment.

"Are you jealous I finally have a cool sister?" He jibed. "She's even a doctor. How awesome is that?"

"Can you stop that and be serious for one moment? I don't even think she's a medical doctor. I'm pretty sure she's merely got her PhD."

His face turned grave in an instant. "Do you think Ava will come on vacation with us? It would be cool to have someone fun around for a change. You've sucked the fun out of every single one."

Rose felt like smacking him across the face. "Can you stop?"

Devon sighed, finally grabbing one of the bottles. "I was just joking around. God, do you have to be so serious all the time," he whined, walking away from her. "Lighten up a little, I was only teasing you. You're still my sister. I just find it kind of cool that I have another one. One who won't try and force me to go to lame-ass museums on the weekends. Or one that tries to act like my mom."

Rose followed after him.

The reason she was serious all the time was because she had to be. Having such a clown for a brother meant all the responsibilities were always on her. Not that Devon cared.

Rose glared at him as he took a serious gulp of whiskey straight from the bottle. "Our father just died, this woman claiming to be our half-sister just shows us and you want me to lighten up? Are you for real?" she asked incredulously.

He actually had the audacity to roll his eyes at her. "I can't speak with you when you act all hysterical," he said, pointing in the general direction at her with his bottle.

"I'm not hysterical, Devon, I'm furious," she pointed out.

"And I didn't do anything wrong to have you unload all your crap on me. If you have problems, speak with your therapist or something and leave me alone," and with that, he stormed out of the room.

Rose could only stare after him. This was so typical of him. He was used to running away each time things became too real for him. She blamed her parents for that. They spoiled him too much, and as a result, Rose had no idea what to do with him.

"What happened? I heard yelling." Adrian appeared a few seconds later.

She immediately went into his arms. "I tried speaking with Devon, and it didn't go well," she complained.

"Well, he's been drinking since noon. You have to accept your brother has a problem. He needs help from a therapist, or maybe AA would do him good."

They parted to sit on the couch.

"I know. I wish he'd see that, but that wasn't what I meant. It's just... this is insane. I can't believe this is my life now. And the way people act around me makes me believe I woke up in some alternate universe because nothing makes sense anymore."

As Rose complained, Adrian started texting with someone, wearing a strange half-smile on his face.

"Adrian, are you even listening to me?"

"Of course."

"What did I say?"

"You saw a movie about an alternate universe."

She gritted her teeth. She was definitely in an alternate universe because all of a sudden even her fiancé was acting like an asshole.

"You are unbelievable," she said getting up and going to her room.

"Rose, where are you going? What happened?" he asked after her.

Perhaps things will start making sense again tomorrow. That was the hope anyway.

EIGHT

Feeling completely fed up with everything and everyone, Rose decided to return to her apartment, at least for a while. Adrian joined her, and despite her doubts when she saw him looking at Ava, he continued to show her compassion and understanding of her crazy family. Maybe she'd been too hard on him?

"Can I get you anything?" he asked, heading to the kitchen.

"I think I just need to lie down and decompress. Is that alright?" Rose asked, feeling vulnerable. She'd been with her family for so long that she didn't even feel like herself anymore.

"Of course, would you like me to run you a bath?" he asked, being very solicitous.

The idea of a hot, relaxing bath sounded even better than her bed. "That would be great," Rose answered.

Adrian headed into the bathroom, and Rose heard the water turn on. What had she been worried about? He was such a fantastic fiancé. He was always looking after her. The grief and the business with Ava were clearly making her erratic. She couldn't let it affect their relationship – she couldn't let him go. She followed him into the room and saw he was lighting a few candles for her, and he'd poured in her favorite bubble bath.

"Thank you, you're the best," she murmured, moving into his embrace.

"It's been a stressful time. In fact, maybe you need some alone time? I can get out of here and go back to my place, let you just process everything, if that's what you need."

Rose bit her lip. The idea of having her place to herself was both welcoming and a bit frightening. She didn't really want him to leave, but he was right. She needed to process not only her dad's death but Ava's appearance. "You don't have to leave..." she said hesitantly.

"I hear a 'but' in your tone," he said with a slight smirk. "It's okay to take time for yourself. Besides, I've got a meeting first thing tomorrow morning. If I stay, I'll just wake you early, and you probably need to sleep in."

"You're sure?" Rose still wasn't sure she wanted him to go, but what he was saying made total sense.

"Yeah, it's fine. I'll text you tomorrow, and we'll figure all this out. Don't worry, Rose, everything is going to work out just as it should." He held her close for a moment and then kissed her gently. "Now, go enjoy your bath, and I'll see you tomorrow."

Rose nodded and smiled as he left the room. As she put her hair up, she heard him leave the apartment and then she turned to the tub and shut down the water. She decided to grab a glass of wine and turn on some classical music before taking her bath.

She knew she was stressed and sleep-deprived, but she was almost sorry that he'd left. As she sank into the tub, she wondered if he was just a little too anxious to leave her. She knew she needed him a lot more than he needed her. She counted on him to be her rock. Her soft place to land, but was she that for him? She didn't know. She tried to be, but these past few days, since her father died, well, she'd become extremely needy.

Was he pulling away? she wondered. *Did he really have an early meeting?* There was no way for her to know if it was true or not. She was probably just being paranoid because of everything with Ava. She was not only doubting herself, she was doubting him, and that couldn't stand. She needed to push those thoughts away and take control before her paranoia pushed him out of her life. She'd ruined so many past relationships by having her father in the back of her mind, telling her to trust no one. And where had that gotten her? She couldn't let herself do that to a guy as sweet as Adrian.

She decided to focus on Ava and what her agenda might be. As she sat there in the cooling water, the scent of lavender surrounding her, she found that she was consumed with anger and resentment toward her supposed half-sister. Ava had not only come into their lives hoping to steal her father's money, but to destroy Rose, and she didn't know what to do about that. She was no match for Ava. Sadness ached in her heart at the thought that Ava was going to take everything from her. Maybe she could just make sure that Ava got a cut of the money, and then she'd go away, but somehow, Rose doubted she would. There was something else behind what Ava was doing, and Rose just couldn't let it go.

Ava was physically perfect, knew how to dress, and talk, and act to accentuate all her attributes. Now she would also have a lot of money to go with that attitude.

Rose groaned loudly. She was sick and tired of her thoughts about Ava because they were making her extremely miserable.

I really shouldn't be that insecure, she chastised herself.

Ava is messing with my head, she is making me crazy, she realized. Rose knew she shouldn't give the other woman that kind of power. She didn't deserve it.

Unfortunately, she couldn't silence that other voice inside of herself completely. It still had questions. Rose was now examining everything, and she had to be vigilant.

She couldn't take anything for granted. She would observe

what was happening around her, she would shake all the foun-
dations to make sure they stood on solid legs, and not just the
people in her family, she would include her colleagues and her
fiancé as well. She wanted to be sure that she was as good to
him as he was to her. She'd need to make an effort to keep him
happy and secure in their relationship and not just be a taker.
She needed to make sure she was making time for him as he had
for her. It was only fair.

It was time to have concrete proof that all her relationships
were on the right path. And those that weren't either got fixed,
or she would let them go. She didn't need them in her life. She
was, of course, thinking about her father's family. Perhaps not
all of them were bad, but those who listened to Melinda and
Joey and their awful gossip, she needed to consider letting go of.

But what if it's not just gossip? Rose thought. *What if what
Ava, Melinda, and Joey were saying was true?*

The thought that Charles may not be her father flashed
through her mind, and her heart ached all over again. She
couldn't think of him as anything other than her father. In every
sense of the word, except for maybe biologically, he was her
father. He'd never treated her as less. He'd always loved and
cared for her. Wasn't that what a father did?

Rose climbed out of the bath and got ready for bed. She lay
beneath her comforter for hours, not sleeping, her mind keeping
her awake as she worried and fretted over things she couldn't
change. As the clock neared four a.m., she finally drifted off to
sleep, but it was a fitful sleep, and she woke in stops and starts.
She'd had some very disturbing dreams, and when the alarm
went off at eight, she couldn't recall them, only that she'd been
left in cold sweats and with a deep feeling that something was
wrong. She felt like staying in bed, forgetting everything, hiding
from the outside world, if only for a little bit longer. However,
her mother was completely relying on her now, so she needed to
get moving.

Taking a deep breath, she got out of bed, quickly showered, and then dressed, driving back to her parents' house. Later that day they would be having the reading of the will. Mr. Merser, her father's lawyer and the executor of the will, would be coming to the house to read it, as his office was rather small and wouldn't accommodate all of the relatives who wanted to be there.

Rose had to brace herself and prepare mentally, and emotionally, knowing Ava would be present as well, though there was no way she would be in the will.

Adrian had texted her that morning to ask if she wanted him there, but she'd said no. She knew that he had meetings scheduled all day, and she didn't want to take him away from work more than necessary. It wasn't fair to him for her to do that. So she thanked him and told him that she'd be okay.

As Ava walked in, Rose had to try really hard not to express all the fury she was feeling toward the woman. She still couldn't believe Ava had actually threatened her.

What a snake.

A few seconds later, Adrian walked in as well.

Smiling, Rose walked over to join him. "What are you doing here?" she asked, happily surprised to see him.

"I know you said you didn't need me, but I felt like I needed to be here, so I rearranged my schedule and came." He kissed her cheek. "I promise I'll just hang back here and stay out of the way unless you need me."

Rose gazed into his eyes and gave him a nod. It was such a sweet gesture and so like him to think of her needs before his own. She was actually relieved he was there because she had a feeling that she was going to need all the support she could get if things went the way half these people thought it should.

"Thank you." She gave him a kiss on the cheek and then went to join her mother in the group of chairs set at the front of the room.

Her mother had rearranged the library like a lecture hall with numerous chairs for the guests and the massive wooden desk for Mr. Merser to sit behind as he read the will facing them all. The chairs her mother had chosen were in the first row, front and center.

Almost as soon as Rose had sat down, Ava took the seat next to her. Rose bit her tongue because, if she didn't, she would ask her what the hell she was thinking. It was insulting for her to sit alongside Rose, Devon, and her mother, as though she was just another one of Charles's children and had every right to be there. Did she have no grace at all?

Does she really expect to be in the will? Why does she think that she's getting any money, considering Dad never bothered to even recognize her as his child in the first place? Perhaps the thought was cruel, but she didn't care. This woman was disrupting her family and had threatened her directly, and Rose had every right to feel angry.

"Good afternoon. My name is Ed Merser, and I was Charles's personal and business lawyer. He's asked me to be executor of his will." He looked out over everyone and then said, "I ask that you all remain seated as I read through his last will and testimony." He cleared his throat and began... "I, Charles Blaisdell, being of sound mind and body, do hereby declare that all of my wealth, business, and personal holdings be split equally between my wife, Thelma Blaisdell, my daughter Rose Blaisdell and my son, Devon Blaisdell, with the exception of a few gratuitous gifts to my staff who have been with me all these many years."

Rose was stunned for a moment. And she wasn't the only one.

However, it wasn't long before all hell broke loose.

"This is a travesty," Aunt Melinda shrieked.

"I can't believe he didn't leave us a single cent," Joey groused.

"Cheap bastard," Nick grumbled.

Mr. Merser waved his hands for everyone to retake their seats. "Please, this is what Charles wanted. Now do hold your tongues and allow me to continue."

He went on to talk about the gratuitous gifts to the staff, which ranged from five to ten thousand to a handful of them, from the housekeeper and personal chef to the gardener and her father's chauffer, but also included several maids who were gifted two thousand each. He then spoke of the accounts, the properties, and the business and how everything was to be divided among the three of them. There were several vacation properties, and while her father had listed which ones went to who, he'd also allowed that, if they wished to trade or sell them, to speak with Mr. Merser about how to go about doing so.

The business was set up in a trust that the three of them were equal partners in, while the business itself would be run by his brother Kenneth as the new president. When Rose's father had run the company, he hadn't taken a salary, but seeing as Kenneth wouldn't have a stake in ownership, he would. Kenneth had been the vice president, so he would be promoted up and his salary would be increased to accommodate all of his new duties. All other staff and salary changes would be brought before the three of them to be approved, as they would be acting as the board of directors for the business.

As to her father's wealth, the amount of money he'd accumulated was staggering and rested upwards of twelve billion dollars. She couldn't even contemplate how much money that actually was.

"And this concludes the reading of the will. Thank you all for coming," Mr. Merser said in the end.

However, nobody was listening to him, as they were too busy complaining among themselves, feeling robbed of the inheritance. Except for Kenneth, who seemed pretty pleased with his promotion and salary increase.

Devon looked at his mother and then at Rose with the biggest grin on his face. Rose felt like hitting him on the head. She couldn't feel happy about the money because in order to get it, her father had died. She would trade it all just to have him back. Unfortunately, she wasn't sure her brother felt the same way.

Ava rose from her seat in a huff. "I will be suing for my portion of the estate," she informed Mr. Merser, "you will be hearing from my lawyer."

Mr. Merser gave her a baleful look and nodded.

Aunt Melinda approached Ava, patting her back. "Of course, you should sue, my dear. It's not fair you were left out while others were so generously awarded for no reason."

Rose rolled her eyes.

"I simply want what's mine," Ava said, as though defending herself.

Aunt Melinda nodded. "Of course, I understand. Charles should take responsibility at least in death if he wasn't so inclined while alive."

Rose wasn't surprised Melinda was bad-mouthing her brother. She always jumped at the opportunity to slander him. Especially if it hurt Rose or her mother in the process.

As they shared their moment, Rose's mother stood and regally walked out of the library. Several relatives commented on how rude that was, how dramatic – but a moment later, she returned with two maids in tow, offering everyone some refreshments.

Rose was proud of her mother. She was always a great hostess, even when her guests were deeply undeserving of such attention. Nobody refused food or drinks, and conversations about what just happened continued. Rose forced herself to stay, even though all she wanted to do was run back to the safety of her apartment with Adrian. Her mother needed her here; who knew what would happen if she left her to these wolves?

As far as she could gather, most of her relatives were encouraging Ava to take the matter to court and contest the will. Rose knew they weren't doing so out of the goodness of their hearts.

This is their revenge because they were left out.

And Ava was just nodding and agreeing to everything that was said. Rose watched as Ava sobbed into the shoulder of one of the aunts about how her father completely forgot about her in his will. She gasped that she couldn't believe he left her with nothing, after everything he put her mother through.

But Rose knew it was all just an act. Ava was a huge manipulator, and it was obvious she would do whatever it took to get her hands on the money. The man she described was not Rose's father, and she couldn't believe his so-called family was allowing this stranger to slander him after his death. Even if she hadn't tried to blackmail Rose, she would still think that.

She looked around to see where Adrian was and hear his thoughts about all that happened.

She spotted him by the door leaning against one of the bookshelves, and he was staring at Ava again, with a strange expression on his face.

Was it longing? Rose wondered.

Filled with anger, and with her ego wounded, Rose gritted her teeth and left the room.

NINE

Her mother, being the gracious host that she was, invited everyone who was at the reading of the will to stay for dinner. A few declined and left in a fury, but the rest, including Ava, Aunt Melinda, her son Joey and his wife, decided to stay.

Rose groaned inwardly, wishing her mother wouldn't worry about appearances so much and simply throw all the leeches out. That was what Rose would do if she was allowed.

Rose stayed away from Adrian, feeling like she was bound to start a fight if they actually talked, and she couldn't do that, not today of all days. Unfortunately, he must have sensed she was avoiding him because he was following her around the house.

Speaking of Ava, that woman actually had the audacity to ask Mr. Merser if he could represent her in her legal matters. She pretended to be a damsel in distress, confessing she had no knowledge of such legal matters and wouldn't even know where to start with contesting the will, and begged for his help.

"It must have been an oversight," she pleaded. "When was the will dated? He only saw the DNA results shortly before he died, surely, I have a case?"

Rose's ears pricked up. "You must be confused." Rose narrowed her eyes. "You told me he never got the chance to see them."

Ava didn't even flinch. "I never said that. If you want to beat me in court, you'd better have some better evidence than whatever you just make up off the top of your head."

Rose went to bite back, but her family's interjections suggesting the names of their lawyers drowned her out.

It was unquestionably an act. But how was it that she was the only one seeing it?

Mr. Merser declined, thankfully, on the grounds of it being a conflict of interest, however he offered to make a list of suitable lawyers she could ask. She thanked him, punctuating her words by touching him on the arm. Rose noted Ava was very physical, especially with men. She already had more than half of Rose's uncles and male cousins wrapped around her little finger. Even Joey seemed to be falling for her charm.

Was touching them a form of manipulation? Probably.

It was as comical as it was tragic how everyone competed among themselves to see who would sit next to Ava during dinner. In the end, Aunt Melinda and Joey won.

Rose was quite surprised when Adrian immediately came to sit next to her. It was on the tip of her tongue to ask if some other seat would suit him better. A place with a better view of Ava. She didn't, but only because she didn't want him to think she was jealous or something worse.

Rose barely exchanged a few words with him because she was still hurt by the look he'd been giving Ava. She couldn't care less if the rest of the family chased after Ava while they completely ignored her, but Adrian was supposed to be hers. He wasn't supposed to be lusting after any other woman, let alone Rose's half-sister. And maybe she was letting her jealousy of the pretty woman get the best of her, but she couldn't help how she was feeling. It was making her think that she'd rushed into this engagement without really knowing if they were right for each other.

Was she sabotaging her relationship by thinking this way? Maybe, but then, in the back of her mind, she could hear her father saying, *Adrian isn't good enough for you. He's just a gold digger. He's going to break your heart.* And now, she was starting to wonder if he was right. Maybe Adrian wasn't the right one for her.

Her father had been right before in the past, but when it came to Adrian, she hadn't listened. She'd been so blinded by the fact that he was handsome and successful and seemed to love everything about her that she'd fallen head over heels for him. But what did she really know about him?

She was starting to think that she would much rather be alone than with the wrong person. So, if Adrian wasn't strong enough to resist one random woman because she was so good-looking and charming, then he definitely wasn't for Rose.

If his love for her was so weak, then they should part.

Shouldn't they?

Rose looked up and noticed that Ava had her eyes on Adrian as she spoke to Joey. She was looking at him like he was being served up for dinner and it made Rose lose her appetite. She gritted her teeth and twisted her fork in her food on her plate, trying to ignore Ava, but the woman laughed as though she could read Rose's mind.

"What are you thinking about so intently?" Adrian whispered in her ear. "Are you okay?"

Rose frowned and slid her gaze to him. She couldn't blurt out that her jealousy of her supposed half-sister was getting to her and making her think he was going to cheat on her. He'd really done nothing to warrant her accusing him of anything other than looking at Ava for a moment. Rose feared it was all in her head, and she was about to lose one of the best relationships she'd ever had because she couldn't control her jealousy. She needed to get herself together.

So, Rose shook her head. "Nothing important," she lied.

It was hard admitting she was, in fact, jealous of Ava. How could she not be? The entire family was eating from the palm of her hand.

On any other occasion, Rose would welcome having someone around who would claim all the attention because Rose really didn't like being in the center of things. But she didn't trust Ava or her intentions. Everything the other women said and did raised Rose's hackles.

She didn't trust Ava. Not one little bit.

Rose felt slightly detached as she watched what was happening around her during dinner. It was more than obvious Ava got her hooks into each and every member of Rose's family. And that was frightening, and infuriating. No matter how crazy it sounded, Rose felt obliged to save her family from the woman. It didn't matter that many of them had treated her badly all her life. Nobody deserved to be played for a fool, or whatever Ava was planning on doing.

That was one of the main problems; besides taking the money, Rose had no idea what Ava really wanted from her family. And Rose knew Ava definitely wanted something. Because if she didn't, if she only cared about the money, then she wouldn't be in that dining room with all of them, manipulating the people around her, making them her allies.

Rose was aware of one thing. She could easily get up and walk out of that room without ever feeling guilty because she didn't owe anyone here anything. And she wouldn't even feel a dent in her wallet if her father's inheritance was split into four equal parts rather than three. It made no real impact on her life, as she would be using her share to fund various charities and art centers and help people who were less fortunate than she was. It would be better if they got a larger donation, of course, but it wasn't about the money. It wasn't even the fact that there was someone claiming to be their sibling that bothered her so much. She wouldn't begrudge any legitimate heir their equal share. This was about Ava in particular. Something about the woman told Rose that she was a liar. A fake, a phony. And if they legitimized her, it would prove all of the awful things she was saying about their father were true. His memory would be ruined. She claimed to have proof, not only that she was Charles's daughter but also that Rose wasn't.

Those thoughts kept her seated. Rose couldn't leave. She couldn't leave her family with the woman. Her intentions weren't pure, she wasn't being honest.

At first, Rose simply thought loyalty and the sense of morals her father instilled in her kept her in place, but as the evening progressed, other feelings inside of Rose emerged.

Rose felt like everyone was rubbing her nose in the fact she wasn't Charles's daughter, while they praised and showered Ava with love and attention at every corner even though she hadn't shown them any actual proof that she was his real daughter. As Joey had said that first day, papers could be faked. But now it seemed they were all just going to take her at her word.

Rose wanted to uncover the truth of what Ava was up to and then rub her family's nose in it. She wanted to be the one saying, *I told you so.* That would be a reward for all the years of being put to the side, mocked, and bullied.

So, although Rose saw this as her chance to get back at her family in a way, she also felt life would be better if Ava never came into their lives in the first place. She needed to find out what Ava was planning. What was her agenda? What made her tick? And most of all, if she really was Charles's daughter.

How to do something like that? Rose couldn't very well ask Ava about her intentions; she would laugh in her face, or simply threaten her again.

Rose could call one of her old college friends, those who

knew Ava, and ask around. However, she didn't like that idea very much. She didn't want Ava being tipped off that Rose was still suspicious of her.

I need a better plan.

Unfortunately, at the moment, she had nothing. But she was not giving up. She was not going down without a fight. Ava thought she could force Rose into compliance.

Father had taught her better than that.

She would fight for her relationships – all of them, including Adrian, and she would fight for her place in the family. Even if all her relatives refused to respect her, she would just force them like her father had. And she would most definitely fight for her inheritance because he'd wanted her to have it.

If her father hadn't left anything to Ava, then there must have been a reason for it. He was always a fair man, and Rose decided to respect his judgment.

After dinner and a lot of wine, Rose decided she had played nice long enough.

She decided to start her silent war against Ava with Adrian. She would show him she was the better woman in every regard. She led him up to her old room with what she hoped was an alluring smile. She was ready to leave for her apartment, but first, she wanted to drive Adrian to distraction so Ava would see who exactly he was engaged to, and she would keep her looks and her paws to herself.

"I'm glad you came over today, I missed you last night." She wrapped her arms around his neck and peppered his lips with kisses.

Adrian grinned and slid his arms around her waist. "I missed you too." He leaned back and looked at her with curiosity. "Are you sure you're okay?"

"Mmm, I'm fine. Maybe too much wine." She smiled, giving

him a look of love. "Drive me home?" she murmured. "Stay the night?"

He leaned down and kissed her passionately as Rose pressed herself up against him. "Of course," he murmured, kissing her more.

Taking his hand, Rose led him back down the stairs, knowing her hair was slightly mussed and her lips bruised from his kissing. She grinned as she waved to everyone and said, "Goodnight, Adrian and I are heading back to my place." She especially enjoyed the look of displeasure on Ava's face.

Later, as they lay on the bed in postcoital bliss, and Adrian softly snored beside her, Rose thought about her next course of action.

She planned on visiting Mr. Merser first thing in the morning to see if there was a way to block Ava from getting anything.

In the morning, Rose returned to the room to see Adrian with his phone in his hand, seated on the side of the bed. She wanted to ask Adrian if he could drive her to the lawyer's office, but he seemed distant, distracted, almost sullen.

"Is something the matter?"

"Work stuff," he brushed it off before quickly dressing.

For some reason, he wasn't looking at her. The same thing happened last night as well, while they made love. He had his eyes closed the whole time. She didn't think anything of it then, too consumed by passion, heated with wine, but now she found it strange. Was there something going on at his job that he was worried about?

She walked over to him, ready to embrace him, when she noticed a strange floral scent on his jacket. It smelled like a woman's perfume, not something she'd wear at all. She always wore something vanilla-based when she wore perfume. She leaned in to get a better whiff of it, and he backed up.

"I have to go," he murmured before rushing out of the room without even giving her a kiss.

"But—" She didn't even get a full sentence out before he was through the apartment door and gone.

Rose couldn't help how her mind immediately went to a place it shouldn't. *Was he having an affair? Was that why he hadn't wanted her close to him in that jacket? Had he been with another woman? One who wore that floral scent?*

It wouldn't be the first time a guy had done that to her, but she really hadn't expected that from Adrian. Her heart hurt at the thought, but she couldn't think of any other reason for him to have run off like that without giving her even a second thought.

The bigger question was, if he was having an affair... who was it with?

Someone at work... or was it Ava?

That thought sent a chill through her heart. *Please don't let that be true.*

TEN

"Please, Rose, speak with your mother before making any major decisions," Mr. Merser implored.

"The woman is an opportunist, Mr. Merser. She's already telling everyone that my father abandoned her and her mother, how much worse could it get? Father made his will, he had an opportunity to include her, and he didn't. He must have had his reasons." Rose was adamant. In a perfect world, Rose wanted Ava kept from getting her hands on any of her father's money. But that wasn't what today was about. Today was about saving her family and maybe her relationship with Adrian.

"I'll warn you, if she has DNA proof, the courts may side with her, even though Charles's will is legal and binding."

"I'm hoping it won't even make it that far, that's why I asked for your help. We don't even know if her DNA proof is real."

He nodded. "Very well. I'll give it to you." He wrote something down and handed her the piece of paper. On it was a phone number, and a street address that felt familiar to her.

"Thank you. Hopefully, I'll be able to find out what she's really after."

"I wish you luck. I don't actually believe that Charles was

capable of doing what she is claiming, Rose. I hope you know that."

Rose was glad to hear that he respected her father and believed he hadn't abandoned Ava and her mother. Not in the way Ava had said, at any rate. It was nice to feel like someone was on her side. She left him then and steeled her nerves for her next mission.

As soon as she left Mr. Merser's office, she hailed a cab and went to the address on the slip of paper. It was time for her and Ava to have an honest chat without prying eyes or ears.

Ava had managed to fool the rest of the family, but not Rose. *That's probably why she threatened me and not someone else,* she thought.

Reaching the correct address, Rose frowned. First of all, now she knew why the address was so familiar to her. It was a hotel she sometimes booked for her out-of-town authors. And second, she found it strange Ava was staying at the hotel in the first place. *Is she already spending money she hasn't inherited yet?* Rose wondered, going inside.

She went to the courtesy phone and dialed the number on the paper. After a moment, Ava answered, and Rose let her know she'd like to speak with her. Ava paused and then gave her the room number to come up.

"This is a surprise," she commented in her usual, nonchalant manner as she opened the door.

"This is a very nice hotel," Rose said, simply to say something.

"I'm here out of necessity. The main water pipe in my apartment burst, ruining everything. I'm staying here until the landlord takes care of it. God only knows how long that will take," she complained.

"How long have you been here?" Rose asked. She knew this hotel was pretty pricy, so it didn't make sense to spend weeks on end in the place just because of a maintenance problem. *Well, not unless you expected to inherit billions...*

"Almost two weeks, why?" Ava arched a brow.

Once again Rose wondered how she could afford to stay in this place for so long. Then again, she was a doctor. Or so she'd said. *Is she a medical doctor? I thought she was the PhD kind. Am I wrong?*

The room Ava was staying in was actually a suite, and pretty lavish at that. It offered a nice view of the city as well. How was she affording it all?

"I will skip all the pleasantries and just ask, what are you doing here, Rose?" Ava asked. She looked mildly surprised, if not annoyed, that Rose was standing there, in front of her. She covered her true feelings rather quickly, which was more proof of how great an actress she was.

Rose sat down in one of the chairs by the window without being offered a seat. She wasn't going to allow Ava to intimidate her this time, or get rid of her that easily.

"You've been to my family home several times now, and I wanted to see where you lived," Rose replied with a small shrug. "Can't say I was expecting this."

"Satisfied?" Ava replied.

"As I said, this is a nice hotel."

"It's agreeable. However, I know you didn't come here so we could trade experiences regarding accommodations."

"That's true," Rose agreed. "I have a favor to ask of you."

Surprise flashed across Ava's face before she raised her eyebrows and stared at her. "A favor?" she repeated.

"Yes."

"I hope it's not for me to drop my claim regarding the inheritance because that's something I would never do. I deserve my share," she said that last part with great vigor, crossing her arms over her chest.

"It's not that, but it's related," Rose said.

"Oh? Tell me what you have in mind."

"Once you take your quarter of the estate, I want you to leave my family alone," Rose said blatantly, then added *my fiancé included*, in her head. Rose had originally wanted to fight and prevent Ava from getting anything; however, if she was to see the back of her, she had to give her something. Even if she wasn't Charles's daughter, if it meant saving her family from Ava's manipulations, then she would do it.

Ava narrowed her eyes at that, looking at Rose as though trying to read her thoughts and figure her out. "What kind of a request is that?" she asked, instead of agreeing.

"A reasonable one," Rose replied simply. And she truly meant it. Ava had no business coming to family gatherings and interacting with them all because she wasn't family. If their father had wanted her to be, then he would have claimed her and brought her home. The fact that he didn't do that spoke volumes to Rose.

And what if he's not really her father and this is all a scam? Rose continued to doubt, but she wanted this woman gone from their lives, and this would be the fastest way to get rid of her.

"Are you jealous of me?" Ava asked, snapping her from her thoughts.

Rose wasn't surprised she picked up on that, but she remained silent.

"Are you worried your family likes me more than you? Is that the reason you made this strange proposition?" she challenged.

Ava was baiting her, and she knew it. Unfortunately, it was working.

Ava sighed. "I understand your concerns, Rose. I truly do, and I can't say they are completely without merit."

"What's that supposed to mean?"

"Your family already likes me better than you. I mean, I've

already been invited to cousin Suzanne's wedding next July," she jibed.

Rose didn't even know she was engaged.

"Unfortunately, you only have yourself to blame, not me."

"And how is that?" Rose asked, raising her chin ever so slightly.

"Well, look at you," Ava said, gesturing in Rose's direction as though that was an explanation enough.

"I'm sorry, I think I'll need more than that."

Ava sighed again. "Despite all your family's money, not to mention the legacy you belong to, you behave and dress like a bland little worker drone. You never participate in your family's activities or go to the fundraisers, and you choose to *work for a living*." She said that last part as though it was a dirty word or something.

When did it become a crime to work for a living? Rose very much liked her job, and wouldn't trade it for being chairwoman of all the charities in the world.

Then again, Ava made a point there. She did stand out in her family, she was different. *Why is that such a bad thing? Because it shows others how bad they are,* she realized.

"Let's face it, Rose, no wonder they all think of you as a loser. Deep down, you know that you don't belong, and everything you do reflects that. That is why I fit with them better than you ever could," she smirked.

The longer Ava talked, the angrier Rose became. At the same time, she started to feel a certain amount of helplessness. Ava was a dangerous adversary.

Going into battle was never Rose's strongest suit. She missed her father. He would know exactly what to do in this situation. But then again, he was the reason she was in this situation in the first place.

"It takes more than clothes to be part of the Blaisdell family," Rose replied. "And although it's true they are all smitten

with you at the moment, that infatuation is completely temporary. They will get bored of you, and then they will see right
through you, as I do."

"And what do you see, Rose?" Ava challenged.

"I see an opportunistic woman who will stop at nothing to
achieve her goals. It's just that I don't know what those goals are
at the moment."

"That's true. And in return, I see a scared little rich girl who
won't be able to stop me."

Rose made a face. "If you're done insulting me, I still need
an answer from you."

"I've grown so tired of this boring conversation. I have no
idea what you're referring to."

"What do you want, Ava?" Rose asked.

"I think I already made myself perfectly clear on that."

"I mean what do you want, besides the money," Rose
corrected. "What do you want from my family?"

"I believe we've already established they're not your family,
Rose," Ava jibed.

"Don't try to deflect, and answer me," Rose insisted.

Without answering, Ava got up from her seat and went to a
writing desk in the corner. From there, she grabbed a piece of
paper from the drawer.

She returned immediately to hand the paper to Rose. Her
eyes scanned the scientific jargon, and then her hands began to
tremble.

"Why are you showing me this, Ava?" Rose asked as she
stared at the DNA test. There it was, in black and white, proof
that her father was not Charles Blaisdell. She felt sick to her
stomach, a million questions racing through her mind.

How Ava got her hands on it was something she'd need to
think about at a later time. She certainly didn't want to ask
because Ava probably wouldn't tell her anyway.

"This is a warning, Rose. Do not try to get in my way, do not try to come to my place and demand answers, or everyone in the family, *my family*," she accentuated, "will get a mailed copy of this report exposing you as the impostor you really are," she threatened.

"And if I refuse to listen to you?" Rose said, feeling defiant. It wasn't as though they didn't already believe that, and even if this report was accurate, Charles had treated her and raised her as his daughter. She hadn't deceived him in any way.

"You won't." Ava smiled with no warmth reaching her eyes, "Now get out. I have work to do."

Although deeply rattled by that exchange, Rose was still aware of one simple truth. Ava had refused to answer her question.

I wonder why?

ELEVEN

Rose left the hotel in a daze. She felt like her whole life went tumbling down for the second time in so many weeks.

It was one thing when Ava simply threatened her with the knowledge that she was not Charles's biological daughter. It was an entirely different thing to hold proof in her hand. She'd thought it was all a bluff, that Ava had been lying about having proof, yet here it was.

Rose felt like she lost something important.

The last sliver of connection she had with the Blaisdell family.

You shouldn't care about some piece of paper. You are still Rose Blaisdell, and nothing and nobody can ever change that, part of her rebelled.

Rose felt paralyzed. There was nothing she could do against Ava. If she tried, Ava would send that report to everybody in the family, turning her relations with the family from bad to worse. And she couldn't allow that. Her mother would be even more devastated and humiliated. Rose had to prevent that at any cost.

What were her options then? To back down? She couldn't
do that either.

I'm stuck.

Ava came prepared for this war. No wonder Rose always
felt five steps behind the woman. Yet the question was why?
Was this some kind of revenge against Rose's family? If that was
the case, then she should have picked a better target. A target
like Charles Blaisdell.

Father died, which leaves me and Devon, Rose realized.
After all, they were legitimate children of Charles Blaisdell
when Ava wasn't. *So, to punish her father for never acknowl-
edging her, she was going to try to destroy me,* she continued to
muse. Rose felt like crying.

She was angry at Ava for doing this to her. She was furious
with her parents, who put her in this position in the first place.
If they were just normal parents, if they hadn't cheated on one
another, then none of this would have happened.

Rose was devastated at the thought she wasn't really
Charles's daughter. But how had Ava gotten a sample of her
DNA to run that test though? Rose wondered. Had Ava
followed her and taken something like a Styrofoam cup she'd
drank out of? A napkin? How did she do it? Rose could barely
function at the thought. She needed to get away from here.
Away from Ava.

Hailing a cab, Rose took her phone out to call Adrian, cry to
him, and share what Ava did to her, and then she paused. It was
obvious that something was going on with him, and that meant
she couldn't count on him as much as she had before.

She couldn't say for sure if something was going on between
Adrian and Ava. She didn't have proof of that, only a feeling.
However, she could not risk telling him something that had
even the slightest chance of getting back to Ava.

Rose spent the entire day in her apartment, alone, thinking

things through, being none the wiser afterward. She needed a plan, a decisive course of action, and she had none. *How to stop that woman?* She had no clue. She needed help from someone who was better at plotting and scheming against high-society enemies. Unfortunately, the only one she knew capable of that was her mother, and Rose didn't want her mother involved.

It's up to me to stop that woman.

With that thought, Rose decided to start digging into Ava's life. Maybe there was something in her past that would help Rose figure out what Ava's end goal was. Arriving back at her apartment, and double locking her doors, she pulled out her laptop and began with a Google search. It didn't reveal anything groundbreaking, just Ava's alma mater and a few medical papers she'd worked on. Then she started looking into the various social media sites, but oddly, it turned out that her profiles were all fairly new, created in just the last few weeks. Already she was friends with various members of the Blaisdell family, which pissed Rose off so much she slammed the lid of her computer closed and shoved it away from her.

Rose hadn't discovered much of anything that could help her, and she didn't know where to go from there. She was way out of her depth, and she'd need more than a basic search to find what she needed.

* * *

Exactly forty days after Rose's father died, her mother held a memorial service for him at the Blaisdell mansion. Her mother invited the entire family, and that meant Ava came as well, much to Rose's chagrin.

The woman continued to ingratiate herself into the family with such ease, it was driving Rose insane. Ava was right, after all. She was a much better fit, and it showed. She was invited to all the biggest, most important family events of the year, not to mention picnics, holidays, and so on.

And Rose wouldn't have that big of a problem with that if her mother wasn't showing affection toward Ava as well. Although her mother would definitely deny it, especially to Rose, it became more than apparent how much she liked having Ava around. And that was only natural, considering how much the two had in common. Ava gushed over her mother's wardrobe and offered her tips on how to give her hair the perfect sheen. She was effusive with her praise at all her mother's events, complimenting everything from the food to the décor. Ava was the perfect daughter her mother never had after all.

And that left a pretty bitter taste in Rose's mouth.

Devon was the same way, playing at being the eager little brother. Luckily, Ava didn't pay him much mind and quite coldly, ruthlessly deflected his attention each time he tried to suck up to her. Unfortunately, that didn't discourage him in the slightest. If anything, it made him want it even more.

Rose knew Ava was doing it on purpose, playing with him in such a manner because, that way, while he was distracted and focused on trying to please her, he couldn't see what she was really doing to the family.

"Maybe you should stop making a fool of yourself," she said to him, taking advantage of a rare moment he wasn't at Ava's side.

"What do you mean?"

"Stop trying to ingratiate yourself with her, it's absurd!" Rose snapped.

He simply rolled his eyes and downed his drink. "What? Are you jealous I like her more than you?"

"Don't be stupid. You don't even know if she's our real sister. All we have is her word for it. Don't you care what she's saying about Dad? All the horrible things she's said he's done to her?"

"Dad's dead, and you don't know how ruthless he really was. You didn't live with him as long as I did."

"I know he loved us and was always there for us!" Rose was adamant.

"Maybe to you," Devon replied.

"If you weren't such a fuck-up—" Rose started and then abruptly stopped as she realized it was the wrong thing to say.

"Screw you, Rose," he snapped, looking genuinely hurt, before storming away.

Rose groaned. She felt like she stepped into some kind of parallel universe, a bizarre world where nothing made sense to her. It was unfathomable to her how members of her family reacted to everything that happened. As in, there was no reaction at all.

They all accepted Charles had this entirely different family, another daughter, as though that was the most normal thing in the world. Even Rose's own mother wasn't as angry as she should be. And that made no sense to Rose. How could they all act the way they were? How could they be so welcoming? How could Devon look at her as just another sister?

And when she tried speaking with her mother about it all, her mom simply waved her hand as though it was all of no importance. She even chastised Rose for making a fuss out of nothing.

"Ava will get her money and leave, and Devon will calm down," she said.

Rose wholeheartedly disagreed.

Since she couldn't reach her mother, Rose tried to talk to her brother. She tried once again to express her concerns about Ava.

Devon looked at her as though she was the crazy one.

"We accepted you even though you're a bastard, so why not her as well," he said simply.

For a split-second, Rose was horrified Devon would say that to her. She wanted to slap him across the face so badly that her palm tingled.

Rose couldn't believe he actually dared to say something like that to her, but looking into his eyes, she realized that he really didn't mean it as an insult, which was even more upsetting. He truly believed that she wasn't his full sister despite the fact that he had known her his entire life.

To Rose, hearing him utter those words with such ease, and carelessness, felt like a knife straight to the heart.

She never belonged, not really. If that paperwork of Ava's was correct, then the man who raised her as his own wasn't her biological father. And that would always stand between them from now on, no matter what.

Who is my real father? Do I know him? Do I want to know him? These thoughts passed through her head.

No, she decided. She didn't want to know who that other man was. She didn't want anything to do with him. He meant nothing to her mother, so he meant nothing to her either.

He must have meant something if she decided to keep you. Rose frowned. She couldn't think like that; it would drive her crazy.

As far as she was concerned, Rose had only one father in this world, and that was Charles Blaisdell. And it didn't matter what others said, what Ava's piece of paper said. *Charles will always be my dad, end of story.*

"Rose? Are you all right? You kind of spaced out for a moment," Devon observed with a strange expression on his face.

"I just needed a moment to process your words. As always, it was a pleasure speaking to you," she mocked.

"I am wise beyond my years."

She rolled her eyes, deciding it was time to go home. She

accomplished nothing trying to persuade her family Ava was bad news. All the same, she wasn't giving up.

The next morning, Adrian texted and asked if they could have a date night. After driving herself ragged with worry, Rose was glad to hear from him and immediately said yes. She was worried about their relationship and wanted to talk to him about it, but she wasn't sure how to bring it up.

Luckily, she didn't have to because he brought it up himself.

"I brought Chinese food, is that okay? I know you like the chicken chow mein."

"That's fine," Rose said, closing the door behind him. She felt funny, like things were off between them, and she didn't know how to get their relationship back on track.

He leaned in to kiss her and she pulled back. He looked hurt for a moment, but then his expression cleared, and he headed for the kitchen. He began to plate their food, and Rose pulled out a bottle of wine.

"In here or the living room?" he murmured, holding the two plates.

"Living room. It's more comfortable." Rose followed him, carrying two glasses. She set them on the table and took the plate he offered her.

They ate in silence for a few minutes, and then Adrian said, "Rose, I don't know what's going on with you. It feels like you've been pulling away from me ever since your dad died. I know you've had trouble dealing with his death, but all I've done is try to be there for you."

His words sounded so heartfelt that Rose immediately felt guilty. She didn't know what to say. Tears filled her eyes and she tried to dash them away. Adrian took her plate and set it on the table next to his own.

"What can I do?"

"I'm sorry, Adrian. I... the other day, when you rushed out of here, I was so worried that you were done with me that I..."

He frowned as he interjected, "That was just work. I told you I had some work stuff going on. I didn't mean to upset you."

Rose sniffled. "It's just Ava... I thought..."

A look of displeasure crossed his face. "You thought I was seeing Ava?"

"No. Yes? I don't know." Rose's voice was soft, and she felt so ashamed.

"You have to let this go, Rose. Ava is only here because she wants what is rightfully hers. A piece of your father's inheritance. That's it. She's not here for me, and I don't care about her. I don't even know her."

"But—" it was on the tip of her tongue to tell him that Ava was blackmailing her.

"No. I mean it, Rose. This obsession of yours has to stop before it ruins us." He ran a hand through his hair in obvious frustration. "You know what, I'm going to go. I can't deal with you being so paranoid about that woman. I'll see you later." With that, he got up and walked out without a backward glance.

Rose was stunned. Had she just tanked the best relationship she'd ever had?

She rushed to her window and looked out, hoping to spot Adrian turning back around and coming back to her. But there was no sign of him.

Rose choked up, tears threatening to pour, but then something caught her eye. Whipping her head around, she saw the silhouette of a woman disappear into a side street. It was hard to tell in the darkness, but she could have sworn she recognized that coat and that hair.

Ava.

Was she here to meet Adrian? Was she just watching her? Was she planning something?

Paranoid, my ass...

Rose vowed then and there that she would beat Ava at whatever game it was she was playing. She was going down. She wasn't going to lose Adrian to a woman like her. She refused.

TWELVE

I can't deal with this anymore, Rose practically screamed, inside her head. She wasn't unstable enough to start doing it out loud; however, that day was fast approaching.

All the same, it was extremely difficult being the only one who saw the truth about Ava. And it only got worse. After making her vow to take Ava down a few nights ago, Rose had gone into town and bought a tracking device. She had managed to slip it under the rear bumper of Ava's car the next day and ever since then she'd been following Ava's movements, but to no avail so far. All Ava had done was go from the hotel to Rose's mother's house and back again. A couple of times, she'd gone shopping downtown, and Rose had followed her at a distance, but still there was nothing to tell her what Ava was up to. Rose was completely frustrated that she was getting nowhere in her investigation of the woman.

On top of all of that, her mother decided to host one of her family dinners. Rose couldn't fathom why her mother insisted they all gather so much, or why she started to include Ava every time they did.

But her mother insisted, which meant Rose was forced to

endure Ava's company more than she liked. Especially considering Ava constantly looked at her with a smug expression on her face, constantly reminding her she had won by just sitting there.

She won one battle, but she definitely won't win the war.

Unfortunately, Ava wasn't the only thorn in Rose's side.

It wasn't a pleasant meal. Like all the others, it was full of snide comments from Aunt Melinda, and small back-stabbings from various other relatives. In other words, it was a typical family dinner.

On her way back from the bathroom, her only escape from her family's craziness, she noted how the door of her father's study was open. That was strange, considering the staff members were under strict orders not to go inside, so she decided to investigate what was going on.

She found Aunt Melinda inside. And for a moment, Rose was touched. Perhaps she was missing her brother after all? And then she saw what was in Melinda's hand.

She was in the process of taking a very expensive Fabergé egg out of its casing. She had a box and a bag prepared, clearly to sneak it out. Rose knew Aunt Melinda always coveted it, and now she was trying to take it while nobody was looking.

That instantly made her see red. *Unbelievable,* the woman had millions and millions of dollars, and yet here she was, stealing from her dead brother.

"What do you think you're doing?" Rose nearly yelled, confronting her aunt.

Fear of being discovered was quickly replaced with irritation and indignation as Aunt Melinda turned. It was just Rose, after all.

"This egg belonged to my mother, and Charles took it without permission. It should be mine now," she argued.

"You aren't allowed to take a single thing from my father's study," Rose said through gritted teeth.

Aunt Melinda's eyes went wide because Rose never stood up to her like this before. She definitely hadn't use that tone of voice before.

"Put it back," she ordered.

Aunt Melinda recovered from her initial shock. "I'm not allowed? Who are you to tell me what I can or cannot do?" Aunt Melinda said, raising her voice.

"I'm one of my father's heirs, unlike you," Rose pointed out. "So put it back, it doesn't belong to you," she repeated.

"You have a lot of nerve speaking to me in such a manner. And I don't care who you think you are, little brat, this is mine and I'm taking it," Aunt Melinda stood her ground.

Rose was about to reply when Joey arrived at the door. "What is happening here?" he inquired coming inside.

Rose groaned inwardly. This was the last thing she needed at the moment: Aunt Melinda's bodyguard coming to her rescue. "I caught your mother stealing."

"Liar," Aunt Melinda snapped instantly. "I did no such thing. I'm only taking what's mine."

"That egg does not belong to you," Rose insisted.

"If my mother says it's hers, then it's hers," Joey rose up to his full height, crossing his meaty arms.

Rose wasn't surprised he had loose notions of propriety, being a criminal and all.

As if summoned, moments later, Devon, her mom, and Adrian joined them. Aunt Melinda sent daggers Rose's way, clearly enraged that she now had too many witnesses to her theft, thanks to her. Rose didn't care. Her aunt needed to be stopped.

"Melinda, why are you holding my wedding present from your mother?" her mom asked calmly.

"I forgot Mother gave it to you, but it should be returned to the family," Aunt Melinda tried to defend.

"It is with the family," Thelma replied, pretty calmly.

"Fine. I was merely reminiscing."

"Reminiscing with a box and a bag at the ready. Mom, she tried to take it," Rose pointed out, refusing to let everyone accept Aunt Melinda's lame explanation.

If looks could kill, Rose would be dead on the floor.

"I know, dear," her mom said, offering a small smile.

"Thelma, you can't seriously believe what that brat is saying," Melinda tried to say more, but her mom raised her hand, stopping her.

"I think it's time for you and your family to leave."

Melinda gritted her teeth, raising her chin ever so slightly as she made a move to leave the room. She was firmly holding the egg.

"Leave the egg on the table," her mom warned.

In a huff, as though thinking Thelma was unreasonable, Aunt Melinda slammed the egg against the table.

Rose and a few others took a collective gasp, waiting to see if it would shatter to pieces. It didn't. It was a true miracle.

"Will you now finally stop inviting these people to dinner?" Rose asked under her breath.

Her mother ignored her.

"I will remember this insult, Thelma," Aunt Melinda said on her way out.

"You got what you deserve," Devon pointed out.

Joey's eyes flashed with fury. "Is that so?"

"Yeah."

Joey nodded. "Then I'll make sure you get what you deserve too."

"Is that a threat?" Devon asked, puffing his chest.

This isn't going to end well, Rose thought, concerned.

"Take it as you will, just don't come crawling to me next time you end up in trouble," Joey spat back.

They continued to talk trash on the way out.

"Just leave, don't make matters worse," Devon replied to him in his easygoing manner.

"You look so tough now, but you cried like a little bitch when Nick's guys were after you," Joey ragged, getting into Devon's face.

What is that about?

Devon said something else that Rose missed because the next thing she knew, Joey punched him in the face. Devon would have fallen, but Adrian managed to hold him upright.

Rose was horrified, rushing to her brother and calling someone to get the first aid kit. "I will call the police right this instant if you don't leave, NOW," she exclaimed. She was done taking crap from the likes of them.

There was a moment of silence that followed her threat, as though all were assessing how serious she was. Rose stood her ground, with her phone in her hand.

They looked at her, clearly stunned by the fierceness in her voice. She was not as weak as they all believed. In the past she avoided conflict as much as possible, but those days were gone. It was time to stand up for herself and for her family.

Sobering up, Joey, his mother, and his wife got into their car and drove away. The car accelerated too quickly, leaving tire marks on the pavement as they pulled out of the drive.

"Thank you, my dear," Rose's mother said to her, kissing her cheek before going back to the house.

Rose had no idea what her mother was thanking her for. Rescuing the egg or for threatening Joey with calling the police. It didn't really matter though. She would take it. It felt good to be a hero for a change.

Rose noted how Ava kept glancing at her on her way inside too. She, too, looked mildly impressed by Rose's show of strength. Rose held her head high. Not that she cared what the other woman thought of her. It was simply good that Ava had the opportunity to see that. Ava wouldn't be dismissing her so easily in the future.

Sadly, her high spirits were short-lived. As though Ava needed to put Rose back into her place after standing up to Aunt Melinda and Joey, she wouldn't stop talking with Rose's mom, even fawning over her. And Thelma was just eating up all the attention Ava was slathering on her. Rose was extremely frustrated to see her mom just accepting this woman like she was her own daughter. She was beginning to think her mother's promise of keeping her enemies closer was just an empty platitude. There was no way her mother was this good of an actress.

Even Devon noticed it and made a snide comment to Rose about how, if she didn't do something about it, she would lose her place in the family.

I already have.

"This turned out to be quite an interesting night," Adrian commented as soon as the two of them were left alone in the kitchen. Her mom had deemed them in need of more wine, and Rose went to fetch it. Adrian joined her.

"What, the part where my aunt tried to rob us? Or are you talking about when Ava flirted with you?" Rose asked, unable to keep her jealousy in.

"What?" Adrian asked, taken aback. "I wasn't flirting with Ava."

"Maybe you weren't, but she certainly was." Rose was hurt that he hadn't rebuffed her attention. *Did he actually like it?*

"Rose. I'm engaged to you."

"I know that. I do. I just don't think she cares."

"Nothing happened, nothing is going to happen. We just talked." He tried to reach for her.

Rose started to giggle and then to touch his arms and his chest in a suggestive manner, the way she saw Ava do during dinner. And then she abruptly stopped, getting serious again. "That is not talking, Adrian, that is flirting," she pointed out.

"You're being ridiculous, Rose," he rumbled. "If she was flirting, I didn't notice."

Unbelievable. I'm being ridiculous.

Yeah, right. Rose crossed her arms over her chest and looked at him. "How could you not notice?"

Adrian smiled. "Because, sweetheart, I only have eyes for you. You are the one I'm marrying. I couldn't give two pennies for her." He drew her in and nuzzled her neck. "Now, let's get your mom her wine and head back out there. Maybe we can leave a bit early and go back to your place?" he offered.

Rose relented. "I just don't like it when she does that. I feel like she doesn't respect the fact you're an engaged man."

"You've got nothing to worry about." He kissed her again and then took the bottle of wine and led her back into the living room.

Rose's gaze traveled around the room. Devon, sporting a nice shiner already, but still in good spirits, had decided to call it a night. That was pretty much everyone's cue that the party was over. Although Rose knew many wanted to stay, to talk about what happened with Melinda and her son, for once, they did the respectful thing and left.

A few minutes later, Rose and Adrian said their goodbyes too, heading back to her place. Adrian made love to her, and then they snuggled close, falling asleep in each other's arms.

* * *

The next morning, her phone ringing woke Rose up.

"Hello?" she answered without bothering to see who it was.

"Oh my God, Rose, it happened again." It was her mother and she sounded hysterical.

"What happened?" Rose demanded, jumping out of bed, instantly awake, ready for action.

"I found Devon in a strange state this morning."

Rose made a face. *How drunk was he?* "Define strange?" she asked as she looked at the bed and noticed Adrian wasn't there. He must have gone into work early and let her sleep. The thought made her smile.

"I don't know. He wouldn't wake up, so I called 911, and they took him away."

"Where?" Rose asked, back on high alert. If Devon had gone with an ambulance, then something really bad had to have happened to him.

"To the ER."

"Are you with him now?"

"Yes. He is in a critical state after suffering a heart attack," her mother explained.

A heart attack? He's only twenty-seven.

"I'm on my way," she reassured.

Although it was wrong of her, one thought passed through her head – *I have to stop waking up like this.*

THIRTEEN

Feeling like a headless chicken, Rose rushed to the hospital. She was scared beyond words. She couldn't understand what was happening.

First, her father died, and then this happened to her brother. What was happening to her family?

By the time Rose arrived at the hospital, her brother's condition had worsened. He was in a coma and had been moved to the ICU.

Her mom practically fell into her arms, sobbing uncontrollably, mumbling unintelligible things, which meant Rose had to hold it together, for both their sakes. It was hard to get to the bottom of things and learn exactly what happened since her mother was in such a hysterical state.

And then the rest of the family started gathering as well. Even Aunt Melinda, Joey, and all the rest came to be with them in the waiting room.

Rose really wanted to ask what the hell they were doing there. They had a lot of nerve showing up after the way they were forced to leave last night, but she held her tongue. She didn't want to cause a scene in the hospital. Plus, if her mother called them, she had to respect that. She could settle all the scores later when her brother was out of danger.

They all mouthed words of comfort, although it sounded more like condolences. Rose wished she could throw them all out. And then, as if things couldn't get any worse, Ava showed up.

"Did you seriously call Ava to come here?" Rose couldn't help asking her mother, starting to see red. Unfortunately, her mother wasn't feeling particularly talkative at that moment, continuing to cry in her arms.

Rose barely managed to put her down to sit in an empty chair, but she couldn't leave her side for a second. Her mother was clinging to her as though she was her life raft.

She wanted to find out what was going on, on so many levels, but had to take care of her mother first.

"Mom, I need to go and find you a doctor, okay? So let me go," Rose tried to speak with her again. She was starting to worry her mother would fall ill from all the stress. Her mother was sixty-five, after all, so things like this could have serious consequences.

Her mother looked at her with pure terror in her eyes. "Oh my God, Rose. How did this happen?" she asked, rhetorically, Rose realized. "First Charles, and now Devon. I can't bear it," she sobbed. "I can't lose him too."

"Mom, I need you to calm down."

Her mom started crying even harder.

"Excuse me," Ava stopped a nurse who was passing by. "My name is Doctor Ava Rothman," she showed the woman an ID as she spoke, "And this woman needs some benzodiazepines. Two milligrams of Lorazepam would suffice," she ordered.

The nurse nodded, then went away in a hurry to do Ava's bidding.

Rose's jaw almost dropped. She knew Ava was a doctor, but

how could she prescribe stuff to people who weren't her patients? Was she allowed to do that?

It appeared that she was because soon her mother was gratefully accepting her sedatives.

Life really wasn't fair. Ava had the brains and the looks. She was a freaking doctor, and soon she would be a billionaire as well. Not that Rose was bitter or anything.

Once her mother got some sedatives in her, she started to calm down, and they all waited for Devon's doctor to come and tell them what was happening with him.

Rose sat there thinking about the research she'd done on Ava. She knew that Ava had studied biochemistry while she was in college. *One day I hope to find a cure for cancer.* Rose recalled one of her quotes from some article where she was asked why her goals set her apart from the rest of her class. She just about snorted. Of course, she wanted to cure cancer. Didn't everyone?

Rose's mother was much calmer now but was still crying, muttering to herself how she couldn't lose Devon too. Rose wished her mother would be slightly more optimistic and not jump to conclusions. Rose remained by her side, ignoring her relatives, ignoring Ava.

At times it felt like a full-time job, preventing her mother from completely falling apart.

And then, to make matters worse, the police showed up. Rose was completely baffled as to why they came and asked to speak with Rose and her mother. However, the reason was revealed immediately. One of the doctors called them because Devon had a huge bruise on his face, and they connected that to his state.

Rose was more than happy to set the record straight. "It happened last night," Rose pointed to her cousin, "Joey hit him."

One of the officers immediately approached Joey to get a statement.

Aunt Melinda huffed at Rose, sending daggers as though she couldn't believe Rose had just sold out her cousin. In return, Rose felt like sticking her tongue out at her. She should feel lucky she didn't mention the theft as well.

Joey got pretty agitated as the officer came to speak with him. "I didn't do anything to him," he defended, pretty vocally.

"So, you deny hitting him?" the officer asked for clarification.

"No, I did, I hit him. But I have nothing to do with him being here," Joey defended.

Rose and her mother still didn't know what was happening to Devon, so to say Joey had nothing to do with it wasn't necessarily true. He might have. They didn't know.

Rose said as much. Joey started growling, before advancing toward her. He had a nasty temper.

"Do you plan on hitting me too?" Rose challenged, but several police officers came between her and her cousin, so she couldn't hear his reply.

A lot of people were talking and shouting at the same time. Mostly the police officers were advising Joey to calm down. Rose saw nurses clustering in doorways, listening to the ruckus they were causing.

"Rose, I can't bear any of this," her mother complained, clutching her chest. This was what Rose was worried about. That her mother would fall ill thanks to all the stress, all the drama.

"Just calm down, all will be sorted soon," she tried to reassure.

"Sir, if you don't calm down, we will be forced to restrain you," one of the officers warned Joey.

"I didn't do anything, damn it," Joey continued to argue.

"Please, Thelma, tell them my son didn't cause this." Aunt Melinda came to her mother's side. "He is innocent."

"We don't know what caused this," Rose was the one who started responding. "We don't know Joey is innocent."

Aunt Melinda gritted her teeth, clearly not pleased that Rose dared to speak with her. Her next words confirmed as much. "I wasn't speaking to you," she snapped.

"Rose is right," her mother stood up to face Melinda. "We don't know what caused this; however, what we do know is that one minute Devon was attacked by his cousin, and the next, he had to be driven to the hospital," she said, her voice shaking, breaking by the end.

"That had nothin' to do with me," Joey went wild.

The police officers had to restrain him because he started acting completely out of control, raging, and shouting all kinds of profanities to Rose and her mother.

And then they started dragging him out to the patrol car, to take him to the station.

"You need to stop this," Aunt Melinda yelled at Rose's mom.

Rose moved to stand between the two women. "My mother doesn't need to do anything," she said adamantly. "We will let the police resolve this issue."

"You were always an evil creature, and now you finally have your revenge," Aunt Melinda snapped at her.

"Do you really think insulting me will help anything?" Rose asked, feeling surprisingly calm despite everything.

"I won't allow you to do this to my son."

"He did it to himself, always causing trouble, but I guess he learned that from his mother," Rose responded.

Aunt Melinda advanced toward her as though to hit her, but Rose stood her ground. She was not afraid of her anymore. From the corner of her eye, she noted Ava smirking at the scene. She must be loving this, that they were at each other's throats.

"Melinda, that is enough," her mom snapped at Melinda, practically pushing her away. "Leave, now," she commanded.

"I won't leave until you right this wrong. My boy is innocent, and if you don't help me, I will ruin you. I know things, Thelma, so don't tempt me," Aunt Melinda warned.

"Do not speak to my mother in that way," Rose defended. "And if that son of yours is responsible for Devon collapsing, I will testify against him. I will speak about your attempted theft as well," Rose threatened, completely losing her temper.

She was done trying to be the bigger person, constantly turning the other cheek. From now on she planned on throwing the first punch if she had to. She would do whatever it took to protect her family.

Melinda looked at her in wide-eyed, utter disbelief. Before she had a chance to say anything, Adrian approached, grabbing her by the arm. "I believe it's best if you leave now, Aunt Melinda," he said in his usual calm, diplomatic manner. She allowed him to escort her out.

Rose had no idea when Adrian arrived. In all the craziness she hadn't noticed him.

Who called him?

Ava smirked at Rose, breaking her chain of thoughts.

"What?" Rose asked, in the same manner she spoke with Melinda.

"I'm impressed you finally found a backbone," she jibed.

Rose approached her. "I've always had one, and you'd be wise to remember that," she said before leaving them all to fetch some water for her mother.

Despite all the bravado, she was shaking inside. Rose was not a confrontational person, so all of this affected her deeply. At the same time, she was very proud of herself. Although this current state was born out of pure necessity, she kind of liked it.

Adrian followed her and whispered, "Why didn't you call me?" as he drew her into his arms.

Rose sighed. "I'm sorry, I should have. How did you know to find me here?"

"I stopped at your mom's house, and the housekeeper told me you were all at the hospital with Devon. I tried to call."

Rose sighed. "I turned my ringer off, I'm sorry." She laid her head on his shoulder.

"It's okay. You good now?" he asked, looking at her.

Rose nodded. She filled a paper cup with water for her mom and the two of them returned to her side.

Eventually, the doctor came to tell them her brother was stable, but remained in a coma. And they still had no idea how it all happened. That was a huge blow for Rose and her mother.

Seeing how there was nothing to be done for the moment, Rose managed to convince her mother they should return home. Someone from the hospital would call them if Devon's condition changed in any way.

Rose felt beyond exhausted putting her mother to bed. The day had drained her, and it was all she could do not to cry.

Is this my life now, just jumping from one tragedy to the next? She really hoped not.

Please, God, let Devon be all right, she prayed.

Once she made sure her mother was dead to the world, so to speak, Rose decided to return to the hospital. She needed to see her brother.

FOURTEEN

"Do you hear me, Devon? I love you, and I need you to wake up," Rose cried, holding her brother's hand the next morning, sitting next to him as all kinds of machines beeped to keep him alive. "Mom and I need you, so come back to us, please."

Unfortunately, there was no reaction from her brother. He looked even younger than his age, lying in that hospital bed. If she didn't know how sick he was, she would assume he was merely sleeping. Despite everything, there was a certain comfort in that.

Rose hoped that at least he wasn't in pain.

Once her visit with her brother was over, Rose lingered in the hospital. The staff had said they were taking him for tests and had welcomed her to stay in the room, but she couldn't. She needed to get out for a while, and it was the perfect time. She had gone for a walk and visited the gift shop, but she couldn't bring herself to leave the premises. She wanted to speak with Devon's doctor to see if there was something that could be done for him. She would bring the best doctors from all over the world to help her brother if she had to.

As she paced around the hospital, a hundred questions and a thousand troubling thoughts passed through her head.

She couldn't believe this was happening to her family. Not so long ago they were all together at one of their family dinners, catching up and arguing amongst themselves.

Then, quite suddenly, her father died. And now her brother was in a coma, and it looked like nobody knew what would happen to him. Would his condition worsen? Would he wake up? All the dice were up in the air, and all she and her mother could do was wait.

Eventually, the nurses noticed her lingering in the hall outside Devon's empty room and asked if everything was alright. She explained that she was waiting for Devon's doctor to arrive so she could speak to him. They assured her they'd let him know she was looking for him.

When he arrived, Rose asked, "Dr. Koy, can you tell me your prognosis? I'm really worried about Devon. We just lost my father, and I can't lose him too."

"For now, Devon is stable," he reassured. "We've been running tests to measure his brain activity, and everything seems normal right now. His body is healing, but he may remain unconscious for some time."

Based on his expression, Rose felt like that would be the only good news he would have for her.

"What's the matter with him, Doctor?"

"Your brother's collapse is a case of Kounis Syndrome, a heart attack caused by a severe allergic reaction," he explained.

"Oh my God," Rose exclaimed in return. "My father died from that same thing not long ago."

"Well, the disease can be hereditary," he replied, flipping through his chart.

"Is my brother going to be okay?"

"Although his brain activity is normal, we do have him on

life support at the moment, and I can't guarantee that his condition will improve any time soon."

In other words, he could stay in a coma forever. "Oh."

"I'm sorry I don't have better news for you."

"Thank you, Doctor," Rose remembered her manners.

Dr. Koy nodded, as if telling her to stay strong, before leaving to deal with some other patients and speak with some other worried families.

Rose's phone started ringing. It was as though her mother sensed the disturbance in the force or something and knew when to call. Rose really didn't want to share what she learned from the doctor, but knew she had no choice. Although she hated that she would be causing her mother additional pain, she answered.

"How is my boy?" Rose's mother demanded.

"The same. He is stable and on life support."

"Is he going to make it?"

"Everyone is doing their best to save him, but Mom, I have some news to share."

"What is it?"

"The same thing that happened to Dad happened to Devon as well," Rose explained to her mother how they appeared to share some strange hereditary disease.

"I had never heard of that disease before in my life, and now I feel that's all I hear about," her mother said in exasperation.

Rose felt the same way. She also thought it was strange how a clearly dormant disease attacked both of them at relatively the same time. She didn't share that with her mother.

Although the doctor tried to reassure her it was all a strange, terrible coincidence, she wasn't so convinced. The timing was too suspicious.

Perhaps this was her father speaking through her. He had been a naturally suspicious man, however, Rose felt like something else was going on here. As time passed by, that feeling only grew, became more dominant, and something she couldn't ignore no matter how much she tried.

Returning home, she shared her suspicions with Adrian. He looked strange as she spoke. She couldn't quite decipher what he was thinking. *Does he think I've completely lost my mind?*

"I think this is no accident, Adrian," she still insisted. "And I don't think some hereditary disease nobody has heard anything about got triggered so suddenly."

Her father was always meticulous and went to his annual checkups without fault, so it was pretty strange to her that none of his previous doctors ever warned him about this Kounis Syndrome. It sounded like a big deal, considering one could die of it so easily. So, it was definitely something he should have known about before his death.

Did he know and decide to hide it from us? She had a moment of doubt. *No,* she banished it immediately.

"The timing is just too convenient. Besides, Devon is too young to be this sick so suddenly from some disease nobody warned us about before."

He took her hand gently, "Have you ever heard of the expression illness doesn't discriminate?"

"Adrian, I'm being serious. It's strange that they both felt ill so suddenly with no previous diagnosis of the disease."

Not to mention all the extended family who were expecting handouts upon his death, as well as Ava, his supposedly long-lost daughter who claims he abandoned her. Rose couldn't help wondering if Ava had something to do with this, somehow.

"What are you saying, Rose?"

"Someone did this to them," she forced herself to say.

Adrian shook his head. "I think you're overthinking things. The simplest solutions are usually the right ones," he pointed out.

"What is your explanation then?" she asked, getting on the defensive.

"You are just processing your grief by creating some problem you can focus on, instead of accepting that your father died of rather natural causes."

That stung.

"I know my father is dead, Adrian. But I can't accept that his death, and Devon in a coma from the same thing, is just some freak of nature accident. I just can't," she stood her ground.

"You have to because there's nothing there. You'll only hurt yourself by not allowing yourself to process all these painful emotions. You need to leave it alone and move on with your life," he said almost harshly.

"When did you stop being supportive?" Words left her mouth even before she was aware of formulating them.

He was always honest with her but never cruel. Now it appeared as though everything Rose said or did irritated him. It was baffling to her because she knew she didn't do anything wrong to be treated in such a manner.

"I am supportive, Rose, you can't see that now, you're too overwhelmed with all that shit."

"It's not shit, Adrian."

"Rose."

"Don't use that tone of voice on me," she snapped angrily. "Something shady is going on, and I'm going to prove it to you," she insisted.

"If Devon was here, he would also tell you how paranoid and unreasonable you sound at the moment."

Too late, he realized his mistake. Rose's eyes flashed with fury. "He is not here, Adrian. He is fighting for his life in a hospital bed, and I'm going to find out why."

She was adamant about that. She would prove to everyone she was right, that her gut feeling wasn't tricking her while in grief.

A small part of her did wonder if Adrian had a point. She

was postponing her grief, she was failing to process her emotions by focusing on something else. That didn't mean she was wrong. That didn't mean she was delusional, as Adrian was suggesting.

"Stop it, Rose," he snapped. "This isn't you. You're making too big of a deal out of nothing, and in the end, you'll only hurt yourself and your mother."

How dare he bring her mother into this? She was doing this for her as well. So they could both know the truth. The real truth. Only that could bring peace of mind, and nothing else.

"A big deal?" she repeated in utter disbelief. "My father dying, and my brother ending up in a coma is not a big deal for you?"

"I didn't mean it like that, and you know it," he was quick to defend. "What happened was a tragedy, there's no doubt about that, however nothing nefarious caused it," he insisted.

"How can you be so sure?" she challenged.

"Because I'm using common sense, Rose, something that you're clearly lacking at the moment. You have to stop allowing these delusions to guide you, it's harmful."

Rose gritted her teeth. "I'm not delusional about this. And I'm not delusional about Ava flirting with you either," she said, completely losing her temper.

"What?" he exclaimed, shaking his head, looking confused by the sudden change of subject.

"You heard me."

"When did you become this jealous type?" he asked, making a face.

She pursed her lips before replying. "Don't make this about me. I'm not the problem, her behavior is." She stood her ground.

"I haven't done anything wrong," he was quick to defend.

Yet.

"So you say."

"You're finding problems where there aren't any, Rose. I don't even know Ava."

You would definitely like to. And then she actually processed what he said.

I don't know Ava.

That was a very strange thing to say, considering that wasn't something mentioned before. Why would he say something like that?

Am I overthinking things?

"Let me make things very simple for you, Adrian," she said, losing patience, tired of arguing and needing this to end. "If you want to be with Ava, be with Ava, just inform me beforehand, so I don't waste time on being with you anymore."

"Waste time," he scoffed. "I'm glad that's how you see our entire relationship."

Once again, Rose felt like he was simply deflecting so he wouldn't have to deal with what he was supposed to – his infatuation with another woman.

Did he sleep with her yet? she thought.

Rose found herself in a very strange state, emotionally speaking. She could clearly see the destruction of her relationship happening, but she was at a loss on how to stop it. All she could do was push forward.

"Let me repeat myself because I really want you to hear me," Rose refused to allow him to change the subject, "if you want to sleep with Ava, at least have the decency to break up with me first."

"Sleep with her," he repeated in a strange tone. He was obviously angry; however there was something else mixed into that as well. "Break up with you? Rose, I really don't understand you," he said with a shake of his head.

At times she didn't understand herself either; however, in this regard, she knew she was right.

"And I don't understand you," she countered.

"You're imagining things," he insisted. "I have no interest in Ava. "

Rose wanted to say something to that, but he continued speaking. He took her hands, touching the diamond ring on her finger. "I want to be with you," he insisted looking straight into her eyes. "I want to marry you, only you."

Rose sighed. She couldn't understand why he insisted on continuing this charade. Why was he denying something so obvious to her?

"If you say so, Adrian," she replied, somewhat defeated, but she still didn't believe him.

"I am saying it. And I will prove it."

"I'm tired of arguing." Especially considering she had more pressing issues to deal with. She would deal with Adrian after discovering what happened to her father and brother.

"Then let's not argue." He leaned in to kiss her, and she let him.

Like everything else in their relationship, that kiss felt strange now as well.

It didn't matter how much Adrian tried to deny the truth. Rose knew the end result would be the same: they would break up and he would be with Ava. This only felt like she was postponing the inevitable. Ava seemed to get whatever she wanted, and Rose knew she wanted Adrian. Even if he didn't recognize that.

She didn't want to lose him, but it was like she could see the future laid out before her, and he wasn't going to be hers. He'd be Ava's instead. She didn't know how to stop that from happening.

FIFTEEN

Two days after Devon collapsed and was rushed to the hospital, the whole family gathered at the Blaisdell mansion. Rose would rather do anything else in this world than be among these people. However, her mother insisted.

To be more precise, Rose suspected that Aunt Melinda demanded a meeting, and was making her mom organize it, but Rose didn't feel like pressing. Her mother was already having a difficult time, and Rose didn't feel like adding to it.

Rose and her mother were very worried about Devon. He was still in the hospital, still in a coma; however, his condition was stable, and Rose really tried to take comfort in that.

It was hard holding her tongue when Aunt Melinda and Joey came over, but she did all the same to keep the peace. She was trying to be a good daughter.

They were all in the living room, while her mom made sure they had some refreshments and that there was enough finger food to go around. To her surprise, after their argument, Adrian came as well.

She was grateful to have him there because she didn't feel

like explaining to anyone, especially to her mother, what was happening between the two of them.

"So, what are we going to do with Devon's share once he dies?" Joey asked out of the blue. "How are we splitting it?"

Rose wanted to rip his heart out. She wanted to pick up a coffee table and hurl it at him.

"How dare you?" she yelled. "My brother is not going to die. And even if he did, you wouldn't be the one getting the money."

She couldn't believe these people, the nerve of them. Rose couldn't stand any of them. It was disgusting that they only cared about the money. It was infuriating they were so shame-less in their greed.

Rose's mother was in a rough state as it was, constantly medicated, although not even that was enough at times, so she really shouldn't be exposed to this. Rose was doing her best to take care of her; however, she couldn't protect her from the likes of Joey, especially since she insisted on calling them all despite their strained relationships. And Rose was being generous, calling it strained. It was a train wreck in reality.

Although Joey had been arrested that day at the hospital, his mother managed to get him out of jail on bail. However, Rose fully planned to fulfill her promise. If the prosecutor asked her to testify against Joey, she most definitely would; there was no doubt about that, because she firmly believed that a man like him belonged behind bars.

Rose would like to see Aunt Melinda in jail as well. Sadly, Rose knew an attempted theft wouldn't be considered a major offense. Nonetheless, Rose would be glad even if the other woman ended up paying a fine or something.

Rose would like nothing more than to simply tell them to go to hell and throw them out, but for some completely strange reason, her mother wanted them around.

When she'd asked, her mother had frowned and said,

"Melinda's been holding something over my head from the past that I'm not proud of. She used it while your father was alive to continue to come to all the family gatherings, and she still uses it now."

"What?" Rose had been taken aback at her mother's words. "What could she possibly have that would make you give in to her, Mom?"

Her mother had shaken her head and refused to speak any further on the subject.

Rose recalled the conversation and wondered again what Melinda could have on her mother.

"My son didn't say anything wrong," Aunt Melinda defended Joey, as was expected. "We should discuss such matters without being so overly emotional." She said that last part looking at Rose.

"Would you be so rational, emotionless, if your son was in question? If we were discussing dividing his money," her mom snapped.

Aunt Melinda pursed her lips.

"None of you would get any of my money," Joey said, brutally honest as ever.

"And yet you expect to get my brother's money," Rose pointed out.

Adrian took her hand in support and squeezed her fingers. She appreciated his effort, but it didn't feel the same as it once had to have him in her corner.

"That is completely different. Devon got that money from *my* brother," Aunt Melinda snapped. "So, it's only sensible we divide it among the closest members of the family."

In other words, she wanted that money for herself, and for her son. *Unbelievable.*

"The most sensible thing would be to not speak about my brother as though he has passed away," Rose said through gritted teeth. She was barely containing her fury. She should have known this evening would turn out like this. Those two couldn't live without stirring some kind of trouble.

Aunt Melinda acted as though Rose hadn't said a word. "Since Devon wasn't married, all he has should go to you, and us," Aunt Melinda said to Rose's mother, staring at Rose as though daring her to step a foot out of line.

"We will not have this discussion now. Devon will be all right," her mother insisted. "So there's no point in even talking about it."

"I'm sorry, Rose," Joey said, although he clearly wasn't. "Devon's obviously not going to make it. And if you ask me, you should just pull the plug on him, not make him suffer, force him to be a vegetable for years."

"Excuse me?" she said incredulously.

"That's the best way," he insisted. "I know it's hard, but we are only trying to make this bad situation a little bit better."

"By telling me I should kill my brother? And then give his money to you?" Rose asked, raising her voice.

"Don't be so overly dramatic," Aunt Melinda snapped at her.

"Mom," Rose pleaded, looking at her mother. She couldn't believe these two. They were nothing but grave robbers. Rose stopped herself there because now she was doing it too. Devon wasn't dead. And he wasn't going to die. He was young and strong, she had to have faith in that. He would wake up and get a chance to live his life to the fullest. And this would all be forgotten.

"Although I see your intentions are completely altruistic," her mom mocked as she raised her chin in defiance, "we won't be having this discussion, not now, not ever."

"And you most certainly won't be getting a cent of my brother's money," Rose added for good measure.

"Like you can stop me, little bastard," Joey snorted.

"Wanna bet, jailbird?" Rose snapped.

Joey's eyes flashed with fury. "You really don't want to start threatening me, Rose, I won't tolerate it," Joey warned. He was such a brute, and it never took him long to resort to violence. He was nothing but an animal.

"Don't you dare speak to my fiancée in such a manner." Adrian, who was very quiet up until that moment, practically exploded, getting into Joey's face.

Rose could only stare at him.

Joey quickly recovered from the initial shock. "What are you going to do about it, pencil pusher?" Joey dared, matching his levels of aggression immediately.

"You really don't want to mess with me, Joey. I may be just a pencil pusher, but I can make your life extremely difficult and miserable."

Rose was surprised by the intensity with which Adrian came to her defense. She wasn't used to seeing him like this. There was a chance she had *never* seen him like this before, come to think about it.

And then the unimaginable happened. Joey actually backed off. He was still talking trash, throwing minor insults at Adrian, but he definitely backed off. Adrian's threat worked.

"Mom, I think it's time for everyone to leave," Rose pointed out.

Her mother nodded. "My daughter is right. You should all leave now. This was clearly a mistake thinking we could spend one night together in a civilized manner."

Rose was relieved her mother had finally realized how toxic these people were and that there was no point in insisting on bringing them all together, expecting some kind of support or compassion from them.

"Remember my warning, Thelma. You can't ignore what's coming forever," were Aunt Melinda's parting words.

It was on the tip of Rose's tongue to say how she would unquestionably remember all Aunt Melinda did of late and then return everything in kind once someone she loved passed away. However, she couldn't utter something that cruel, even to that woman.

Once they all went home, Rose took a deep breath, releasing some of the tension.

"Are you okay?" Adrian asked, looking concerned.

Not by a long shot. "Thank you for dealing with Joey for me," she said instead.

Adrian smiled. "No need to thank me. I will always have your back, no matter what."

Rose truly wished that to be true, but she wholeheartedly doubted it. There was this rift between them that made her question everything, doubting his reasons for staying with her.

Is he with me because of the money? Wasn't that always the case? Was he like the rest of them, but knew how to hide it better?

It was true that was something she worried about at the beginning of their relationship. That was why she never spoke about her family with him and never explained what her father did for a living, all in the hopes he wouldn't discover how wealthy her family was until she was ready.

And then, over time, Adrian managed to put all her worries at ease. It appeared as though he truly loved her for who she was. It appeared he was completely okay that she worked as an editor and didn't own much. Now all those old insecurities came out to play, and she wasn't sure about anything anymore.

"Something Joey said really triggered me. What if he or someone else on his behalf did this to Devon and Dad intentionally? What if all of this happened because someone wants all the money for himself?"

"What? Now you think Joey killed your father and tried to do the same to Devon to get all the money? When he wasn't even in the will in the first place? Do you hear yourself? Do you know how ridiculous that sounds?" he chastised.

When he put it like that, it did sound a bit strange, but she wasn't prepared to dismiss it so easily. Besides, Joey wasn't the only one salivating over those billions of dollars. That was a lot of money, and even people who weren't criminals would be tempted to do something for the prospect of becoming wealthy beyond reason.

"I know how it sounds. That doesn't make it impossible."

"Rose, you have to get all these crazy ideas out of your system. You're starting to worry me. Stop it!"

Will they lock me up in some mental hospital if I continue to speak like this? Will Adrian, as a lawyer, help out? She reminded herself with what ease he just threatened Joey.

Rose had no idea what possessed her to have all those thoughts, but they definitely acted as a warning. She needed to be more careful in the future. If she was right and something was happening inside this family, then she needed to be cautious with whom she shared her suspicions. And that included Adrian. She couldn't trust him anymore. She couldn't trust anyone.

"Maybe you're right," she forced herself to say. "Maybe I'm trying to find justifications where there are none. What happened to Dad was a freakish accident and nothing more."

"I'm glad to hear you say that," he said, sighing in relief, hugging her, and kissing her forehead. "I know it's hard, but we'll make it through this, I promise."

Later that night, Rose couldn't stop stressing about Adrian, or why he was so adamant her theories had no merit. Why couldn't he humor her a bit, and help her discover the truth instead of being so rigid?

But she was most disturbed by how easily she'd decided he couldn't be trusted and lied to him. *Is it finally time to break up with him?* she couldn't help wondering.

Am I the problem?

SIXTEEN

Rose was surprised to see that Ava didn't leave the mansion with the rest of the family.

She is not family.

Neither are you.

Ava left the living room with the rest, but then she clearly decided to linger, to explore the house. Rose found her sitting in her old bedroom, at her desk, having a drink.

Did she hear my discussion with Adrian? was the first thing that came to Rose's mind, though, it was shortly replaced with something else. Seeing her sitting at her desk, in her room, in her space, filled her with anger.

"What are you doing in here?" she demanded, gritting her teeth. She could not fathom why her mother insisted on including Ava in all their family affairs. Then again, there were a lot of things she didn't understand about her mother. That was just something she had to learn to live with.

"Having a drink," Ava stated the obvious, "And contemplating a few things. This family is a train wreck, isn't it?" she said almost conversationally.

Rose wasn't going to do this with her. She wasn't going to sit there with her and have a friendly chat. Ava made it completely clear from the start that they should be enemies.

"You have no business being here."

Ava simply gave her a look, taking a sip of her drink. She was drinking whiskey, probably her father's, Rose noted.

"Everyone else left, so we would like to be left alone now," Rose tried again, still being pretty civil. Because she knew if she lost her temper again, Ava would threaten her with exposure.

Ava smirked, setting her drink to the side. "Everyone?" she challenged. "Did Adrian leave too?" she asked sweetly.

Rose was about to snap before catching herself in time. It was obvious Ava was baiting her. She really was a true snake.

"I know what you are doing, and it's not going to work," Rose said instead.

To that, Ava laughed. "You think you know, but in reality, you have no clue."

"What's that supposed to mean?" Rose demanded. As far as she was concerned, it was time to place all the cards on the table.

"You know, you and your 'family'," she mocked the word, "will lose the lawsuit if things continue."

Rose knew that although Ava constantly threatened to take them all to court for her part of the inheritance, she hadn't actually filed anything. As far as Rose knew, she didn't even have a lawyer yet. Mr. Merser would inform her if there were any developments in that regard. This brought up the question: what was Ava actually doing here? If it was just about the money, she wouldn't be wasting time like this.

She also wondered where this confidence came from. Was she emboldened by what happened to Devon? Rose couldn't rule that out.

"Are we just chatting, or do you have a point to make?" Rose countered. "Either way, a little advice, you suck at it regardless."

Ava didn't like that but masked it quickly. "I have a proposition for you."

"Okay, let's hear it," Rose replied still standing by the door. She refused to sit down, wanting to make it clear how unwelcome the other woman was, especially in her room.

No matter what Ava had to say, Rose had no intention of accepting it. There would be no negotiations with a terrorist.

"I will drop my lawsuit if we settle for giving me half of Charles's inheritance."

Although she delivered that in all seriousness, Rose had to laugh. What she was suggesting was completely ridiculous.

"Let me get this straight. Although you haven't even filed a lawsuit yet, you want to settle for half?"

"Yes."

This woman is incredible. "Ava, you have no real case to speak of," Rose tried to reason with her.

"I have proof," she insisted.

"Yes, you have a piece of paper stating you are Charles's daughter, but he never bothered to claim you or put you in his will. Do you see where I'm going with this?" Rose questioned.

Ava's eyes flashed with fury. "Do you want to test how much a piece of paper could make a difference? We can try it on your case first," she threatened instantly.

For some reason, the threat simply didn't have the same effect as before. Rose had no idea what changed in her head, but she liked it. "No need to get your feathers all riled up. My point is why do you think you deserve half?" Rose asked.

"Because I do," Ava stated. "You grew up with all of this, while I had nothing. You got horse riding camp and family vacations, while my mom and I had barely enough to scrape by. You were catered to by a full staff while I spent some nights watching my mom go hungry so I could eat. You got to go to an Ivy League college with your doting dad paying all of your bills for some degree I doubt you even use, whereas I'm up to my ears in med school debt, and I'm actually *helping* people. He ignored me and left me and my mom to fend for ourselves. And when I told him about the DNA test, he just pushed me away. Belittled me and said I was nothing but trash." Her jaw ticked.

Despite her impassioned speech, Rose wasn't impressed. Her father would never have done any of that. He was an honorable man, and something about what Ava was saying was bugging her. There was something off about it.

Since Rose said nothing, she continued. "I want seven billion dollars, more or less, and I think that's very fair of me," she insisted.

Rose was so stunned that she could only stare at the other woman. She was shocked and slightly amused by her audacity, and her greed.

What other leverage does she think she has? Rose had to wonder. Even if she did take them to court, she would never get half, so what made her come here and demand something like that in the first place? Rose simply didn't get it.

That was not what she asked.

"Only seven billion?" Rose mocked. "What will you do with such a small amount of money?"

"I have a much bigger need for it than someone like you could ever understand," she said snidely.

Rose made a face. "What do you mean someone like me?"

"Rose?" Adrian appeared at the door. "I heard voices," he explained, looking between the two of them. There was a slight tinge of fear in his eyes.

Is he afraid I am confronting Ava because of him?

"We're just chatting," Rose explained, hoping he would excuse himself and leave.

"What are you chatting about?" Adrian asked, coming deeper inside the room.

Rose groaned inwardly.

"Ava is just about to tell me what she would do with seven

billion dollars," Rose explained, seeing how Adrian had no intentions of leaving.

"Seven billion?" Adrian muttered the number, clearly not understanding anything.

"She wants more than half, not a quarter," Rose clarified.

Adrian's eyes widened. And then he recovered, clearly realizing how rude he was. "What will you do? Will you travel all over the world, and visit the ancient cradles of civilization? That's what I would do." He tried to lighten the atmosphere.

"I have much bigger plans," Ava said, raising her chin ever so slightly.

"Like what?" Adrian asked with interest.

Rose gritted her teeth. Ava could talk about the difference between the colors coral and peach, and he would still have that same awed expression on his face.

"As I'm sure I mentioned before, I work at a research facility, and to put it plainly, that money could be put to much better use helping the world than in some brat's trust fund," she said, her tone rude.

"That is a very noble cause, Ava," Adrian complimented. It was obvious there was something else he wanted to say, add a few more praises, before remembering Rose was there too, and stopped himself in time.

It was on the tip of Rose's tongue to ask if they would like some privacy and leave them alone. Adrian was unbelievable. And he had the audacity to claim he wasn't interested in Ava.

It was clear that he wanted to kiss her then and there, especially after hearing how she claimed she would be spending her inheritance on saving the world. *Seven billion dollars for the institute she worked for? She had to be joking...*

"Do you have any more questions for me? Are you ready to settle now?" Ava asked Rose.

"I cannot give you an answer now. However, you've defi-

nitely given me a lot to think about," Rose replied diplo-
matically.

There was no way in hell Rose would hand over that kind of
money to her, no matter how noble her cause appeared to be.
Rose couldn't trust a word Ava said; she'd caught her in a lie
before, and it seemed too convenient that she'd switched gears
now. As far as she was concerned, the best-case scenario for Ava
was that she could walk away with three billion and not a cent
more. Seven was simply too much. Hell, the three was too
much, but if it made her go away, Rose was swayed.

She wants Devon's part as well, Rose realized. *She is a
vulture, a scavenger like the rest of the family.*

"Don't think too long, I'm not a patient person."

"And yet you chose to be a researcher, how curious," Rose
noted.

"I'm sure that Rose, Thelma, and you will come to some
kind of an arrangement," Adrian offered, always trying to be a
diplomat.

"You forgot Devon," Rose pointed out angrily. It was infuriating how quickly they all were ready to write her brother off,
Adrian included as it turned out. Rose didn't plan on giving up.
She would never give up hoping he would wake up, and return
to them.

"I know, Rose, but..." he stopped, clearly not knowing how
to continue.

"I think it's time for you to leave," although Rose turned to
look at Ava as she said that, she meant Adrian as well. She
couldn't look at him at the moment with how mad she was.

Ava got up from the chair very slowly, seductively. Rose felt
like rolling her eyes. She had no idea why she bothered to put
on a show. Adrian was her only audience, and he was already
salivating at her.

"Of course," Ava said, "however, I want to say goodnight to
Thelma first."

"She already retired to her room," Rose explained, losing patience.

"That's okay, I know the way," Ava said, leaving Rose's bedroom.

True to her words, she started walking down the hall toward Rose's mother's room.

Rose went after her, silently fuming at her every gesture. It was infuriating how Ava behaved as though she owned the place. *She definitely knows her way around*, Rose grumbled to herself.

Ava knocked discreetly against the door before entering. "I just wanted to say goodnight before leaving."

"How very kind of you," her mother replied, allowing Ava to kiss her on the cheek.

Rose didn't fail to notice how Ava behaved completely differently around her mom than when she was all alone with Rose.

"Keep me posted how Devon is," she added on her way out.

"Of course."

"Goodnight, Mom, I'll be leaving too," Rose said.

"Goodnight, dear."

There were no goodbyes offered to Rose by Ava, not that she cared. Ava simply left. And it was good seeing her back for a change. *What a bitch.*

Yeah, sure, she is all sweet and full of concern about Devon in front of Mom, yet somehow failed to mention she wants seven billion dollars, Rose argued in her thoughts, showing Ava out. The other woman clearly wanted Rose to do her dirty work. Rose had no intention of obliging.

If Ava wanted that kind of money, she would have to ask for it from Thelma herself and let her see she was nothing but an opportunistic snake like the rest of them. It would be difficult to keep her mask on when they all knew she was all about the money.

"I thought of leaving as well," Adrian said, snapping her from her thoughts.

Rose could see Ava's car driving away from the house.

Is he going to meet her?

"Okay, bye," Rose said coldly, walking away from him.

"Rose? Is everything all right? Are you angry with me?"

"It's fine. Just leave, Adrian."

He did as she said. A few months back he would have followed her to find out what was wrong, but not anymore. And she didn't want him to either. Left all alone, she grabbed her keys and drove to her apartment, resuming her musings about Ava.

The courage to ask that much money from Rose's family, firmly believing she had every right, was astounding. And the reason she gave for needing that kind of money was equally ridiculous.

She was acting like she was Mother Teresa or something. No doubt that would get her some sympathy points from the family. Then again, that could be a double-edged sword, considering how selfish they all were; giving away money and doing things for others wasn't in their true nature. They all pretended to care, they all sacrificed a small portion of their fortune and donated to all kinds of charities as part of a PR strategy. However, that was all for show.

While Ava worked her way within the family and manipulated feelings with her noble story, Rose watched her closely, fully knowing Ava was keeping an eye on her as well.

They were both ready for that first strike.

The question was, who would make the first move?

SEVENTEEN

Rose spent a good portion of the night going over everything in her head. By morning, she had come to the realization that she was miserable. She hadn't been happy since her father died, and Ava had come into her life. Ava was like Oleander. Beautiful and deadly poisonous, even to the touch for some people. She'd infiltrated Rose's life and was taking over.

Rose glanced at the dot on her phone screen as she kept track of where Ava was. She remained at her hotel, which wasn't surprising given how early it was. Her mind turned back to Adrian, wondering where he was now. She questioned where it had all gone wrong with him. Was it her? Had she changed? Had what she wanted out of life changed? Or was it Adrian who had changed? She was certainly seeing things in him she hadn't before, and that disturbed her.

Had he always been like that with other women, overly friendly, staring at them? Or was it just Ava? It didn't really matter, she supposed, because it was a character flaw that she wasn't sure she could live with. Not when she could never be truly sure that he wasn't just biding his time to get to the money, like so many others.

Then what was she still doing in this relationship with him? It was obvious it wasn't working. For either of them. Was she petty, keeping him to herself when she knew he would rather be with someone like Ava? Or was the fear of being alone right now and dealing with everything by herself preventing her from cutting that cord?

At the same time, the sad reality was that she was already alone. Adrian wasn't an ally, which meant she would have to do everything on her own anyway.

Maybe I can find some outside help, she had a sudden thought. Since she couldn't rely on anyone inside the family to help her out in discovering what the hell was going on, perhaps she could find someone on the outside.

There was only one logical solution. She needed to hire a PI who could start digging into everything and would find the evidence she so desperately needed. Evidence that could help her expose Ava and rub everyone's nose in the fact she was right from the start.

And what if he can't find anything? What if Adrian is right, and this is all just in my head? She had a moment of doubt that she quickly dismissed. She would cross that bridge when or if there was a need for it, not sooner.

She decided to find a lawyer first. Mr. Merser was a great lawyer, her father had trusted him, but she wanted someone completely unconnected to her family for this. She didn't want word of what she was doing to get back to her mom or anyone else in the family. She couldn't very well ask her friends or colleagues for recommendations, so she started searching online. She couldn't explain why, but she wanted someone younger, who did a lot of public service cases.

Basically, she wanted someone with a soul, not simply a shark who was hungry for power, and money. She didn't want someone who cared only about winning. She wanted someone who would be invested in discovering the truth like she was.

Was that a bit insecure of her? Probably, but she stumbled on someone she thought had potential and decided to make an appointment.

His name was Alex Min, and he was prepared to listen to her.

The next morning, she arrived at his office, and he welcomed her in.

"What can I do for you, Ms. Blaisdell?" he asked.

While she explained her situation revolving around her father's death, her brother ending up in a coma after the same diagnosis, a new half-sister appearing, and their general struggle around the inheritance, he seemed deeply worried and sympathetic.

"First, I would agree with your assessment of the situation. That is a lot of coincidence, and with the kind of money involved, it's good to be skeptical of these kinds of things. I would suggest you hire a private investigator who can get to the bottom of these suspicious occurrences in your life."

Rose was glad to have someone who finally agreed with her. "Do you have someone trustworthy I could speak with?"

Mr. Min nodded. "There is someone my office retains from time to time. He also collaborates with the police on certain cases, so I know he is very reliable and discreet."

"That's exactly what I need."

He handed her a business card.

"Gregory Falcone," she read out loud.

"That's right. He is one of the best," he assured her.

For some reason, she had a good feeling about this guy, Gregory. Which was a good thing too, as he was her last hope, after all, to prove to others, and to herself, that she hadn't completely lost her mind.

"Could you set up a meeting with him? I would like to speak with him, and perhaps hire him, as soon as possible."

"Of course," the lawyer replied. "I will make that call right away."

As Rose left his office, she had a spring in her step. Nothing would stop her now.

EIGHTEEN

Rose couldn't explain why, but she felt a bit nervous going to see Gregory Falcone. Maybe it was because she had lied to Adrian again, not wanting him to know she was going to hire a PI. There was so much at stake, and she couldn't take any chances.

Gregory was nothing like she expected. He was in his forties, on the tallish side, really soft-spoken, with a thin build and a kind face. His brown hair was floppy and graying, his nose was long, and his eyes brown. He looked more like a schoolteacher than a PI. She decided to trust him.

"What can I do for you, Ms. Blaisdell?" he asked in a very calm and professional manner.

Rose decided to tell Gregory everything. It would be foolish to hide anything from him if she expected any kind of help from him. If she wanted this mystery solved, she had to put all her cards on the table.

Rose surprised even herself with the ease with which she managed to get everything out. She told Gregory about her father, how he died from some strange, rare disease. Then she told him about her brother being in a coma from that same ailment. She told him her suspicions of her half-sister who appeared quite out of the blue and demanded half of the inheritance.

"I just need someone to investigate these things, so I'll know once and for all if I'm losing my mind, or not," Rose said quite honestly.

Gregory looked at her long and hard before replying. In those moments Rose was certain he was about to turn her down. Luckily, she was wrong.

"I take no pleasure saying this, but I think you might be right," he said eventually. "Usually, when people follow their guts, they are right."

"Does that mean you will accept the case?" Rose wanted to know, feeling almost giddy that now two people seemed to have her back in this.

"Yes, I will," he replied simply.

Rose nodded, so relieved that he had agreed. She was finally speaking with someone who not only believed her but someone who could help her. Then again, there was a chance he was doing all of this only for the money. As she had that thought, part of her rebelled. Gregory really didn't seem like the type who would take advantage of her. He worked for the police as well; surely there was a level of trust there?

"What's the first step?" she asked, unable to hide her excitement completely. "Is there anything you need from me?"

"Here are my thoughts," he started. "First, we need to do a second autopsy on your father. And we need to get a specific doctor who will do a thorough examination of your brother," he suggested glumly.

Rose realized that he was completely right. She should have thought about something like that on her own, in the first place. It would be prudent to get a second opinion about everything. At the same time, that didn't mean she liked it. Although she wasn't superstitious, she didn't like the feeling of disturbing the dead. Nonetheless, she was prepared to do it, if it meant getting to the bottom of things and discovering the truth.

And then something came to mind. "My father is already buried," she pointed out.

How am I to organize another autopsy if he's already underground? she thought, horrified.

"We will have to exhume him," Gregory replied simply, as though they were discussing the most common thing in the world and not something as disturbing as violating her father's resting place.

"I don't know if I can do that," she replied honestly.

"That's the only way, to know for sure," he was adamant.

Rose remained quiet.

"I know that something like this is difficult to accept, but after all that has happened to you and your family, I believe that you deserve to know the truth, and this is the path toward it."

Rose needed a moment to process that. If she wanted to discover the truth, to learn if she was right about everything, then she had to get her hands dirty, and quite literally.

"How is something like that done?" Rose asked eventually. "I will never get approval from my mother if I ask," she added as an afterthought.

"Well, it might be legally ambiguous, but could you get her to sign permission without telling her what it's for? There is a way to do it discreetly and without any objections from the authorities. At least not any that would be timely."

Rose thought about it and realized she could actually give her mom the papers to sign and tell her they were for the lawyer. Her mom most likely wouldn't bother reading them. It was a bit shady, but Rose needed answers, and this was the best way to get them. "I'll see what I can do."

He explained they could exhume her father, do a second autopsy with a different coroner, and then rebury him before anyone was the wiser. Rose had to admit that Gregory was very clever. Then again, he did this kind of thing for a living and clearly had a lot of experience. Something about his calm manner put her at ease.

Once they finished discussing her father and started making arrangements for her brother, it was obvious Gregory had something more to say, but was hesitant.

"Is there something else that we need to discuss?" she prompted.

"If I could be so forward, I would also suggest something else," he hedged.

"Do whatever you think is best," Rose replied simply. She knew that for this to work she had to trust this man completely.

"I would like to start surveilling your fiancé, Adrian. You said you'd only been together six months?" he said without beating around the bush.

Rose was taken aback by that. She hadn't realized she'd shared that much. All the stress was creating gaps in her memory, but recovered quickly.

He is really offering a full round service, she joked to herself, even though she felt anything but jovial.

"I wouldn't want you wasting time on that when there's so much more I need to know regarding my father and brother," she explained.

"The offer stands if you change your mind. I'm offering because you never know what people are hiding, and given your status, it might be wise to err on the side of caution," he said, not pressing the issue, although it was more than obvious that he wanted to do that for her.

"Thank you, I'll keep it in mind."

Rose was grateful, but she thought they needed to focus on what was more important at the moment, which was discovering what actually happened to her father and her brother. Although she was shaken that someone else brought up suspi-

cions about Adrian's intentions, she was more than capable of
dealing with Adrian on her own. Or so she hoped.

"Based on your experience and what you heard so far, what
do you think happened here?" Rose had to ask, returning them
to the main subject.

"It's hard to say at the moment," he hedged, "however, I
definitely suspect some form of foul play."

"Do you think someone killed my father and tried to do the
same to my brother?" Rose asked, fixing him with her direct
gaze. That was what interested her the most, after all.

He didn't flinch, "Unfortunately, because of the money at
stake, that would be my first thought."

It was a strange feeling of relief that someone else was
seeing what she was seeing, even when they were discussing
something so unthinkable as her father's murder.

Rose nodded again. "Okay, then that's what I need to be
your priority, to discover who did this to them." So, this person
could pay for what they did.

"I need you to tell me everything about all the people in
your life who could have a motive to do something like this, so
we can perhaps find the most likely suspects," he explained.

Rose was more than happy to oblige. She started with her
father's family. Although Rose personally believed that Aunt
Melinda and her son Joey had the most to gain, she still covered
all the rest of her relatives, not wanting to leave anyone out,
because this wasn't about her personal animosities, this was
about discovering the truth.

Once they covered the family, friends, and colleagues of her
father and her brother, which was rather extensive, Gregory
was still not done asking questions, and Rose liked that he was
thorough. It gave her hope that he would be the one to find the
guilty party, no matter what.

"Tell me everything you know about Ava," he asked next.

"I really don't know that much, actually," she confessed.

And Rose realized that was by design. She didn't want to know anything about her because if any of what Ava said was true, then her father's betrayal would hurt even harder. At the same time, she knew she made a mistake acting like that because it was prudent to know your enemy. Her father taught her that at a young age and her mother had recently reminded her of it.

"It doesn't matter, any details could help, even from back when the two of you were in college together," Gregory replied in a reassuring manner.

Rose did her best, but sadly, as she said to him, she didn't know that much. They were not friends in college, and they certainly weren't friends now.

"As far as I know she works for a research company. She's a doctor. She's demanding half the inheritance because she wants to fund her research for some cure. She has DNA results that prove she is my father's biological child."

"Hmmm."

You need to be completely honest with this man, she snapped at herself when her mind turned to the other DNA test. "She's also blackmailing me to not go against her," Rose added.

That piqued his interest, and he asked for more details, so she told him about her own DNA results.

"That's interesting," he commented.

"You think it means something?" she asked.

"Perhaps. Perhaps not. That could only be a reassurance on her part that she gets what she believes belongs to her," he explained.

"All the same, I would like you to dig as much as possible about her because even if she had nothing to do with my father's passing, the evidence against her could be used in the lawsuit," Rose explained.

"Of course," Gregory reassured, all the while taking notes.

"Oh, and I should probably tell you... I put a tracker on her car." Rose felt her cheeks heat.

Gregory smiled. "You did? Have you found her doing anything strange? Going anywhere odd?"

Rose sighed. "Well, not yet. But maybe it will be useful? I'll give you the login information so you can use it." She grabbed a pad of Post-its from his desk and a pen and wrote it down.

"That could be really helpful." His smile widened as he took the paper from her.

Rose hoped that with Gregory's help, she would gather enough evidence against Ava to prove she was a fraud so her family wouldn't have to give a cent to her from her father's inheritance. Even if she wasn't a killer, Rose really didn't like her and hated the idea of splitting money with her. A person like her didn't deserve it. And it didn't matter that she presented herself as this noble savior. Rose wasn't buying it. Ava was a snake and nothing else.

"I will do my best to have something for you in the next couple of days, at least about Ava," Gregory reassured.

"Thank you very much," Rose replied honestly.

"It's my pleasure. And don't take this the wrong way, but I need to express how serious this matter is and that everything discussed has to stay between us," he stressed the words.

"Of course." She nodded.

"I know it's hard, but we will get to the bottom of things," Gregory said on her way out.

"I know we will," she said, and she meant it. With him by her side, she was feeling optimistic.

Once again, Gregory looked like there was more he wanted to say and hesitated if he should.

"Thank you for everything. I'll get that signed release to you as soon as possible," Rose added, hoping that would be an invitation for him to speak his mind.

"Rose, I hope you don't mind me asking, but are you all right?" he asked, taking her aback.

Of course, she wasn't all right. Her life, her family, was a complete mess. And she definitely started to hate that question. However, at the same time, when Gregory asked her that, she didn't resent it that much. Perhaps that was the reason she decided to reply honestly to him.

"I am far from all right, but I'm managing." Because she didn't have any other choice. She had to be the strong one in the family because if she completely broke down then they were all doomed. That sounded a bit overdramatic, but it was true. She was the only one doing the work, she was the only one interested in discovering the truth.

"I understand. And if you need anyone to speak with, know that I'm one phone call away."

Even though they were strangers who just met, Rose truly appreciated his offer. Although it was out of character, she found herself trusting him.

"Thank you," she said.

"I will call you as soon as I have something," he said gently, opening the door for her.

"Good."

Rose left Gregory's office feeling slightly better than before, unburdened in a way. It would be great to have some real information soon. Not simply regarding Ava, but about everything.

And then Ava wouldn't be ten steps ahead of her anymore. Having Gregory by her side would be a game changer.

That thought almost put a smile on her face.

NINETEEN

Rose felt much better, mentally and emotionally, after hiring Gregory. Having someone in her corner helped her continue pushing forward, and acted like the energy infuser she needed. Gregory would give her the answers she so desperately needed; she was sure of that.

She headed toward her mother's house so that she could get the exhumation permission signed. She was in town and decided to drive past Ava's hotel, just to check. She hadn't thought to look at the tracker before leaving Gregory's office, so when she pulled up to a stoplight, Rose grabbed her phone out and looked at it. Ava's car was on the move.

Where is she going? She pulled up the map and noticed the road she was on would take Ava to the hospital. Was she going to go finish off Devon?

Panic filled Rose as she pressed on the gas when the light changed. She had to stop her. She sped down the street, turning left onto the road Ava was on, hoping to catch up to her. Rose glanced at the dot as it moved, but instead of going straight as you would if you were going to the hospital, Ava turned. Rose eased up on the gas, as her fear for Devon subsided.

She slowed a bit but made the same turn Ava had. She was probably a minute or two behind her. As she followed the tracker, she watched it stop and stay in one place. Rose looked around, and a feeling of dread filled her. She knew where she was. This was Adrian's neighborhood. And as she got closer to his apartment building, Rose noticed Ava's car parked on the curb.

What was Ava doing here?

Reaching his building, she parked her car and got out. She barely made a few steps when she stopped in her tracks, shocked. Right in front of Adrian's building, on the steps in front of the main entrance, was Ava herself. And she wasn't alone. Adrian was there as well, glued to her body as though they shared skin, while they kissed passionately.

All kinds of thoughts, and all kinds of emotions, passed through her head in those moments.

I knew it. I knew it, she thought furiously. She had half a mind to get back in her car and run them over. It wasn't a reasonable, sane thought, but it was there just the same.

Despite knowing that Adrian wasn't the right man for her, she'd never thought in a million years that he would do this to her. She felt like the last six months—almost seven— had been a lie. He felt like a completely different person to her. Had she ever known him at all? Had he only been using her for the money? Had he known who she was all along? Rose gasped for breath, feeling a full-blown panic attack coming on. Had he decided that Ava was the better catch because she was demanding half of the Blaisdell fortune? Did he think Ava could win and she'd share the money with him?

Rose was reeling as she stood there watching them. Ava and Adrian acted as though they were a couple of teenagers with one another. Although Rose believed her emotions regarding Adrian were pretty much resolved, she was wrong, and her eyes filled with tears. She couldn't believe that bastard had the audacity to lie to her. He'd made her feel crazy, and jealous, said she was obsessed with Ava and her flirting, when in reality she was right all along. He was cheating on her with the woman they'd been fighting about this whole time.

Gregory was right. She didn't know Adrian as well as she'd thought she did. She had a gut feeling about this, and it didn't let her down. *Way to go, me.*

Rose was frozen in place, watching the two of them make out in the middle of the street, as though they couldn't even wait to get inside to be in each other's arms.

She wanted to run away, to cry in her room, alone. She never wanted to see the man in her life ever again. She never wanted to see Ava again either.

Unfortunately, life didn't work that way. Even if she broke up with Adrian then and there, she still had to deal with Ava one way or another. That made everything more complicated.

Rose let go of the shock and panic that filled her, drew her chin up, and started marching forward. Before that, she made sure no tears would fall down her face. She wasn't going to allow those two to see how much seeing them together rattled her. Instead of running away, she was going to confront them, deal with them, and be done with them once and for all.

"I knew it. I fucking knew it," Rose started as she approached. She wasn't big on profanities, but she felt like this situation required it.

Clearly recognizing her voice, the pair parted. Adrian's eyes widened in shock. He was caught red-handed, so to speak; he wasn't going to be able to weasel his way out of this. He wouldn't be able to blame Rose for what happened, and that cheered her up a bit despite the situation.

"Rose," he stammered her name, looking startled, which was very uncommon for him. Adrian was never one to be at a loss for words.

Ava, on the other hand, simply smirked. She looked pretty

unbothered that her affair had been discovered. More to the point, she clearly liked that Rose finally learned the truth, that Ava managed to steal Adrian from her. That only infuriated Rose further.

"Rose," Adrian tried again, but Rose decided that bastard didn't deserve to talk.

"I knew it! I knew it was more than her just flirting with you, and I was right, you bastard. And you dared to make it seem as though I was imagining things," she seethed.

"It's not what you think, it just happened. Ava dropped by and it just kind of happened," he tried to make excuses for himself.

Rose wasn't buying it. She wasn't that stupid or gullible. This wasn't a first kiss type of scenario.

"Stop lying," she snapped.

"Rose, I'm sorry, I, I..." He looked at Ava as though asking for help.

The other woman fixed her lipstick, snapping her compact shut.

Rose gritted her teeth. "I don't care if you are sorry." Because she knew he wasn't. He was only sorry he got caught. He was sorry he wouldn't be able to deceive her anymore, and nothing else. "I don't want to see you ever again, it's over." She instantly felt better saying that. "You are a weak-willed, cowardly liar, and I am disgusted by you," she threw in his face.

All the while, Ava just stood there enjoying the spectacle without bothering to say anything or defend her lover. Then again, what was there to say anyway? It was pretty clear, at least to Rose.

"I never lied to you, this happened... unexpectedly," Adrian continued.

Rose scoffed. "Yeah, right. Do you really think I'm that stupid?" she asked rhetorically. "I knew this would happen.

And like the true coward you are, you didn't have the decency to break up with me first before jumping into her bed."

Unfortunately, the treacherous tears reappeared in her eyes, but it couldn't be helped, she was that furious, at Adrian, at Ava, but mostly at herself, because if she had only broken up with him a while ago, once she realized the relationship was over, she wouldn't be in this situation in the first place. In the end, she only had herself to blame.

"You know, I never asked for any of this," Adrian said, starting to get angry. "I never wanted this to happen to me, to any of us," he tried to defend.

Rose looked at him incredulously. "Right, so now you are a victim; that's rich. You are disgusting, Adrian, and no matter what you say, the fact remains that you are an opportunistic man whore who will do whatever it takes, say whatever it takes to advance in life," Rose said, aiming to inflict as much pain as possible.

He definitely didn't like hearing that. His next words confirmed as much.

"I'm disgusting? Do you know how painful it is to be with you? Do you know how infuriating it is to be with someone as weak as you are? Someone who is nothing but a doormat. You're a paranoid bitch who dragged me into your family drama."

It really stung hearing all that, but Rose decided to stand her ground. "I can see you are tongue-deep in my family drama without any problems," Rose deadpanned.

Ava started laughing at that. It was obvious how amused she was that Rose was breaking up with her fiancé in such a public manner, and even happier that she was the cause of it.

Before Rose could hit back at Ava, the flash of cameras stopped her in her tracks. Whipping round, she noticed a gaggle of paparazzi who had seen her and Adrian having a full-blown yelling and screaming public break-up. But she hardly noticed them, as Ava's laugh had disturbed her more than anything else that had happened that day. Not even all of Adrian's insults had the same impact on her because it was no ordinary laugh. It was a proper mad scientist laugh, as though they were her lab rats that did something right for a change; there was no other way to describe it.

The whole situation felt unreal. Not just because Rose and Adrian were breaking up in such a loud and public way but also because they had a peculiar spectator, Ava, who looked like she wanted to take notes, laughing in that freakish manner.

Is this just an experiment for her? Rose had a sudden thought. *Am I merely a lab rat to her?*

"You are completely crazy; you know that, right?" Adrian snapped. "No wonder I had to be with someone else when life with you is so unbearable," he complained, clearly angry.

Rose wasn't that surprised he resorted to insults because he had no real arguments to defend his disgusting behavior. Rose's father was right about him from the start. Adrian only cared about the money. And he clearly realized that if he switched to Ava, he would have even more of it.

She said as much, even knowing it would be splashed all over the tabloids. She just didn't care any longer. "You have no credibility anymore. You're a liar. And that means your words mean nothing, your insults mean nothing. You have no real arguments, only garbage."

Adrian snorted. "You want arguments? How about you constantly whining about everything," he threw in her face. "I would go mad staying with you; that's a fact."

Rose rolled her eyes. "You did stay with me, and that says a lot about you and your character. About your ulterior motives. And it's obvious to me you would just keep lying to me if I didn't discover the truth," she pointed out. "You are nothing but a gold digger," she added, disgusted. "My father was right about you; you are a mediocre lawyer whose only accomplishment in life would be marrying someone rich."

Rose had gotten very angry at her father when he told her that to her face about Adrian. She didn't want to believe that, but unfortunately, he was right. He was right about so many things, yet she was stupid, foolish, naive, and refused to listen to him. What she would give now to have him by her side, to listen to his pieces of advice.

"I'm done listening to you anymore," Adrian replied, raising his chin. He turned to look at Ava. "Come on, let's go," he said to her, offering his hand.

Ava glanced at Rose before accepting it, and together, they started climbing toward the entrance of the building, leaving Rose all alone in the middle of the street, upset and deeply disturbed.

On the one hand, she knew this was for the better; on the other, she didn't like the fact she was played for a fool. It would take her a long time to get over this insult, she was aware of that.

Something else occurred to her. "Hey, Adrian," she called after him.

Part of her was surprised that he stopped to look at her. She was glad that he did because otherwise, she wouldn't be able to do what she needed to do. She took the ring from her finger. "Take your cheap ass ring back," she yelled throwing the thing at him. She never liked that ring anyway.

The ring bounced off his chest, and then onto the steps, falling downward as more camera flashes caught the moment. Adrian started chasing after it, in panic. He managed to get it before it ended up in the gutter. Rose made a face seeing that. It would be amusing to see Adrian getting his hands and his clothes dirty. And he would most definitely do everything in his power to get it back. Money, wealth, that was what was important to him after all. He proved that much.

"Thank you for saving me the trip to ask for it back from you," he said trying to save some dignity.

"Of course, I'm giving it back. If I want a proper ring, I'll buy it for myself," she pointed out proudly.

He smirked. "You'll have to, because nobody in their right mind will ever want to marry you, be with you, love you," he threw in her face, returning to Ava and going inside the building.

On their way inside, Ava whispered something in his ear, and he laughed.

Once they were gone, Rose held herself together so she wouldn't completely break apart in front of the paparazzi. She knew if they saw it, they'd say it was because she was so heart-broken, but that wasn't what had her in an emotional wreck. It was the humiliation of it all, and his parting words that did the trick. Especially since that was something she believed deep down inside, too

Finally making it to the privacy of her car, she started sobbing, thankful for the tinted windows to keep out the prying eyes of the reporters. Nobody needed to see her acting the fool over a man like Adrian.

Rose had no idea how she got to her parents' house. Her mother looked startled to see her in such a state. Rose fell into her arms, still crying.

"Rose, what happened?" her mother demanded.

"I caught Adrian cheating on me, with Ava," she said through sobs. "I broke up with him."

Rose could feel her mother shaking her head. "It was bound to happen," she murmured mostly to herself.

Rose broke away so she could look at her. "It was bound to happen?" she repeated incredulously.

Her mother took the bottle of pills from her pocket, and washed one down with something that Rose hoped was a plain orange juice. It was a tranquilizer, of course.

"I mean, your father and I did warn you about him, sweetheart," Rose's mother explained calmly, like they were discussing the weather.

"Why didn't you make me listen?" Rose sobbed.

"It wasn't up to me to interfere, and you were in love, what could I have said that would have deterred you?" her mother replied simply.

Rose sniffled. "I don't think I'm upset because I loved him. I'm more upset at being humiliated by him." She wiped her eyes. "It's going to be all over the tabloids."

Her mother tilted her head and looked at her. "How? Did he go to the press?"

"Worse, they were there for our break-up on the street in front of his apartment building. He and Ava were all over each other."

"Oh, Rose." Her mother frowned.

"I'm going to my room." She needed to be alone.

Rose groaned, imagining how others would react when they heard this news. She could just picture Aunt Melinda jumping for joy when she heard.

Rose practically fell onto her bed, pulling the cover over her head. There was no way she would be able to sleep, but at least with time, she managed to put her crying under control. Once she got all of that out of her system, she was able to function once again.

Instead of feeling heartbroken or in pain, she was pissed off. She was angry Adrian made a fool out of her. *How dare he?* she asked herself over and over. *How dare she?* She couldn't even tell whether there was ever anything real between them. The more she thought about Adrian and Ava together, the angrier she got. Rose wanted revenge for what happened to her, plain and simple.

Rose would make sure Ava paid for everything bad she did in her life. Even if Rose ended up being exposed as illegitimate because of that DNA test result, she wasn't going to back down.

Not now. Not after Ava did everything in her power to make an enemy out of her.

She had nothing to lose anymore.

Her family already ostracized her, so what did she have left to fear of losing anyway? Even if she went down with Ava as well, it would be all worth it, putting that bitch where she belonged.

And it went without saying that Adrian would also get what he deserved along the way. They were both despicable people, they were both guilty, and Rose would find a way to make them pay.

That was a promise.

TWENTY

Rose spent the next several days getting her thoughts and feelings about everything that went down with Adrian under control. She wasn't so much hurt and brokenhearted over him as she was humiliated, and that seemed almost harder to get over somehow.

And when the news hit the tabloids, Aunt Melinda came by her mom's house to gloat and carry on, gleeful at how things had fallen out between Rose and Adrian. It was to be expected that she would act in such a way, but that didn't make it any less painful to endure. Surprisingly, Joey offered to take him out, but Rose didn't want him dead, just away from her and her family, so she declined. Part of her figured that Joey just liked hurting people, and it would have been an excuse for him to do it. Still, it almost made her feel like he still accepted her as part of the family, despite his mother's claim and Ava's too, that she wasn't.

In the meantime, she'd managed to get her mom to sign the exhumation permission by telling her they were just legal formalities. It wasn't exactly a lie; it was just a legal formality that Rose needed to find out what exactly happened to her father.

As soon as she had it, she took it over to Gregory's office where she also informed him that she was no longer engaged to the lying bastard who was now seeing her half-sister. She'd used a bit more colorful language at the time, especially when he said he'd unfortunately seen the tabloids, but he'd also said he was proud of her. That had made her blush. Something about the man was just familiar, comfortable. In a way, it felt as though she'd known him her whole life with how she opened up to him. It was refreshing.

They began texting and calling each other almost every day. Mostly to talk about what he'd found, but occasionally, they talked about other things. Sometimes it was just a quick hello. It felt good to have someone to do that with. Rose really didn't have very many friends.

Two weeks later, Gregory called to let her know he managed to take care of everything. Rose's heart beat faster, knowing he meant all that nasty business with her father's remains.

A judge was contacted, and the body was exhumed and then transported to a private lab for the second autopsy. Gregory had a friend who was a coroner, who agreed to do this favor for them. For the right price, of course.

Rose was pretty much amazed it all happened without anyone in her family being the wiser, which was a good thing because her mother would blow a gasket if she realized she'd given permission for Rose to have that done.

It was of utmost importance that Gregory and Rose gather the evidence without anyone discovering what they were doing in the first place. She didn't want her mom tipped off until it was all said and done, and she couldn't get too mad at Rose for deceiving her. Rose was hoping she would be too caught up in the evidence they discovered to be upset with how it was obtained. She also didn't want anyone else in the family to find out about it because there were certain members— Aunt Melinda— who would be more than happy to go blabbing to Ava and Adrian about what she was up to before she was ready to tell anyone.

And the killer— if there was one—would surely try to stop Rose from discovering the truth. She was sure that the guilty party would be especially interested in sabotaging them during this process, which was precisely why Rose was happy it hadn't come to that. That it was all done discreetly.

It didn't take long for their coroner to do the second autopsy. Filled with anxiety, Rose waited for his results. At the same time, it was arranged for a specialist to visit Devon, to see if he could figure out what had happened to him.

A few days later, Gregory called and asked Rose to visit him in his office because he had some news to share with her. She went immediately. It wasn't like she had anything better to do these days than stress and think about her disaster of a life.

"Like I told you over the phone, I found something out," he said as she entered.

She liked that about him. "What did you find?" she asked while sitting down.

"I have the autopsy report."

"Is it good or bad news?"

"It depends on perspective," he hedged.

"Tell me," she prompted.

"As you know, my friend Doctor Martinez agreed to do an autopsy on your father, while Doctor Michaelson did a full examination on your brother, and both came to the same conclusion. In your father, it was difficult because his blood had been drained, so he tested the bone marrow, where it was found, but in your brother, it was still in his bloodstream," he explained.

Rose was confused. "What does that mean?" she asked.

"As you know, your father died from Kounis Syndrome brought on by an allergic reaction."

"Yes, I know that, but I don't understand what he might have encountered that would have triggered it. It doesn't make sense."

"Well, Dr. Martinez and Dr. Michaelson both discovered large quantities of apitoxin in your father and brother."

"Apitoxin?" Rose questioned. "What is that?"

"It is commonly known as bee venom. Your father and brother were both highly allergic."

"So they were stung by bees? That doesn't make any sense. It's cold out and don't bees hibernate in the winter? They weren't outside when this happened anyway. Father was at home, getting ready for bed. Devon was too, actually."

"I can understand why you're confused. They found no bee sting anywhere on either of them, yet there was a large amount of apitoxin in your father's system, and your brother had almost as much in his. Could either of them have used a cream or gel that was made with bee venom for arthritis without knowing they were allergic?"

Rose frowned, trying to wrap her mind around this new piece of information. "I don't think so. My father didn't have arthritis, and neither does Devon. And why would they use something with venom in it?"

Gregory shook his head. "Surprisingly, for some people, bee venom gives people with arthritis some relief. Some of them actually have bees purposely sting them."

Rose couldn't even imagine doing that. However, that wasn't what was bothering her in that moment. "Gregory, if they didn't have any bee stings and didn't use any kind of cream or gel with it, how did they get such large doses of the venom in their systems?"

"I need to ask you... is there anyone who might have known about their allergies?"

Rose sucked in a ragged breath. Was he saying what she

thought he might be saying? "Do you think someone intentionally poisoned them?"

"I'm afraid that might be exactly what's happened, and then made it look like Kounis Syndrome," Gregory replied.

So, it was a good news/bad news kind of a situation.

"Who would do such a thing?" Rose wondered out loud. More importantly, who would do this to her father, and her brother? *Is it possible they share a common enemy?* What was the motive for this? All kinds of questions passed through her head. But there was really only one answer. Money. They both had it, and somebody wanted it.

"I don't know at the moment; however, I'll have more information soon," he reassured.

"Is there a way to discover where this bee venom came from?" Rose asked next.

"Dr. Michaelson is trying to isolate the venom and test it. It seems there are different compositions of venom depending on the exact type of bee it came from. It might be possible to discover what apiary developed the venom and who bought it, if we're lucky."

While she listened to Gregory speak, one thought was front and center in her mind. She was right from the start. Her gut feeling was telling her someone did this to her family on purpose, and now she had proof.

Unfortunately, that didn't make her feel any better because knowing that didn't change anything; her father was still dead, and her brother was still in a coma. And Rose was sure that even if she shared this news with her mother, she wouldn't believe her. Because she wasn't ready to listen. However, in time, Rose hoped that would change. In the meantime, she would gather as much evidence as possible. She would do everything in her power to discover and bring this killer to justice.

"What's on your mind, Rose?" Gregory snapped her from her thoughts.

"I was just thinking how it doesn't make me feel any better knowing I was right. Someone intentionally caused harm to my father and brother," she replied honestly.

"Knowing someone intentionally poisoned them can't be easy; however, there is a good side to it all as well."

"What is it?" she asked because she failed to see it.

"By knowing this was no accident, we will continue digging, and we will find the guilty party, and make them pay for crimes committed."

"That's true," she allowed.

Someone within her circle killed her father and tried to do the same to her brother, and that made her feel quite rattled. Was it Ava? Or maybe one of the relatives? She couldn't be sure yet. More worrisome was how was she to act from now on? She didn't want to alert the killer that they were onto them with how they'd managed to do this, but she was afraid.

"What is our next course of action?" she asked, simply to stop herself from thinking.

"I'll wait for Dr. Michaelson to finish his research regarding the venom, and then I'll gather all the evidence and go to the police," he informed. "It's time we involve them in this because this person needs to be criminally charged after all."

Rose couldn't agree more. "Once they take over the case will you still be able to help out?" Rose wanted to know. She enjoyed talking to him and felt like they'd gotten to be friends. She didn't want to lose that.

"That's up to you, of course."

"Yes," she replied, her cheeks beginning to flush, "I would like you to stay involved, until the end, until we find the killer."

She would feel much better knowing Gregory was on the case as well. After all, the police didn't even question whether it was a murder in the first place.

"I must warn you. Despite what movies portray, there's a chance that won't happen overnight."

"I understand."

"And there's something else. This person is clearly dangerous and will do everything in their power to elude the police, so be extra careful. We aren't out of the woods yet. This is just the first step in the right direction."

"I'll be careful and keep pretending as though nothing's out of the ordinary."

"Good, but considering you and I both believe that your father's money is the motive for his murder and for your brother's current condition, I think you and your mom should both take extra precautions," he replied.

He made a good point. "I'll do what I can. I'm not sure how to deal with my mom. I can't tell her yet about Dad and Devon, not without more evidence, but I can keep an eye on her and check her room for anything that might have been tainted."

"Since we don't know how your father and brother were poisoned with the venom, I'd say watch what you ingest. The venom is actually colorless and odorless in liquid form, so be vigilant."

That was a scary thing to hear. How would she know if it was in her food or drink? She'd have to make sure it was sealed prior to drinking it or eating it. "Got it." Rose nodded.

"Also, I want you to be prepared for whoever is doing this to your immediate family to attempt to pin your father's death and your brother's situation on you or your mother."

Rose hadn't thought of that and suddenly felt worried about that being a possibility. "What can I do?"

"Figure out where both of you were at the time and who might have been around you, so that they can give you an alibi."

Rose frowned. She wasn't sure that she could find someone in the family willing to provide her with one, maybe one of the staff? She'd have to think about it, but considering they didn't know yet how her father and brother were poisoned, trying to find someone to vouch for her during that time might be difficult, and she said as much.

"I see your point, but still, it's good to keep it in mind, and be wary."

"I will. Thank you, Gregory." She smiled and gave him a wave as she left his office.

Rose left the building feeling kind of strange. Her emotions were all over the place. On one hand, she was relieved they were moving forward; on the other hand, she was frightened of what that actually meant. This person, this killer, already proved how dangerous they were, and that meant they could most definitely hurt Rose, or her mother, or anyone else for that matter if they got in his way.

And that meant that Rose and Gregory couldn't allow themselves to make any mistakes.

Although she didn't discuss it with Gregory because she didn't want to cloud his judgment, her main suspect was, of course, Ava.

Ava arrived at a very convenient time, and it was more than obvious she had a grudge against Rose's entire family. She certainly wanted to destroy them all, not simply take the money. And that kind of hate could make people do almost anything.

More to the point, her father died from an allergy to bee venom, and Ava was a doctor who might be able to access medical records and find something like that. If anyone in Rose's circle of suspects was knowledgeable about such things, it was Ava. *Who better to know how to poison a person with bee venom and trigger something like Kounis Syndrome than a doctor?* She was a biochemist and probably had access to all different kinds of things, including this venom, especially if it was being used in various pain relief products. For all Rose knew, the research facility she worked at could be testing these allergens for various medical purposes. Rose decided to do an internet search and see how accessible it was.

A moment later, her heart dropped into her stomach. You can buy it online from various sources easily. It wasn't just available to researchers. Anyone could get their hands on it.

Including Joey, she realized. But had he known about her dad's allergy? About Devon's?

Unfortunately, that led her to a third option. Her brother. Devon could have done it without realizing he was also allergic, she hypothesized.

Would he have killed his own father and then accidentally poisoned himself too? Rose had to wonder. It was terrifying and most troubling to think her brother might have killed their father; sadly, at this point, she couldn't rule anything out. So, no matter how much it pained her, her brother had to be on the suspect list as well, because she had no proof stating otherwise, which meant she had to doubt everyone.

Even

Mom? She dismissed that because her mother definitely didn't have what it took to kill someone. No matter how angry she was at her husband for cheating on her, she would never resort to killing him. And she would most definitely not poison her son. She loved Devon more than anyone else in this world. And that was a fact.

Realizing that two heads were better than one, Rose decided to text Gregory and share her thoughts about the list of possible suspects.

I can't stop thinking about what you discovered, and my main suspects are Ava, Joey, and possibly even my brother

Your cousin Joey?

Yes, as I mentioned when I gave you my family's history, he's been in prison, and he's never afraid to get his hands dirty or bloody

That's right. I remember, but I hadn't gotten to him on my list yet. I will move him up on the suspect list and look into him more deeply

Feeling like there was more to say and really wanting to hear his voice, Rose dialed his number.

"Yes?" he answered instantly.

"Look into Ava first," she advised. Rose could not explain why, but her money was on Ava, so to speak. Ava seemed to have the best means and motives to want Rose's father and brother out of the picture.

"Rose, Ava may be a blackmailer and possibly a con artist, but there's a big leap between that and being a murderer," Gregory cautioned. "She may just be taking advantage of the situation."

That was what Rose suspected at the beginning. Things had definitely changed since then.

"I know. Hear me out though, considering she's a doctor, a biochemist, and I'm sure knows her way around all kinds of poisons and probably can access peoples medical files. Not to mention she definitely held a grudge against my father. She is the prime suspect, at least in my book."

"You could be right. Though I'm not sure about how she'd have access to their medical records without their authorization, I suppose it's possible." He sounded thoughtful and then added, "Don't worry, Rose, I will check her out to see exactly what she can do, and we'll get whoever did this. I will be thorough. And with some time, the evidence will unquestionably point us in the right direction."

"It certainly will."

TWENTY-ONE

It had been another week, and Rose couldn't keep silent about what she knew any longer, despite Gregory asking her to keep it between them. She needed to tell her family that her father was murdered. She needed to look in each one of their faces and see who could have done this. It was eating away at her, and she couldn't let it go. She couldn't wait for Gregory to dig deeper into each of them. She wanted answers now. She needed them desperately.

Gregory had taken the information to the police the day before, and he'd informed Rose that the cops would be coming by to question everyone anyway, so she thought it might be better to have everyone in one place for them to do that. Besides, if they all came to her mom's early enough, maybe she could speak to them as a group, and suss out who had done this before they arrived.

So, she organized one of her mother's family gatherings. Of course, she had to make it look as though the invitation came from her mom, not her, because they wouldn't attend otherwise. She even included Ava and Adrian in the invitation, mainly because Ava was her number one suspect in all of this. She even shared her plan with Gregory, who said he would pass the information along to the police, so they'd know where to find everyone and at what time.

He'd spent the past week digging into each of her family members, but so far, he'd found no leads on the venom that had been used to kill her father. He wasn't giving up, though, and he still had Ava to look into. He'd done a deep dive into Joey's life, and that had taken him days to get through. It seemed Joey was very well connected in certain criminal circles in the city, but there wasn't anything to tie him directly to Rose's father's death.

Gregory warned her when she proposed this plan, in the hopes of drawing out the killer, to be very careful of who she accused. He'd even said he was worried about her pissing Joey off too much when it didn't look like he was the one they were looking for. Rose had told him she would be careful, but she was determined to find whoever had done this.

Now, she stood with a satisfied smile on her face as each of her relatives arrived.

"Why am I here, Thelma?" Aunt Melinda questioned.

"I have no idea," her mom replied, seeming bewildered that the family had all arrived at her home at the same time. "I wasn't expecting to see you all today."

Aunt Melinda began to protest, but Rose silenced her.

"I'm the one who invited everyone for lunch," Rose explained. "I have some news to share with you."

"Oh, let me guess, you're finally coming out," Joey deadpanned.

Quite a few people laughed at that, Rose decided to ignore him.

"No, no, I got it, you're devoting your life to God and joining a convent," Joey corrected himself, still trying to crack a smile out of the room.

Rose waited for them all to get their jokes out of the way but remained serious. When it was quiet, she said, "I wanted to inform you all that I've hired a private investigator to research what really happened to my father and Devon."

That made them all shut up and pay attention. Rose was pleased her words had the desired effect. At the same time, she could see that quite a few people looked at her disapprovingly. Her mother included.

Rose continued, "After a closer examination of my father's remains and Devon's lab results, a couple of specialists have come to the conclusion that they were both poisoned with bee venom. They weren't stung. What happened to them was no accident. My father was murdered, and someone has attempted to murder Devon."

"Bee venom? How was something like that missed the first time around?" her mother questioned.

"The coroner didn't look for what kind of allergy triggered the inflammation that caused the Kounis Syndrome. I wanted to know exactly what it was that affected both Dad and Devon. It was venom."

Rose glanced at Adrian with defiance. She wanted to say, *I told you so.* He looked as though he was about to be sick.

She was actually surprised that she felt nothing even remotely tender for him, considering she was supposed to marry the man. Now, all she felt was anger and disgust when she looked at him.

The entire group started speaking, speculating, and throwing shade at one another, but they stopped dead when Rose clapped her hands to get their attention.

"Oh, and I forgot to mention the best part... the killer is one of you," Rose added with disgust. Gregory had advised her to be cautious, to not reveal her hand too much, yet here she was rattling the hornet's nest.

She wasn't sorry she did it. *Who knows, perhaps the killer will be stupid enough to reveal themselves today.*

"Well, if nobody's brave enough to say it, then I will," Adrian started, much to Rose's surprise. "It's obvious that Joey did it. He's the criminal in the family, after all."

That was unexpected, Rose thought.

Joey instantly jumped to his feet, his face going dark, ready to fight. "What the fuck did you just say about me? That I did it?" he boomed. "Why would I do such a thing? I have nothing to gain!"

It is interesting he didn't say, I'm innocent. I didn't kill anyone, Rose noted, but then again, that wasn't Joey's style.

"Your mother does," Nick pointed out.

"If I wanted someone dead, I definitely wouldn't use bee venom as a poison like some pussy," Joey sneered.

That's true enough. Joey would most likely shoot them, or beat them to death, Rose thought, watching everyone.

"Speaking of Melinda, perhaps she did it herself," Nick continued as he stared at Melinda. "You had to know your brother was allergic to bees. Makes sense to me."

"Did you just honestly accuse me of poisoning my own brother, Nick?" Aunt Melinda replied, getting riled up as well.

"You've often said how you couldn't wait for him to drop dead," Nick stood his ground.

"I didn't mean it!" Aunt Melinda exclaimed.

"Yeah, right. You've coveted everything Charles had. You've always resented that he turned Grandpa's money into a billion-dollar business."

"I bet Devon did it because he knew he would squander his share of the inheritance and needed more money that Charles wouldn't give to him," Joey started to hypothesize.

Rose sucked in a breath at that. He was voicing her own initial fears about her brother.

"And then accidentally poisoned himself as well, being an idiot," Aunt Melinda added, backing up her son.

Rose frowned. She couldn't let that stand. "My brother did not kill our father," she snapped.

"I agree. My sweet Devon would never do such a thing. But I can't say the same for the rest of you," her mother spoke out, taking everyone by surprise, Rose included.

Rose would have sworn her mother would live in denial, but she was relieved to see her accepting the truth.

The people in the room continued to accuse one another for the next couple of minutes. And it went beyond the murder of Charles Blaisdell and the attempted murder of Devon. All kinds of dirty laundry came to light. Ava, Rose observed, seemed to be taking it all in with quiet amusement, but she kept her mouth shut, and nobody seemed to be accusing her of murdering Charles, which irked Rose a little.

After saying what she had to say, Rose had fallen silent as well and simply observed people around her. She was still trying to see if she could spot the killer. It was proving more difficult than expected since the woman she actually suspected seemed calm and untouchable. Then again, this was real life, not a movie; Gregory had warned her about that. That nothing would be as obvious as she hoped it would be. Which was unfortunate.

Rose checked the time, knowing that pretty soon the cops would join the party as well. She and Gregory had discussed him joining her too but decided that he should stay in the shadows for the time being so the killer wouldn't be aware of his identity, and he could continue investigating unbothered.

Knowing that they would want to speak with the entire family, Rose suggested she gather everyone so they would have the opportunity to speak with the entire family at once. That way, they would all be caught off guard, without stories prepared and, most importantly, without lawyers. The detectives in charge of the case had agreed it was a good idea.

And then the doorbell rang. "Perfect timing," Rose commented as she nodded at the housekeeper to let them in.

A few people looked at her in confusion as she headed for the foyer to greet them.

Detective Noel St. James, a man in his forties, was huge, with a rumbling voice, very dark skin, a shaved head, and deep brown eyes. His every gesture, every movement, breathed confidence. He demanded respect by his presence alone. The room went dead silent as he and a few other officers joined them.

Rose wanted to grin at seeing the shock, awe, and dread on her relatives' faces.

"Did you know about this, Rose?" her mother demanded, looking quite irked.

That somewhat surprised Rose. Didn't her mother want to find the person responsible? What was she so afraid of? What was she hiding? Was this simply about the family's reputation? Or was there something else at stake? All those questions passed through Rose's head.

Instead of answering out loud, Rose simply nodded.

Pretty much everything that was said before the police arrived was repeated, meaning all kinds of accusations were flying around the room as the police started asking questions.

"Yes, I have a record," Rose heard Joey grumbling at one of the officers, "but poisoning someone isn't my style."

Is that really how he wants to defend himself? passed through Rose's head. *Wouldn't that be like admitting you have already killed someone?*

"I'm not smart enough to organize all this shit," Joey continued. "I'm more of a heat of the moment kind of guy," he defended. "Besides, I didn't know Uncle Charles was allergic."

Rose almost smiled at that because it was definitely a unique defense. *I'm not smart enough to pull this off and basically admitting that if he were going to kill someone, it would be a spur of the moment thing.* She wondered how a judge would react hearing that.

Although Rose knew it was very wrong of her, she was enjoying this moment immensely. Seeing her entire family squirm under scrutiny was priceless.

She had already given her statement to the police, so they didn't speak with her. She was free to observe and listen to others.

Ava claimed ignorance to everything. She acted as though she had just arrived and had no clue what was happening. As though none of this had anything to do with her.

At the same time, it was strange seeing Adrian squirm while being questioned. Was he embarrassed he had to admit that he was with Rose first before hooking up with Ava?

"It really doesn't take much in the way of brains to drop poison into someone's food or drink," Detective St. James pointed out to Joey, snapping Rose from her thoughts.

"Yeah, but how would I get something like bee venom anyway?" Joey challenged.

"Mr. Oldman, you're not on trial. We're merely asking questions at this stage."

"It's a legitimate question," Joey insisted.

"It can easily be purchased online," the detective said without beating around the bush. "And even if you didn't order it yourself, one of your buddies from the Malcone family could have gotten a hold of it for you, just like they do for other substances I'm sure you get from them."

That was exactly what Rose believed could have happened. The rest of her family had always known and turned a blind eye to the fact that Joey was a drug dealer. Rose had known too, but she hadn't been able to go against the family and turn him in, not before. Now was a different story. Still, hearing he was connected to a powerful mob family was frightening.

"I would never do such a thing," Joey insisted.

Eventually, Joey was taken away to the police station for further questioning after it was revealed he attacked Devon on the night he fell ill.

All the same, Joey remained adamant he knew nothing about the poisoning.

"I had nothing to do with it. I'm being framed," he yelled, as two police officers escorted him out.

"Mr. Oldman, we will sort everything out at the station," the detective replied in a calm manner.

And then Joey made a bad situation worse by hitting one of the police officers, which was very typical of him. After that, they stopped being nice, and calm. And Rose knew he would end up being detained even if he was proven innocent, because attacking a police officer was a serious offense, especially to other police officers. They would make him pay no matter what. Not that Rose felt sorry for him, not one bit.

Rose also made sure to mention how she caught Aunt Melinda attempting to steal things from around the house a few weeks back. The detective's attention was piqued by that because it could definitely be viewed as a motive. Aunt Melinda was taken away for questioning as well. Mother and son, side-by-side, were handcuffed in a police car, and Rose was seriously tempted to get her phone to take a picture so she could enjoy it later.

The rest of the family started gossiping immediately. Although they were generally shocked by what happened that day, they were also not that surprised to see Melinda and Joey go down. It seemed they couldn't wait to start tearing the two of them apart.

Rose was very much amused by the turn of events, but her smile faded when she caught sight of Ava, watching all of them with a look of smugness.

As much as Rose enjoyed watching Melinda and Joey being

pulled in for further questioning, she knew in her gut that they weren't to blame. She narrowed her gaze on Ava. She might have fooled the police this time around, but she wasn't going to fool her and Gregory.

Enjoy it while it lasts, Ava; I'm going to wipe that smug look off your face soon, Rose thought with a glare.

TWENTY-TWO

Rose's family, including her mother, were now convinced Charles and Devon were poisoned by Joey and Melinda. But Rose felt like they had all jumped to conclusions without looking at the bigger picture. She knew in her heart something wasn't right.

Of course, Rose couldn't completely rule out that Joey and Aunt Melinda were the guilty parties; they were bad apples, but she didn't really think they were capable of pulling this off.

Detective St. James reassured her they were doing their due diligence, following evidence, being thorough, and so on when she called to get an update on the case. Joey and Melinda were both being held for seventy-two hours while they continued to look into things. Joey was also being charged with assault, so he was likely to go to jail, at least for a little while.

As grateful as she was that they were being investigated, she really wanted them to look more into Ava and was glad that Gregory was working on the case alongside the police as well. It was reassuring to her that the complete truth would come out.

She met Gregory for coffee and shared what had happened the day before at the family gathering and with the police. "I'm worried they're focusing too much on Joey and Aunt Melinda," she said.

"Joey and Melinda will be able to clear their name if they are truly innocent, and then the police will definitely move on to searching for other suspects. Meaning, they will move on to Ava, or as much as I know you don't want to hear it, Devon."

Although, on some level, she could understand that the problem was she was too impatient, her gut feeling was telling her it was Ava. She was afraid if she wasn't arrested soon, she would find a way to get out of it or maybe even go after someone else in the family. And that was something Rose couldn't allow. That was something Rose wouldn't be able to live with.

"Although I understand your point of view, this is something you need to accept and let play out," Gregory advised.

"But I know they didn't do it, Gregory. Joey was right in what he said," Rose insisted. "He's more of a heat of the moment, beat the shit out of them kind of guy. I know he's a dealer, but he's more likely to use his fists than to poison someone, let alone my dad and Devon."

"I tend to agree with you, and that is what my research on him says, but you can't know that for sure," Gregory cautioned. "If I've learned anything on this job, it's that people can always surprise you, in a bad way."

Rose shook her head. "I know that. And I do think if they had the opportunity to kill my dad, they would have, but I don't believe they are smart enough to use bee venom to trigger something like Kounis Syndrome," she pointed out. "Knowing Joey, if he were to actually plan to murder someone, he would probably arrange a car accident, or a mugging gone wrong. He's a physical kind of guy, you know?"

Gregory nodded, and for a moment she thought that meant he agreed with her, and then he said, "Or that's exactly what they want you to think. It's a great way to create reasonable doubt. People are unpredictable, Rose, and are capable of great horrors if motivated enough."

Rose knew he spoke from experience, but she still had her doubts. Why would Melinda and Joey decide to kill Charles now?

It wasn't as though they hadn't had plenty of opportunities over the years. They had a lot of their own money, so why now? What possible motive would drive them to do this to her father now and not when he and Melinda first had their falling out? It didn't make much sense to Rose.

There was one person who had recently come into their lives who could have orchestrated all of this. Ava.

She said as much. "The police should look into Ava, she had means and motive, and she appeared right after my father died, claiming an inheritance."

Am I really the only one who sees how very well it all fits together?

Ava probably hated her father because he abandoned her and her mom and wanted to take revenge. Killing him and taking all his money was definitely the best revenge.

"Not to mention she is actually smart enough to pull something like this off," Rose added, as an afterthought.

"That is all true," Gregory allowed, "However, how could she have poisoned your father if she wasn't around before he was murdered?"

Rose had to admit that his question had merit.

"She was definitely around though," Rose remembered. "Ava told me that she met with him to tell him he was her father a few weeks before Christmas. He didn't believe her and demanded she get a DNA test. Though I have to say, she's lied a few times about when and how often she met him. At first, she said he had died before she got the results, but later she said that she showed him the results, and he didn't believe her, so I don't know when she met with him exactly. I wish I'd realized she changed her story at the time, but I was upset and didn't know what it was that bothered me about it until later."

"Okay, so let's say she did meet with him after getting the test results; that had to be at least a few days prior to his death, correct?"

Rose thought about it and then nodded. "Yes, I think so."

"Well, if she poisoned him then, he would have died much sooner and not on New Year's Eve," Gregory countered. He definitely had a point there.

"I only have her word that she didn't see him after that. She could have seen him that day, and we just don't know it," Rose replied, thinking of other ways Ava could have done it. Then something struck her. "Perhaps she had help."

"You think she had an accomplice?" Gregory asked, intrigued.

"Why not?" Rose challenged. "That can't be so far-fetched, it happens. And maybe the person who helped her didn't know what he was doing in the first place. The specialist did say the poison could have been administered in any number of ways, so she could have paid someone to deliver something to my father, something he could have used before he died," Rose theorized.

"I guess it could have happened that way, but it is somewhat risky. Too many things could have gone wrong with that plan, someone else could have gotten a hold of it," Gregory warned.

Rose didn't care. She knew she was right. Ava was the one behind all of this. Her showing up was just too big of a coincidence for her. "That might be true, but it wouldn't have affected them if they weren't allergic, right?"

"True, and you might be right about the angle with the accomplice. I'll look into it," he allowed.

"Have you discovered if she is capable of getting medical records or what she does as a biochemist?" Rose asked.

"I haven't been able to determine if she'd be able to do that yet. I'm looking into the research facility she is employed with;

however, like any medical institution, they are extremely paranoid, with tight security, so it's going to take me a little bit longer
to get someone to talk," he explained, much to her chagrin.

"Don't worry, Rose, I will keep digging," he reassured. "If
she had something to do with your father's death, I will find
out."

Rose had no doubts about that. She simply wished the
police thought the same way. "You know there is one more thing
that I find suspicious," she said.

"What is it?"

"I called Mr. Merser to get an update on the lawsuit Ava is
filing. He informed me she's hired Adrian to represent her."

"Why is that strange? They are together now, after all,"
Gregory said.

"Perhaps you're right, but it seems odd to me when he's not
that kind of lawyer. He's a corporate lawyer. It's how we met.
He was representing an author and helped with the contracts."

"That's not too big of a stretch though; her wanting part of
the inheritance and filing a suit for it could technically fall in his
wheelhouse. I can check on what kind of law he actually prac-
tices, but at the end of the day, she can have anyone with a law
degree advise her. It could just be that she's comfortable with
him because he knows the situation, and she's dating him."

"Maybe I'm just looking for more connections and chasing
ghosts," she said reluctantly. Then again, something at the back
of her mind was telling her it was all connected; she just
couldn't see how at that moment.

"How are you feeling, regarding them?" Gregory shuffled
the papers on his desk. "It can't be easy seeing them together."

"Actually, I'm fine. I'm not loving the fact that he dumped
me for her in particular; however, I'm not heartbroken about it.
Adrian was never the right man for me, and I think deep down,
I knew that."

"I'm glad to hear that." Gregory made a small pause before

continuing. "You know, I hate to bring it up, but with the right representation and that DNA test result, Ava has a pretty good chance of winning her claim, even though your dad had a specific last will and testament. Juries tend to look down on what they believe to be deadbeat dads," Gregory pointed out.

"Yeah, I know," Rose sighed, "If she wins, she will get a quarter of my father's estate, which works out to about three billion dollars. So you see, she has the biggest motive, the most to gain with my father out of the picture."

Because if Charles Blaisdell was still around, she wouldn't be getting a cent.

"That is true," he allowed.

"Who knows, perhaps as you said last week, Mom and I are next on her hit list so she can claim it all," Rose added, trying to sound logical and hiding the worry in her voice.

"You know, I'm not ready to say with utmost certainty Ava is the mastermind behind it all. Whoever did do it is clearly focused on the money. So, it would be safe to assume that after eliminating your father and trying to eliminate your brother, you and your mom would be next on the list because that way the whole inheritance would be up for grabs."

And who would get it all if we all died? Ava.

"So, what am I supposed to do now?"

"I will continue digging, and the police will continue doing the same, and together we will discover who is trying to harm you and your family."

That was somewhat reassuring.

"In the meantime, do everything in your power to keep yourself and your mother safe," Gregory advised.

If only my mother will cooperate, Rose thought.

TWENTY-THREE

"Mom, is this a good time to have a chat with you?" Rose started carefully, knowing how her mother could get.

"What is it, Rose?"

Rose didn't even know where to start. Her mother was so delicate that the wrong word could set her off, so perhaps there was no good way to do this. Better to rip the Band-Aid off, she supposed.

"I've spoken with the private investigator I hired, and he's advised that we should be more careful from now on."

"Why?"

"Because the person who harmed Devon and killed Dad is still out there, so we need to be cautious. And you should definitely stop orchestrating family gatherings," she said.

Rose hoped her mother would be more inclined to accept this advice if it came from someone else, and not her.

"Anything else?" her mother asked, sounding a bit irked, although Rose couldn't understand why.

She wasn't about to ask; she was sure it would only lead to another argument, and she was really tired of fighting with her mother. Besides, she had a feeling she knew what this was about.

It wasn't like it was Rose's fault the killer was on the loose.

"Yes," Rose continued, ignoring her mother's tone. "We should stay away from Ava as well. We can't trust her, not now."

Instantly, her mother made a face. "Honestly, Rose, you need to stop hating Ava just because you feel insecure," her mother chastised.

It's good to know you think I'm inferior to Ava, Mom. Not.

"This isn't about me, Mom. This is about the fact someone killed Dad and tried to kill Devon, and she is the most likely suspect," Rose practically exploded.

"Now you will use any excuse to continue your animosity toward her. Remember, you shouldn't hate the woman, but the man who left you for her."

Rose looked at her incredulously. "This isn't about Adrian. I couldn't give two cents that he's with her now. I'm saying this because she might be dangerous. Gregory is investigating her, and until I get a full report, I don't want you to take unnecessary risks," Rose explained, as calmly as possible, hoping that her mother would actually listen to her for a change.

Her mother looked at her, narrowing her eyes. "You're using this private investigator to fuel your insecurities. Honestly, Rose, I expected more from you."

Rose gritted her teeth. Her mother was absolutely infuriating at times. "For the last time, this is not about me, it's about discovering the truth," Rose insisted. "And the truth is that Ava has a twelve billion dollar motive to hurt us."

"Whatever you say, dear," her mother said in a dismissing manner, which only infuriated her more.

"Why won't you believe me?" Rose demanded. "Haven't I proven this far that I was right?"

"Is that what this is about? You want the satisfaction of

being right? Of being able to tell me, I told you so?" her mother practically accused her.

"All I'm asking is for a bit of reasonable doubt toward Ava on your part," Rose replied, trying really hard to remain calm. She didn't want this escalating into a full-blown fight.

"I'm trying, but this obsession of yours with Ava is alarming."

"This obsession of mine is what made us discover the truth. If it wasn't for me, we wouldn't even know Father and Devon were poisoned," Rose stressed the words, once again feeling ridiculous she had to point out the obvious.

"I'm sure that the truth would have come out either way, even without your meddling," her mother said, completely diminishing her role, and her efforts in all of this.

That really hurt. Rose had no idea why her mother constantly did that, had to put her down, had to diminish her.

"Yeah, right," she snorted sarcastically. "Nobody even knew it was a murder to begin with. Nobody was even suspicious."

"That may be true, but if you keep digging, maybe people will suspect you or I were the ones to hurt them. We are the only other beneficiaries, remember?" her mother said with a sigh. "Either way, you need to let the police deal with finding the person responsible, and not meddle, or play around with that private investigator of yours."

There were so many things wrong with that sentence.

"I'm not stopping my search for the truth," Rose was adamant, and her mother should be aware that she wasn't going to stop until the guilty party was in prison.

"As far as I'm concerned, the truth is already out, and the people responsible caught."

In other words, Rose's mother believed that Aunt Melinda and Joey killed her dad and attempted to kill Devon. No wonder she didn't want to listen to her. Her mother wanted it to be Aunt Melinda because she was her biggest nemesis. And she had the audacity to say Rose's emotions were clouding her judgment. *That's rich.*

"I can't believe Melinda stooped so low. It's disgusting. Their father must be turning in his grave for this disgrace."

At that, Rose knew that there was no convincing her mother that Ava was the actual killer. She would have to find out for herself when the cops released Aunt Melinda and Joey.

As for Rose, she saw dangers around every corner. Because her father's and brother's allergies were used against them, she had herself tested and found that she had the same allergies. So, considering her father and brother had been poisoned with bee venom, she became suspicious that Ava might try to poison her next. Because of that, she refused to eat or drink anything that she didn't open or prepare herself.

That wasn't the only thing she did to protect herself. She also ate exclusively in her old room or at her apartment, where she'd had the locks changed since Adrian had a key to her place. And then, when it was time to join the family in the dining room, she simply pretended to eat. She hated not eating what her mother's chef prepared, but she wasn't about to take any chances with her life.

Although she wanted to refuse to take part in those charades and stop participating in family gatherings altogether, she knew she couldn't. Though her mother refused to listen and continued to behave recklessly, Rose felt obliged to save her, even from herself. That was why she endured every gathering, so that she could watch over her.

If anyone noticed she wasn't eating or drinking anything served to her, there wasn't a comment on it, which only infused her paranoia more. There was a killer among them.

Rose had to double her efforts to stay vigilant. She watched what her mother ate or drank like a hawk, and, like a complete lunatic, she was replacing as much of it as possible, putting fresh products and unopened bottles in her mother's hand when no one was looking, all in the hope of keeping the two of them alive until Gregory discovered the killer. She wasn't even sure that her mom had any allergies, but she didn't want to take any chances. After all, what was to stop the killer from finding another way to poison her?

It had been Gregory's suggestion that she change the locks on her apartment, though she was rarely there anymore, feeling like she should be around her mother, watching over her as much as possible. He'd also taught her the basics of how to make sure nobody was following her. It was daunting that this had become her life now. She felt like she was in some kind of spy movie, or a thriller, and just like the main characters, she had no idea what was going on, or how all of this was going to end.

Living like that, in constant stress and fear, waiting for the other shoe to drop, was beyond tiring, especially since Gregory was her only support. They had started spending so much time together that he had become her confidante as well.

It was surprising how much she trusted the man, considering what Adrian and a number of other men had done to her confidence. The biggest difference was that Gregory had earned her trust, and it was obvious how much he trusted her too. Because, as much as she opened up to him about her life, he had also opened up to her about his.

Whenever he wasn't out in the field, so to speak, trying to save her family, Gregory was with her. They went to get coffee, or dinner, or simply walked around the park, and talked about everything going on in their lives.

"I feel like I'm going crazy when I'm around them," she confessed, exhaling in frustration. Once again, she was complaining about her family. She was aware she did it a lot, but Gregory didn't seem to mind. "Maybe I am crazy, for expecting them to change. For expecting my mom to trust me."

"Rose, you're not crazy," Gregory insisted. "You're

extremely brave, and you've shown how strong you are weathering everything on your own."

I don't feel brave or strong, she thought.

"This whole situation you're in is impossible," he continued speaking, unaware of her musings. "Don't let anyone tell you otherwise."

"Thank you for letting me vent. I just don't understand them, and it gets to me."

"Hopefully, my contact will have something soon, and I'll have more info for you," he tried to reassure her.

"Thank you, Gregory. I don't know what I'd do without you."

Gregory reached for her hand and held it in his as they stood in the park. "It's my pleasure that I can help, Rose. I will discover what happened to your father and brother because you are the most deserving person I've met in a long time, and I can't bear to see you suffering like this."

His heartfelt confession really touched her, and the look in his eyes told her he was sincere in his words. She couldn't resist and tossed her arms around his neck, hugging him. A moment later, his arms slipped around her back, and he pulled her close, holding her tightly to him. It felt nice being wrapped in someone's arms again; however, it went beyond that. It meant so much more because it was *him.*

What is happening to me? she wondered. *Am I falling for my private detective?*

She would have to be careful. She couldn't face another heartbreak, not yet.

TWENTY-FOUR

When Rose arrived back at the mansion, she was surprised to find several crime scene technicians there with a warrant, sweeping the entire house for evidence of foul play.

She was surprised because Detective St. James hadn't told her anything about them coming to do such a thing.

Rose was very impressed by how efficient those technicians were. They went throughout the entire house, starting from the bottom, and meticulously working their way to the upper levels of the mansion.

Although Rose was extremely curious to see it all, to observe their process, she stayed out of their way. Her mother, on the other hand, fussed the entire time. She acted like she would have to be the one cleaning the whole house after they finished, which would never be the case, not in a million years, not when she had an entire household staff to take care of such things.

"What do you need from me, Detective?" her mother asked as they settled into the living room the next day.

"I've received the results from all the samples we collected from your house yesterday," he replied.

"What did you find?" Rose asked impatiently. She knew that he definitely found something. Otherwise, he wouldn't be there, sitting in the living room. He had much better things to do than have a social visit with them.

"We found the bee venom that was used to murder your husband in his study."

Rose was relieved. She hadn't touched anything from the study. Hoping to preserve her father's things as much as possible.

"Where?" Rose asked. She knew she would have to be the one asking all the questions because her mother looked beyond startled, and perhaps even a bit brain-fogged.

"That particular sample was found in the brandy snifter."

Someone spiked his drink. That made sense. Rose's father liked to have a glass of brandy every night as a nightcap. Everybody knew that. He was very predictable in that manner.

Something else occurred to her as well. Devon had been going through their dad's liquor cabinet, drinking his way through it. *He didn't do it.* He wouldn't drink the stuff if he knew it was already spiked with that poison. With this new piece of information, Devon was cleared. That was good news.

Who put the poison in the liquor to begin with though? That was the real question. That was the only question that mattered.

At that moment, Rose remembered that she'd caught Aunt Melinda trying to steal that Fabergé egg from the study. She'd had the opportunity to spike the drink at that time, but her father was already dead by then. She could have still done it to harm someone else in the family though. Everyone knew Devon was a lush. It wasn't surprising he'd raided Dad's liquor cabinet and ended up in a coma.

Rose decided to share her thoughts with the detective, at least in part.

Detective St. James nodded. "We also found traces of the bee venom in the glass in Devon's game room."

That makes sense. "He drank from the same bottle Dad did," Rose stated the obvious.

Rose's mother started crying at that.

"That is the assumption we're working with," the detective agreed.

"Have either Melinda or Joey admitted their crimes?" her mother wanted to know, after dabbing her eyes with a silk handkerchief.

"Not yet. They've lawyered up, and are refusing to talk, but I'll keep you posted on any developments," he reassured.

Rose wasn't completely buying that, which was precisely why she planned on having a chat with Gregory later. She wanted to know if Detective St. James was keeping anything from them. Rose had to know everything. Only that way would she be able to protect her family.

"We would be most grateful," Rose's mother replied.

Shortly after he left, and once Rose's mother returned to the living room, she looked at Rose like she was surprised she was still there.

"What?" Rose asked.

"Why aren't you changing?" her mother demanded.

"Changing for what?" she asked, genuinely confused.

"Have you forgotten about our meeting with Mr. Merser?"

"I don't need to change for that, I'm ready to go whenever you are," she reassured.

Her mother looked as though she was debating if she should start yet another argument about Rose's wardrobe choices but kept quiet. About forty-five minutes later they were on their way to meet with Mr. Merser in his office.

Rose still hasn't informed anyone how she had someone else now protecting her interests, Alex Min. She liked the idea of having someone unfamiliar with the inner workings of her family representing her. She had nothing against Mr. Merser, he was a nice man, but she needed someone her mother and the rest of the family didn't have access to.

This meeting with Mr. Merser was quick, as he had a very specific goal: to see if they could find a mutually acceptable agreement with Ava. Her mother remained adamant that the inheritance be split four ways, with the business and properties remaining exactly as Charles specified and that Ava would get the money equivalent to those. Mr. Merser had said that was a more than fair offer, and that was what he'd take to the table.

Rose had never shared that Ava had tried to negotiate her own deal with her, asking for seven billion. Maybe that was a mistake, but if Rose had her way, Ava would get nothing.

And that wasn't simply because she was potentially a murderer. Rose was infuriated by everything Ava said or did. It was disgusting how she flaunted Adrian in front of her. Ava was all over Adrian whenever Rose was around, as though it was imperative for her to hurt Rose, to humiliate her and make her feel jealous. The funny thing was, she wasn't bothered by it. *At least not very much.*

Truth be told, she wouldn't want to be with such a weak man, but she couldn't deny it was a blow to her ego that she'd allowed him to fool her for so long. She had started doubting herself because of him, and that was unforgivable.

That was why, no matter what Ava did with Adrian in front of Rose, she would endure it. She would ignore it as much as possible. All the same, what really pissed her off was Ava's constant kissing up to Rose's mother, and other relatives.

And they all let her. That was the most problematic part. Ava was invited to birthday parties and all kinds of other events, and she went shopping with some female relatives, while Rose was never invited to any of those things. Rose tried to be the bigger person about it, but at the same time, part of her really wanted to let Ava destroy them all so they could get exactly what they deserved.

Rose took such behavior from Ava as more proof she was guilty of something and was trying to secure her spot within the family. She was trying to sway as many people as possible so she would get as much money as possible in the end.

Whether Ava was a killer or not, and Rose would bet her entire inheritance that she was, she wasn't going to allow her to achieve any of her goals.

Ava was a killer and a con artist, and that was why Rose refused to leave her mother's side anytime Ava was around. Despite all of Ava's taunting, Rose was going to stay strong, because she had no other choice, her life was on the line, her mother's life as well.

Unfortunately, considering her mother was refusing to believe her, Rose's job of protecting her was that much harder. As though to prove a point, her mom started spending even more time with Ava than before. They got coffee together, they went shopping together, and there was nothing Rose could do about it. She started feeling estranged from her mother, not simply because her mother refused to listen to her, or see the truth, but because she refused Rose's help to begin with. Rose constantly felt like she was fighting uphill.

Rose had no idea how to change that. She had no idea how to force her mother to see the truth. It didn't help that the police acted as though they already had the true killers in their sights, and it seemed like they refused to investigate anyone else. They obviously believed that Aunt Melinda and Joey were the guilty parties, and they just hadn't secured the proof yet. While they were all looking at Melinda and Joey, who hadn't been charged and were released from custody but told not to leave town, nobody was watching what Ava was doing. And that was terrifying to Rose.

Rose was pretty disappointed in Detective St. James for

being so narrow-minded. She had expected more from someone who had such a long career in law enforcement. To him, Aunt Melinda and Joey killing Charles for money simply made sense albeit they weren't even in the will. Rose could argue that Ava killing Charles for the same thing made more sense, but the only one listening to her was Gregory.

The detective's biggest argument was that Aunt Melinda and Joey were frequent guests in the house. Joey was a criminal, after all, with many shady contacts, and it looked like he was in major debt to the Malcone family, so they most likely had the means and opportunity to poison her dad and Devon, without anyone being suspicious of them.

And now the whole family had turned against them, telling the police all kinds of dirt about them, because, over the years, they'd managed to antagonize most of them. That was what happened within the Blaisdell family, they easily turned against one another, which only solidified the detective's belief that he was focused on the right people.

"And after speaking to your father's personal lawyer, we discovered that Joey had initially been in your father's will, but he changed it just a few months ago. According to Mr. Merser, your father found out about some of Joey's activities and decided to drop him from the will."

Rose frowned. She hadn't known that. "What do you mean? Father was going to leave Joey money?"

"Yes, a quarter of a million dollars, it seems. There were also supposed to be inheritances for each of his siblings, but when he rewrote his will back in October, he decided to leave it all to your mother, you, and Devon aside from a few smaller monetary gifts to staff," Detective St. James shared.

Rose was floored. She'd had no idea that her father had originally planned to give money to anyone other than them, not that she really cared, except now it seemed Joey had more of a motive than she'd thought. "Did Joey know that my father was going to leave him money?" she questioned.

"I can't answer that. Right now, he's not speaking, and even if he were to answer, I don't know that I'd believe him." He shrugged.

Rose had no idea what to think now. Was she completely wrong about Ava? Had Joey done this to get his hands on part of the money? Had Melinda tried to help him? Was her mother right? That thought blew her mind.

"And don't forget, you yourself said your aunt resorted to trying to steal from your mother's house the instant her brother was in the ground," he pointed out.

He was right. They were despicable people, who had no shame, and only cared about money, but all the same, despite learning what she had, Rose couldn't believe they'd try to kill her father. Something in her gut told her that Ava was the one behind it, but Detective St. James wasn't interested in looking into her.

All that meant was that Gregory was her only hope, because it had become apparent that she couldn't rely on Detective St. James to continue digging.

She really hoped Gregory would have some news for her soon so she could stop being her mother's watchdog all the time, and focus, at least a little bit, on herself, because she felt like she was unraveling, and she wouldn't be able to keep it together for too long.

TWENTY-FIVE

Upon receiving a message from Gregory a few days later, Rose grabbed her purse and hurried out of the house. Driving to the park, she quickly found a spot to park and got out to meet him. She found him sitting on a bench, his face marred with a worried frown.

"What's the matter, Gregory?" she asked without beating around the bush.

"I'm afraid you were right, Rose; St. James has no interest in looking into other suspects. He believes Joey is the one behind your dad's death and your brother's attempted murder, and he's got a pretty good case, actually."

Rose suspected that much; however, hearing it from a proven source was very disappointing and infuriating as well because Rose truly believed he was making a mistake.

"I knew it," she replied glumly.

"I mean, I can almost agree with him, except poisoning them isn't really Joey's MO. I really don't think Melinda or her son, no matter how criminally connected he is, would kill your dad and then try to kill Devon with something as random as bee venom. He's not that smart, for one thing. From all my research into him, he's more of a hands-on kind of guy and would probably have chosen a mugging scenario or something along those lines to kill someone," he spoke with vigor.

"Exactly," she agreed. "That's where I get hung up on the case too. I get that Joey has connections to various criminal organizations, but that doesn't mean he'd kill my dad. And if the mob wanted my father dead, why hadn't they tried to kill him before? It doesn't make sense to me."

Gregory sighed. "I have to admit that my opinion of St. James has really changed because of this case. He's become sloppy and jaded over the years."

"So, what can we do to steer him, steer the police in the..." Rose wanted to say, 'in the right direction', but although her gut feeling was telling her Ava was the real culprit, she had a sudden moment of doubt.

After all, she had no real proof. More to the point, personal animosity could be clouding her judgment. Rose had certainly been wrong about Adrian, so no matter what, she had to keep an open mind because she didn't want to make the same mistake twice. "Different direction," she settled to say eventually.

"St. James needs to see that not everything is as black and white as he wants it to be," Gregory replied, still deep in thought.

"Okay, how to make that happen?"

"I'll continue working with the police, while I dig and explore all options, see where all the evidence might take us," Gregory replied with a small shrug.

Rose nodded. She trusted Gregory. If anyone could get to the truth, she knew it was him. "What do you need from me?"

They discussed expenses and the private lab he wanted to send the samples of bee venom to in order to determine what facility it came from, and Rose told him she didn't care how much it cost. She would spend her entire inheritance if it got her the answer to who killed her dad and hurt her brother.

After they finished discussing that, Gregory seemed to hesitate for a moment. He gave her a shy look and then said, "Do you want to visit the specialist at the lab with me? Maybe after he takes a look, he'll be able to give us something new to go on."

A few days later, they were in the private laboratory of his friend Dr. Michaelson.

"There are several facilities around the country that are working on various medical uses for bee venom, as well as for use in beauty products that are said to regenerate the skin, give a person a youthful glow."

"So have you isolated which facility this venom is from?" Rose asked.

"Based on some of the proteins and enzymes in the venom sample, we've narrowed it down to the eastern region of the US. That gives us about thirty facilities to look into who are known to use these bees. I'm still testing, and I'm hopeful I can narrow it down a bit more fairly soon."

"Would that include the research facility that Ava works at?" I asked, looking at Gregory.

"She works at Pinecrest Research Institute. Are they on your list?" Gregory shared.

Dr. Michaelson paused for a moment and then nodded. "I believe they are on the list, but I can't say for certain that this venom came from them yet."

As we left Dr. Michaelson a few minutes later, and headed to the car, Gregory admitted, "The more we learn about all this the more inclined I am to believe that someone with experience, with medical knowledge, is behind it all."

"It's Ava," she said simply. "It fits."

"Initially, I merely did a cursory check on her, but now I'm doing a thorough background and credit check on her," Gregory acknowledged.

"Something will surface then, I'm sure of it," Rose was adamant.

"Do you want to come back to the office with me? Maybe you can help me research?"

"I'd like that," Rose replied, thinking about Ava. "You know, Ava's been very secretive about her past, other than telling us that her mom and my dad met in Cancun. That's pretty much all she gave me. Oh, and that her mom died recently. I know she went to the same college as me, but beyond that, I don't have a clue."

"Let's go." He directed her to his car and drove to his office.

Once they were there, they ordered Chinese take-out and then got to work on the two computers in the office. Gregory had access to websites and searches that Rose had never seen before. He got her started looking into Ava's mother, Karin, and what happened to her, while he dug into Ava's background after college.

Rose had found Karin's obituary, but there wasn't much said in it, other than she was survived by her only daughter, Ava. There was nothing about her being from Cancun, or Mexico or anything really. Just that she'd worked as a house-keeper at one of the hotels in the city right before she died. Rose decided to keep digging into Karin's past to see if she could find a connection to her dad.

A couple of hours later, Gregory looked up and said, "Rose, look at this."

Rose got up from her chair and moved to his side so she could see the computer screen. "What did you find?"

"It looks like Ava worked for a DNA testing facility for a couple of years."

Rose was floored. She stared at the screen to see exactly what that facility was known for. *It is no wonder she had a DNA test ready if she worked at such a facility,* she mused. Then something else came to mind. If she worked there, if she had equipment and knowledge on her side, then who was to say she didn't take advantage of that? Who was to say she didn't fake those results, so she could con Rose's family and take the money? Rose had no doubt in her mind that Ava was capable of something like that. She was that cold-hearted, she was that ruthless.

She decided to share her thoughts with Gregory. "If she worked in that kind of place, could she have faked those DNA tests?"

"That's a real possibility. I also found something else," he shared and pulled up another screen.

"What else?"

"Ava worked at County General for a while, about two years ago. Isn't that where your family doctor, Dr. Moss, works?"

Rose nodded. "So, it is possible that she was able to access my dad's records and find out that he had an allergy to bees?"

Gregory's gaze met hers. "I think that is entirely plausible."

"But that would mean she's been planning this for a very long time, right?" Rose pondered. "If she somehow fudged those DNA results, to make it look like she's related to us, to make it look like I'm—" Rose started to hyperventilate.

Gregory jumped up from his chair and came over to her. "Are you okay?"

Rose shook her head, gasping for breath. The thought that she was actually Charles's daughter was overwhelming and filled her with joy, but also panic. It was like too many emotions passed through her at once, and she couldn't get a handle on any of it.

"Just breathe, Rose. Put your head between your knees and take slow, deep breaths," Gregory suggested, rubbing her back.

Rose did as he said, and after a couple of seconds her heart rate began to slow, and she could function again. She sat back up and looked at him, smiling. "Thanks, just had a moment."

"I get it. We're one step closer to proving Ava is the one behind all of this." He smiled gently at her. "Did you find anything on her mother?" he asked.

"Just that she died about a year ago from breast cancer. And I found that she worked as a housekeeper for the Omni for about six years before she died. I haven't found a connection to Cancun though. She was born here. I was about to look into her previous employment when you called me over."

"Well, let's see what you find," he said, retaking his seat and moving over next to her.

Rose began searching again and then gasped. "Look at this!"

"She worked in housekeeping at Blaisdell Elite Enterprises. Your father's company."

Rose nodded, her mind going a million miles a minute.

"So the affair is possible then," Gregory said, his voice soft.

Rose knew his words were true. "Unfortunately, I guess it is. I still don't buy it though. Why say they met in Cancun when her mom obviously worked for my dad's company for twelve years? It doesn't make sense."

"That's a good point," Gregory agreed. "Why did Karin leave BEE? Her salary was pretty good, from what that says, and there's a five-year gap between her leaving there and eventually going to work for the Omni..." He pulled the keyboard toward him and started typing.

"What are you looking for?"

"What I'm doing is highly illegal, but..." He kept typing. "I'm in... now I need to find..."

Rose watched in fascination as he scrolled through emails. "Wait, is that my father's email account?"

"His business account, yes." He kept scrolling and then paused and clicked to open a specific email.

Rose leaned in closer to him and read the email. "She was begging him to take her back." Rose's heart just about broke reading that. It looked like proof that her father had been having an affair with Karin.

"Look, I'll keep digging. Maybe I can find more proof in these emails." He glanced at the clock and then back to Rose. "It's late though. I should probably get you home."

Rose yawned and nodded, but she was slightly disappointed because she wanted to keep digging, and a part of her just wanted to stay with Gregory. "Yeah, probably," she murmured, her heart still feeling a little fragile at this latest discovery.

He smiled. "I promise I will keep working on this over the next few days, and I'll keep you updated."

Rose smiled back; she believed him. "Okay."

She walked out to his car with him, and when he dropped her at her mom's house, she waved to him until he pulled away before going inside. Finally, she felt as though they were making some progress.

As the days went by, Rose started to sleep a little bit better, despite everything, despite all the dangers, feeling that Gregory was close to pulling all the pieces together, seeing the bigger picture, and discovering the complete truth.

Am I wrong for putting so much trust in one man?

TWENTY-SIX

"I have some bad news," Mr. Merser shared over the phone.

Rose wasn't sure what he was referring to. Had Ava filed to take all of her father's estate or something? Still, she kept quiet and allowed her mother to speak.

"What is it, Mr. Merser?"

"The police have decided not to file murder charges against Joey."

Rose drew in a sharp breath. Was it possible that Gregory had finally convinced St. James that they were on the wrong track? He hadn't said anything about talking to St. James. "What does that mean?" Rose asked carefully.

"It means that the police no longer consider him a suspect in your father's murder. It turns out he has a firm alibi," he explained.

Rose felt like her head just exploded. *What proof did they find to rule Joey out as a suspect?* The bee venom could have been added at any time to that brandy snifter, and he had access to the house – not that she thought he was guilty, but still. Was this talk about an alibi just an excuse to explain them changing the direction of the case? What was Detective St. James going to do now? All kinds of questions swirled inside her head.

"That is good news, Mr. Merser. Now the police will focus on someone else." *Someone like Ava.*

But will they? she wondered.

I have to have faith that they will. And if they don't, Gregory will keep pushing them in the right direction.

Rose's mother commented, "That is ridiculous!"

"What about the assault charges?" Rose asked.

Just because she didn't believe Joey had anything to do with her father's passing didn't mean she wanted him completely off the hook. He enabled his mother to steal, he assaulted Devon, and he threatened Rose. Not to mention, he attacked the cops too. He had to be accountable for all those things. Behaviors, especially those kinds, had to have consequences.

"The charges for the assault and battery of your brother, and for attacking police officers remain," he informed them.

"Good," she replied, before adding. "What about Melinda?"

"Yes, Mr. Merser, what about Melinda?" Rose's mother interjected. "Please tell me she, at least, is going to get what she deserves."

Rose felt like rolling her eyes at that.

"According to Detective St. James, they are still focusing on her. She had access to the study, and she did attempt to steal from you. They are trying to find how she acquired the substance, but at the moment, she's keeping her mouth shut, and her lawyer is keeping them from questioning her too harshly."

Rose had mixed feelings. On the one hand, the petty part of her wanted Aunt Melinda humiliated and bothered. On the other, she knew she shouldn't end up in prison for something she didn't do.

"What a pity," her mother said. Obviously, Rose's mother had no sympathy toward Melinda. Unfortunately, her mom continued to believe Aunt Melinda and Joey were guilty. That was because she refused to listen to Rose and accept Ava was behind it all.

"Thank you for letting us know, Mr. Merser, we appreciate it," she added as she stood and left the room, leaving Rose holding her phone.

Rose expressed her thanks as well, minding her manners.

"Rose, before I let you go, I needed to speak with you."

Rose frowned. She didn't know what he had to discuss with her personally. "Oh?"

"Yes, Mr. Cosgrove approached me on behalf of Ava."

Adrian, she thought sourly. "What did he have to say?"

"He claimed you reached an agreement with Ms. Rothman for a settlement of seven billion dollars."

Rose was shocked. The nerve of them. "That's a lie. Ava asked for that amount, but I never agreed to it," she replied sternly. "And don't you dare say anything about this ridiculousness to my mother," she warned.

"Very well, I didn't think you had. I will deal with them."

Rose breathed a sigh of relief. "Thank you."

As Rose hung up the phone, she heard a crash in one of the back rooms. Fearing some reporter or worse had broken in, she rushed to see what it was. She'd been doing her best to ignore the paparazzi, but they'd been all over them since her father's death and had, of course, had a field day over her break-up with Adrian. On occasion, Rose had even noticed them following her as though she was some celebrity debutante. It was annoying, to say the least, but she put up with it and ignored them for the most part. Now, though, if one was breaking in, she'd have to call the cops.

She stopped short in the doorway to see her mom with her hands on an antique vase, ready to throw it at the wall. "Mom! What are you doing?" she gasped.

Tears streamed down her face. "They're letting them get

away with it! They killed Charles, and they've tried to kill my boy, and they're getting away with it!" she screeched.

Rose took a calming breath and reached for the vase. "I know you can't see it at the moment, but this is good news."

That immediately stopped her mother in her tracks, which was a good thing, considering, with her hands now empty, she was reaching for a very expensive painting.

She looked at Rose in shock. "How can you say that?" she demanded. "Those killers belong in jail. They took your father away from me, and your brother. Or don't you care about that anymore?" she practically accused.

"I care about punishing the real killer," Rose hedged. "And that is Ava, not Aunt Melinda or Joey," she pointed out.

Her mother screamed and dug her fingers into her hair, yanking on it with frustration.

"Mom, all the evidence points in that direction," Rose insisted, choosing to ignore her mother's tantrum.

"I don't want to hear that nonsense again," her mother stressed.

"It's not nonsense," Rose stood her ground. "The evidence against Ava is piling up, and you are the only one who's refusing to see it because you're blinded by this hate toward Aunt Melinda."

Rose couldn't understand why her mother was so insistent that Aunt Melinda was the one behind it all. Sure, Melinda was a bitch who constantly belittled her and ridiculed her, gossiped about Rose, and made horrible snide comments behind their backs, but for the longest time, her mom had just put up with it for the sake of family peace. She didn't understand now why her mother believed Melinda would actually resort to murdering her brother for money when she had her own. It might not be in the billions, but it wasn't as though she was poor either.

Her mother stared at her for a moment, looking as though

she was going to speak, but then simply screamed again and rushed out of the room. Rose shook her head. She didn't follow after her. She didn't see the point. And to be honest, she couldn't care less if her mom demolished the entire house. It wasn't like Rose was emotionally attached to anything in it, especially since it looked more like a museum, or an art gallery, than a home.

Grabbing her things, Rose left the house. She couldn't be around her mother when she was acting like that. And it was still completely mind-boggling to her that her mother would rather demolish the entire house than believe Rose.

Driving aimlessly, Rose came to a decision. It might be a bad idea, but in her mind, it was the only way forward.

She headed for Aunt Melinda's house.

TWENTY-SEVEN

Aunt Melinda lived in a completely ostentatious house that was only slightly smaller than Rose's parents' mansion. Rose knew Melinda always resented that fact because, in her mind, bigger was always better.

Rose was let inside by a maid and told to go to the sunroom because the mistress of the house liked to drink her coffee there. Although Rose hadn't stepped foot inside that house in years, she still knew her way around it pretty well. She still recognized the cupboard Joey had shoved her in when she was seven, and the painfully decorated drawing room where they'd sat around during some tedious lunch.

Aunt Melinda scoffed once she saw her. "Did you come to accuse me of killing someone else now? Your favorite pet, for example?" she said snidely, instead of greeting her in a normal manner.

"You might be a thief, but I never believed you killed Dad in the first place," Rose pointed out.

"Your mother does, but she's always hated me."

Rose had always wondered why there was so much animosity between Melinda and her mother. She knew there was something there, but she didn't know what, and she doubted she would get the truth from Melinda now. Eventually, she would discover what that thing between them was, but for now, she needed an ally. Even if that ally was someone she didn't really like. "That's true," she agreed, "but I'm not my mother."

"Clearly. At least Thelma has some class," she countered, wrinkling her nose.

"If you're done insulting me, I want to tell you why I came here today," Rose said, refusing to allow Aunt Melinda to suck her into some petty argument when she had bigger fish to fry.

Aunt Melinda gave her a look, as though she wasn't pleased, however she remained quiet.

That's the best I can hope for, I guess, she thought.

"I know who the real killer is," Rose said without preamble.

Aunt Melinda opened her mouth as though to say something and promptly closed it. Rose knew the other woman well enough to guess she was about to say something insulting or sarcastic, but for some reason, she thought better of it.

Am I growing on her? Rose joked.

"And how did you come across such information?" Aunt Melinda asked instead.

"I'm still working with that PI I told all of you about."

"Then who did it?"

Rose hesitated for a microsecond before responding. "Ava."

Immediately, Aunt Melinda started laughing.

"Before you completely dismiss it, just hear me out," Rose rushed to say.

Surprisingly, Aunt Melinda sobered up. "Very well, let's hear it then. What's your smoking gun?" she challenged.

Rose knew she only had this one chance to convince Aunt Melinda she was right, so she decided to tell her everything that she knew, everything that Gregory had managed to discover so far.

"We all knew from the start that Ava is a doctor; however, what we didn't know was that she worked for County General, where she had access to our family medical records. From there, she went on to work for a DNA facility, where she could fabricate DNA results to say she was related to us…" Rose started at the beginning, not wanting to miss anything that might convince Melinda of the truth. Rose still believed that Ava was lying about being Charles's daughter, despite the fact that Ava's mother probably did have an affair with her dad.

Aunt Melinda had a lot of questions, and Rose was more than happy to answer them to the best of her abilities.

"She also had access to bee venom through Pinecrest Research, where she currently works…"

Rose was pleased to see that the more she talked, the more interested Aunt Melinda looked. It was obvious she was at least intrigued, if not anything else. Rose would have to do some more convincing before she believed her completely.

"…She also demanded I convince the family to give her seven billion dollars."

To that, Aunt Melinda burst out laughing again. "That's insane," she commented through the cackles.

Rose knew her aunt would find that tidbit particularly amusing. She cared about the money the most, after all, and would never agree to some stranger getting that much of it.

By the time Rose finished her narrative, Aunt Melinda was nodding her head as though she too was finally seeing things clearly. Luckily, she realized that what Rose was saying made sense.

"I thought you were just acting out, being jealous, but you may be onto something," Aunt Melinda allowed.

This was as close to being praised as Rose ever got from her.

"My gut feeling has told me something was wrong with her from the moment she entered our lives, and I was right," Rose replied, unapologetic.

Aunt Melinda nodded again. "Have the police verified all these claims?"

"Why would they? When they have you as a suspect," Rose replied, letting her irritations and frustrations be plain on her face.

"Right," Aunt Melinda muttered. "So, what do you want from me?" she went straight to the point. "Do you want me to call Joey? I could have him take care of her."

The idea that Melinda would condone her son doing something heinous to anyone was a bit disturbing, but she didn't want to touch that at the moment. "To be honest, no. What I want is *your* help," Rose said honestly, and in a pretty concise manner, she told her aunt what she expected from her.

When the moment of truth came, her aunt made a decision, she grabbed the phone and started dialing. Part of Rose was really shocked she actually managed to sway the other woman; the rest was simply relieved.

Without wasting any time, Aunt Melinda dialed 911, from one of Joey's easily disposable phones. Rose's plan was simple: to tip off the police about Ava. Aunt Melinda pretty much told the police everything Rose told her, stressing how Ava had knowledge, access, and means to commit a murder and attempt another one. Granted, Gregory had given them some of the information, but she wasn't sure he'd shared everything yet. Rose fretted for a moment that she hadn't told Gregory what she was up to and realized she'd need to let him know what she'd done.

"Will it be enough?" Aunt Melinda asked after finishing the conversation. For good measure, she dumped the phone into her drink, ruining it in the process.

"I don't know," Rose replied honestly. "But Gregory is still working on it too," she reassured. "And please don't tell anyone who he is," she added as an afterthought.

She didn't want anyone to know Gregory was still snooping

around, although she was pretty sure the cat would soon be out of the bag.

"And you tell no one how I helped you today," Aunt Melinda warned.

"Of course, I won't. Who would believe me anyway?"

Aunt Melinda heard her and agreed.

Rose called Gregory as she left her aunt's house. "Hey," she said into the phone as she drove.

"What's up?" he asked, sounding slightly distracted. "Everything okay?"

"Yes, but I need to... I did something, and I needed to share." She was hesitant because she didn't want to make him mad.

"Oh?" He sounded interested and slightly intrigued. "What did you do?"

Rose explained her visit with Melinda and what she'd done. "So... what do you think?"

"Could work. Maybe draw them out to make a move. You need to be extra careful now," he offered. "I'll get in touch with St. James and back up what your aunt told them with the proof I found."

Rose was relieved that he was so calm about what she'd done. He didn't explode or tell her she was stupid for doing it, he just adapted and pushed forward with their investigation. She really liked that about him. "Thanks, Gregory."

"You stay safe, okay? I'm going to bet St. James will be conducting more interviews of everyone now, but that doesn't mean you're out of the woods yet."

"I know. I will," Rose replied, liking that he was concerned about her. "Did you find any more information about Karin?"

"I did, in fact. Turns out she was fired for theft. There were internal emails about equipment going missing, laptops and the like. After a thorough investigation, it was discovered that Karin had been stealing them and pawning them for cash. Your father didn't press charges, but he did fire her."

"Oh, wow. Why would she do that? Was it to get back at my dad for not helping with Ava?"

"That's just it. I'm not so sure that email we read was about them breaking up romantically, Rose. I think she was begging for her job back."

"Will you keep digging? I want to know for sure one way or another."

"Absolutely, I will. I'll talk to you soon," he said before hanging up.

For the first time in a while, Rose felt her heart swell with hope. Hope that they would catch Ava, that they would prove that she wasn't Charles's daughter. Of course, that left Rose with the question of why Ava had done all of this in the first place. Was it all about the money?

It didn't take long for the police to ask all the Blaisdells to speak with them again. This time around they were all summoned to the police station. Rose cheered once she saw Adrian and Ava were asked to come as well. *Her days are numbered.*

Gregory was there too, and Rose pretended not to know him while he was with the police, helping on the case. They both agreed it would be better if nobody knew who he was, because that would make his investigation a little bit easier.

Rose stood by the vending machine, trying to decide what to grab to eat, starving after the endless waiting around. The interviews were taking too long, she thought, when Adrian approached her. She did her best to ignore him, but unfortunately, it was apparent he had something to say to her.

"Why do you keep looking at her like that?" he snapped. "Why do you hate her so much?" he continued. "I decided to leave you... me! She had nothing to do with it, so stop trying to sabotage her every step of the way."

There were so many things wrong with that little speech of his; however, Rose decided to stick to the basics.

"While I'm tickled that you think I have no right to be upset that you cheated on me with her, this actually has nothing to do with you and me, Adrian," she said, looking him straight in the eyes, to make sure he was actually hearing what she was saying. "No matter what you think, I don't care about you anymore, and I definitely don't care that you're with her. However, I think she's a murderer, I think she killed my father, and for that, I will forever hate her guts. I'll do everything in my power to put her in jail," she said, completely losing her temper.

Adrian looked at her so rattled, that for a split second, she believed he would merely storm away without saying anything. She was wrong.

Adrian managed to recover quickly. "You're out of your mind. And each day without you, having to deal with you, shows me I made the right decision."

Did he actually think that something like that would hurt her? He clearly didn't know her very well. Probably as much as she didn't know him.

"I don't care about your opinion," she replied calmly, smiling at him.

"I will sue you if you continue to slander my fiancée."

Rose did her best not to flinch at his words. The two of them deserved each other. "Be my guest. And let me give you some advice. Watch your back, Adrian, because that woman will definitely drag you down with her." Rose walked away, her chin held high.

Rose took a seat next to her mother, waiting her turn to speak with the lead detective. She knew she shouldn't have saidthat. She'd revealed her hand. There was no doubt in her mind that Adrian would tell Ava everything she'd said. Then again, the police already knew all of it, so sooner or later, Ava would find out Rose had been secretly researching her all this time.

Preferably, it would be later though.

And if she was extra lucky, Adrian would simply think she was bitter and dismiss everything, like before.

She really hoped so, because this was extremely foolish, not to mention dangerous, of her. *Gregory's going to be angry with me for having words with Adrian,* she thought glumly.

I need to find a way to fix this.

How?

TWENTY-EIGHT

After leaving the police station and heading for her apartment, Rose found Ava waiting for her outside of her apartment door.

Oh, no.

Rose didn't have to guess twice who gave Ava her address. Adrian was a complete bastard. And since Ava was there, it was a safe bet he had already shared what she'd said.

She knows I think she's a killer, Rose thought as a very powerful uneasiness started to spread through her body. She was glad that she'd changed the locks on her apartment and that this interaction wasn't happening inside her space but in the hallway.

Adrian really was a spineless, opportunistic cretin. She could say even far worse things than that; however, she was choosing her words with care, not wanting to succumb to all those negative emotions like resentment and anger.

Although she was done with him, the betrayal still hurt. Especially this one because he knew how much she valued her privacy.

Rose truly felt like strangling Adrian, but then again, he was her mistake. Her father had warned her about him. More to the point, he had point-blank told her Adrian was only in it for the money, and she hadn't believed him. She had practically accused him of wanting to keep her alone and chaste for the rest of her life.

I was such an idiot.

Unfortunately, that cheater wasn't beside his fiancée at the moment. Apparently, Ava had come to speak with her alone.

"What a nice surprise," Rose said, deciding to use Ava's words from when they met at the hotel.

Ava scowled. It was obvious she didn't appreciate that joke.

"If you don't back the fuck off, I will release the DNA results to the public, and then I will have my lawyer contest your right to the inheritance," she threatened.

By her lawyer, she meant Adrian. Rose had no doubts he was good at what he did, but he wasn't that kind of lawyer, and Ava knew it. Besides, she was sure he was no match for Alex Min. After all, Rose hired only the best.

Rose started laughing. "I really don't think we are on the same page here," she commented. More to the point, Rose now had a very good reason to believe that the DNA test result Ava had was a fake, she just didn't want Ava to know that she knew.

Rose's reaction threw Ava off guard for a moment. "Why are you laughing? I am dead serious," she practically screeched.

"I know you are, I just don't care," Rose replied with a small shrug.

"You will care when I strip you of everything you have," she said haughtily.

"Look, Ava, I've already given my statement to the police, so there's no use threatening me now. The damage is already done," Rose jibed. It was as though Ava forgot Rose wasn't motivated by money like the rest of her family. She didn't care about the money, never had, but even so, there was no way Ava could take her inheritance from her.

"I have no interest in indulging your delusions, my lawyer

already took care of everything, no matter your smear campaign against me, I have an alibi," she said all in one breath.

For some reason, Rose wasn't buying any of it.

"However, for putting me through all that, I will most definitely ruin your life. That's a promise."

"Good luck with that," Rose replied, unfazed.

"I tried to be fair with you, but now, I will get your share as well, because you're a spoiled little brat who can't handle when someone takes her toys. Face it, Rose, I'm just better than you. I'm the one who deserves Adrian, the family, the money, all of it."

Rose rolled her eyes. It started to be apparent that Ava was suffering from delusions of grandeur.

"Whatever, Ava, I'm not afraid of you anymore." And she meant it. Rose had a good lawyer, and she had evidence on her side; in any case, Charles Blaisdell legitimized her, his name was on her birth certificate, and he was named as her father. At this point it didn't matter if they shared the same blood or not, he was her father, and he put her in his will, end of story. She wished she'd remembered all of that when Ava first made her threats.

At the same time, she didn't even know why she was indulging Ava. This petty squabble about the inheritance would never reach the court, because long before that, Rose would make sure she ended up in jail for murder. She said as much. It was time to reveal all the cards, and for Ava to be afraid for a change.

In one swift move, Ava pushed Rose against the hallway wall, pulling out a knife, and pressing it against her neck.

Rose almost blacked out. Her heart was beating like crazy, and her palms started to sweat. Unfortunately, she had failed to comprehend how dangerous the other woman was.

I shouldn't have taunted her like that. She's already killed one person and tried to kill another. It was obvious she was willing to do anything to get her hands on the inheritance, and that also meant removing all the obstacles from her path. Ava said as much. And, at the moment, Rose was the biggest obstacle.

Rose started to panic. Her instincts told her she needed to run away from this dangerous situation, but the cold blade of the knife stopped her from moving an inch.

It was hard to remain calm, in place, but she forced herself to stop freaking out because she didn't want to get cut, at least not by accident. She was definitely worried now.

"What are you doing?" she demanded, putting some bravado into her voice as she stared into Ava's fac, contorted in rage. She couldn't believe she ever considered her beautiful when now all her ugliness was plain to see.

"I want to make myself loud and clear now, you little brat. If you don't stop poking around, if you don't get out of my way, I will fucking kill you," she threatened without missing a beat.

And Rose truly believed her when she said that. Ava's stare was murderous.

But something inside of Rose snapped because the next thing she knew, she said, "Well, you'll have to kill me, because I have no intention of getting out of your way. I won't stop. I will never stop. I will protect what's left of my family, and I'll prove you killed my father, and put my brother in a coma, you psychotic bitch," Rose said all in one breath because, to be fair, she didn't know if she would have another available.

Rose had no idea where this sudden courage, sudden defiance came from, but here it was, and she wasn't sorry for utilizing it.

To Rose's utmost shock, Ava started laughing. "Your family? You can't mean Melinda, Joey, and the likes of them?" she practically mocked.

"I mean all of my family," Rose replied stubbornly.

Ava shook her head. Rose noted that the pressure of the

blade against her neck loosened ever so slightly, but she remained still.

"You can't be serious," Ava said. "You risk your life while fully knowing they would never do the same for you?" she asked incredulously. "If so, you're an even bigger idiot than I originally believed."

Rose was very much aware of how undeserving, and ungrateful, some of her family were. She really didn't need Ava to tell her that.

"I am serious, and I would risk my life for them, family is family," Rose remained adamant.

"You're a fool. They're on my side now. They belong to me."

"I wouldn't be so sure of that."

Ava laughed. "Those rotten, greedy, backstabbing bastards are so stupid they will believe everything I tell them."

"If you say so," Rose replied stubbornly, done with this argument.

Ava looked at her with something that was pretty close to pity, among other things. "Adrian was right about you, you're completely unhinged."

Coming from someone like Ava, that almost sounded like a compliment.

"Maybe I am, but what's your excuse?"

"Excuse me?" Ava asked, clearly caught off guard.

"Why are you doing all of this? Why did you target my family? Are you motivated by greed, or something else entirely?" Rose demanded.

Part of her was pretty much aware she was in no position to demand anything, yet she couldn't stop her mouth speaking all the same. She needed to know. And she felt like this was the best opportunity she would ever have for discovering the truth, for figuring out what made the other woman tick.

Rose needed to know *why* her father had to die.

Ava jerked as though Rose had just insulted her gravely. "I'm taking my revenge against your family for ruining mine," she said, moving away from Rose, dropping the knife to the floor, and then practically running away.

Rose had no intention of chasing after her, especially considering she couldn't move her legs. She was very much aware she almost died today, but for whatever reason, Ava hadn't followed through.

Lowering herself down to sit on the floor by her apartment door, with shaky hands, Rose pulled her phone out and dialed Gregory. It went straight to voicemail.

He was clearly working.

"I'm really glad you gave me that camera," she said, leaving a message for him before disconnecting.

Rose looked at the camera Gregory had installed in the doorbell by her apartment door. When he first proposed something like that to her, for her safety, she had found it a bit silly, but she'd acquiesced.

She didn't think of it as silly anymore.

Rose frowned. Unfortunately, when she inspected it, it looked like it might have taken some damage. Ava had slammed her into it at full force, and the lens looked a little worse for wear.

Taking a few deep breaths, calming herself down, Rose opened the door to her apartment. She went in and got a screwdriver to open the camera and inspect the little device. She noticed that the lens was broken; however, when she went to the computer to check the recording, the audio was still intact, and though the video was blurry, it recorded everything. The entire exchange between Ava and Rose.

I've got you, she thought victoriously.

TWENTY-NINE

There was a specific place in hell for people like Adrian. Rose was sure of that.

Even if she managed to aim all her anger, frustration, hate, and even fear, toward Ava, for what that woman did to her and her family, Rose realized that there would still be enough fury left over for Adrian as well.

She had really made a mistake with that one. She couldn't believe she ever loved that man, trusted that man. Worse than that, she had wanted to marry that man, which now felt almost unfathomable. Then again, it was better she'd learned the truth about him now than after the wedding. *Now that would be an utter disaster,* she tried to comfort herself. It was somewhat working.

What was holding her back from exploding was the fact she only had herself to blame. She lost her temper with him, revealed her hand, and, as a result, Ava almost killed her. Rose still had no idea what stopped the other woman from slitting her throat.

Maybe she didn't want to ruin her Dior power suit with my blood, she thought sarcastically.

It was obvious now that Adrian told Ava everything about Rose. And not just about their last interaction, but everything in general. For example, where she lived, what she liked, disliked, what she was like as a person, and so on. How else to explain how Ava was always so many steps ahead of her?

None of that mattered anymore; to a degree, all Ava's cards were revealed. Ava knew Rose suspected her, and in return, Rose now had proof of Ava assaulting her. Or so she hoped. She had to have faith that Gregory would be able to salvage the recording.

Not even the police would be able to ignore something like that. Detective St. James would be forced to look into Ava more closely, whether he wanted it or not. Considering everything, that felt like a small victory.

I need Gregory to find something else too, the smoking gun, she continued to muse, *that would completely shatter the advantage Ava had so far and put her straight behind bars.*

Rose knew they were running out of time. There was no doubt in Rose's mind that pushing Ava against the corner would only make her more dangerous. Her little show-and-tell with a knife proved that much. Then again, she was already dangerous enough.

That bitch pulled the knife on Rose, in the middle of her apartment hallway. Anyone could have come out and seen her at any time. That, right there, showed that Ava felt she had nothing to lose. She acted all smug and superior, but there was clearly something deeply wrong with her.

Unwillingly, Rose patted her neck. At times she could swear she could still feel the cold steel against her skin. She shuddered. *Ava almost killed me today.* Only then did she truly start to realize the gravity, the danger, of the situation she was in.

And they all dared to call me crazy, she thought. Rose was right about Ava from the start.

Rose almost ended up dead as well in her pursuit of the truth, but that was beside the point. She couldn't think about it because it would be her undoing, and she needed to be strong for the time being.

Gregory came to see her as soon as he got her message.

"What happened?" he demanded, clearly seeing how shaken up she was.

There was a pretty good chance she was in shock because her thoughts made no sense. Rose was feeling all over the place, and she was strangely focused on unimportant things instead of the fact she almost died.

I didn't die, that has to count for something, she thought.

"Are there any other cameras around the building that we could maybe look into?" she asked, instead of answering his question. She couldn't recall if there were any security cameras in her apartment building. Maybe there was one in the hallway that would provide a clearer picture of what occurred—one not marred by the cracked lens of her doorbell camera.

Gregory frowned. "I can look it up. Why? What's happened?"

Rose took a deep breath before answering. "Ava paid me a visit, and she threatened me with a knife," she explained, trying to appear as calm as possible.

Gregory was instantly on high alert. "Are you all right?" he demanded, running his hands over her arms, studying her, checking her out to see if she was injured in any way.

"I'm a bit shaken but unharmed," she reassured instantly.

Gregory took a deep breath. "Tell me everything that happened."

She did. "I made an error in judgment with Adrian. I hinted at my suspicions of Ava to him, and as I got home, she was waiting for me. When she threatened me, I lost my temper. We got into an argument, and the next thing I knew, she had me pinned against the wall, with a knife at my throat."

Gregory cursed. "If she's become that desperate, then that means we're close to discovering something."

"I really hope so," she said, once again massaging her neck, although there was nothing on it.

Rose would hate if what she went through today was for nothing. Because it was more than obvious that Ava had snapped. She was afraid of something, and it wasn't about reputation or inheritance. It was all about revenge. *But revenge for what?* Rose wondered. Had her dad actually abandoned Ava? Was that the reason Ava was set on destroying them? Rose couldn't be sure. All Rose knew was that Ava was afraid she would lose her freedom before she accomplished her goal of destroying Rose's family. All the same, she was dangerous and needed to be stopped no matter what.

"For the time being, you shouldn't stay at your apartment, considering she knows where you live now," Gregory cautioned, pulling her out of her thoughts.

Rose nodded. But that also meant she couldn't go to her mom's either.

"I'll check myself into a hotel," Rose replied.

"Pay with cash and use a fake name."

Rose was stunned by that. She wasn't a criminal. Why wouldn't she be able to just use her debit card?

Gregory must have read the thoughts right from her face because he said, "You can never be too careful with a determined killer on the loose. You could easily be found by using your card."

Well, when you put it that way... "I'll do that then," she agreed. "And before I forget, could you maybe check this out for me," she handed him the thumb drive she'd made of the video feed from the doorbell camera.

"You caught your altercation with Ava on the camera?"

"Yes, I think so. Most of it anyway, but the video is a little blurry."

"What happened to it?"

"I think it got messed up when she slammed me into the door," she explained, almost apologetically. "I don't think she knew there was a camera in it, thank goodness."

"I think I can get it cleaned up. I know a tech guy who is really good at stuff like that."

As far as Rose was concerned, that was a piece of pretty good news. "Great."

After he put the thumb drive into his pocket, Gregory said, "There's something else I wanted to share with you, a discovery, if you will."

Rose had no idea where this was going. "Okay," she replied slowly.

"Based on everything that's happened, taking into account what transpired today, I'm starting to suspect that Adrian has been helping Ava from the start," he shared.

"What?" Rose exclaimed.

To be fair, before Gregory arrived, she, too, thought of Adrian and what a treacherous piece of shit he was, feeding Ava with information about Rose. However, apparently, she didn't put all the pieces together. *Is it really possible Adrian was in cahoots with Ava all this time?*

"Remember when we discussed Ava having an accomplice?"

"Yeah, but we couldn't pinpoint who that person might be."

They even speculated Ava simply bribed some caterer working at the New Year's Eve party to spike her father's drink and poison him that way.

"I think that person might be Adrian. It all fits when you think about it. He was at the New Year's Eve party, and he was around when Devon got ill as well, not that anyone had to specifically poison him, he could have just poured brandy from the same decanter," he pointed out.

More to the point, Adrian had been the one who convinced

Rose to attend the stupid party in the first place. She hadn't even wanted to go. That horrified her.

"But we met over seven months ago," she rebelled.

"I know. Unfortunately, this looks to me like they've been playing a long con," he explained.

Rose placed a hand over her mouth as she thought back over their entire relationship. "Oh my God," she muttered as she realized Gregory was right. She already knew from their investigations that Ava had been planning this for a long time, so, of course, Adrian was part of that plan.

"I did some digging into him—" Gregory held up his hand to stop Rose from interjecting, "I know you told me not to worry about him, but something about him just stuck out to me. But you'll be glad I did. He's not who he says he is."

That stopped Rose's spiraling thoughts. "What do you mean?" Rose frowned.

"Adrian Cosgrove is an alias. His real name is Adrian Franks. He does have a law degree, and he worked for that same DNA facility that Ava worked at."

"What?!" Rose was fuming. He really had known Ava the whole time.

"About a year ago, he changed his name and went to work for Darlington Law Offices, where he exclusively went to work with authors. My theory is he was looking to find an 'in' to the publishing house you worked for. Didn't you find it odd that you were called in so early in the process before the author even signed the deal?"

Rose thought about it and then shook her head. "No, not really. It's happened before with high-profile authors. They want to know every single person that is going to have their hands on their books."

"Hmmm. I guess I didn't really think of it like that. Well, still, I think that was why he took that particular job. So he could get close to you."

"So he did know who I was, who my family were before we even met."

Rose should have known. It wasn't as though she'd changed her name. She still went by Rose Blaisdell, but she'd been naive enough to think that she could just claim a loose family connection to her father. There were plenty of Blaisdells out there who weren't rich, and she'd thought she could just pass herself off as one of them. Apparently not. Now she wondered if everyone she worked with had known exactly who she was.

"I was so stupid," she murmured.

"No, in any other situation, I'm sure you probably could have claimed to be just a cousin, not the heiress to the Blaisdell fortune, at least you could have before your father died. The paparazzi have pretty much outed you now though."

Rose shook her head. All she'd ever wanted was to live a normal life. She had never wanted the falseness and flattery of being a billionaire heiress. She'd gone to school, gotten a job, all on her own merits. She lived in a modest apartment building and drove a standard economy car. She didn't even dress in designer clothes unless she was forced into it by her mother for some family function. And it was all for nothing.

"So they set this up together." Rose felt as though she'd been blindsided.

"Yes, I believe Adrian has been her partner from the start. Especially considering how easily he was stolen away from a smart, pretty, good, and warmhearted girl like you," he added softly.

Rose couldn't speak for a moment. All kinds of thoughts, ramifications, and consequences were passing through her head. If Gregory was right, then this was all her fault. Her father was dead because of her. Devon was in a coma because of her. And that realization was almost unbearable.

Gregory clearly misunderstood her silence because he continued to persuade her. "You said it yourself that he was very loving and supportive from the moment you met. That he professed his undying love and expressed a desire to marry you shortly after you started dating. He was clearly love-bombing you, so you would fall in love with him, and invite him into your family. And then, all of a sudden, he was with her. It doesn't make sense unless you look at the bigger picture. He was with her first. They came up with this cruel plan together."

Rose's eyes filled with tears.

Is that how Ava managed to get a hold of my DNA too? Did Adrian steal it, or did she just make a fake test result at that lab? That thought had been bothering her since Ava showed her the DNA report on her and her dad. If it was real, how did she get Rose's DNA to test it? Rose stopped herself there because each thought was scarier than the previous one. More horrible too.

"I will get to the bottom of this, I promise, Rose, but I have to say something else."

She looked at him, although she wasn't sure she would be able to comprehend anything else at the moment.

"Adrian is an idiot either way."

She didn't see that one coming. That comment made her smile.

"I agree," she replied dryly because if she didn't joke, she would start crying for sure.

I'm to blame. It's my fault.

Gregory helped her pack a bag and then drove her to a hotel. She barely recalled stopping by the bank to take out cash beforehand, nor the name he'd registered her under. It didn't matter to her, not when she felt like being anyone else right now.

All she could think was that all of this, everything, was her fault. She'd brought Adrian into her family. Introduced him to her dad, to her brother, her mom... and he'd tried to destroy them all. Her soul was hurting at the thoughts running through her mind.

It was one thing to think Adrian left her because he fell out of love, or because he found someone better suited, someone who looked better and had more money than her. It was something else entirely to realize they weren't actually together in the first place. It was all a lie from the start. It was all just a devious plan to weasel his way into her family, so he could exploit it, so he could destroy it, alongside Ava.

He had pretended from the start because he had an agenda. Realizing he was with Ava from the beginning that he was actively helping her to achieve her plan, and murder members of Rose's family, was excruciating.

I'm such a fool, her soul cried over and over.

Her father had been right. She should have listened to him. She should have trusted him.

She had definitely learned her lesson the hard way, and for that experience, she only had to lose her father, and almost lose her brother.

When the truth gets out, Mom will never be able to forgive me.

She will never speak to me again, Rose realized, and to make matters worse, Rose wouldn't fight it. Because in the end, her mother would be right.

I'm to blame.

THIRTY

The next morning brought new problems.

Ava made good on her threats. She sent the DNA test result to everyone in the family. It didn't matter that it was probably fake, they all thought it was real.

As expected, Aunt Melinda jumped at the opportunity to contest the will.

I guess our little alliance is over, Rose thought sarcastically.

Somewhere along the line, Rose realized that she was handling this a lot better than she expected. *A brush with death would do that to a person, it puts everything into perspective.* So, Rose really couldn't care less about all the petty squabbles, she only cared about sending Ava to prison.

Sadly, she was the only one who thought like that. The rest treated Rose's illegitimacy as a nuclear bomb that just exploded in their backyard, as though that was the biggest scandal imaginable.

Rose immediately went to see her mother.

"I told you that woman is a snake, do you believe me now?" Rose snapped, not being able to contain her fury. She didn't want to either. She was angry with her mother, frustrated, and disappointed as well.

"Melinda already hired an attorney to contest the will," her mother said, ignoring all the rest.

Rose was already aware of that fact; her lawyer, Alex Min, had informed her immediately.

"Is that really all you care about?" Rose asked incredulously.

"I care about your father's legacy, about our *family* legacy."

Rose had no idea what that meant anymore. "So, what are we going to do?" Rose asked, although if she stopped to think about it, she would realize how redundant that question actually was.

Her mother organized a family meeting.

All gathered— and Rose really meant all— like sharks, the Blaisdell clan clearly sensed blood in the water and rushed to see who was going to be devoured.

Ava looked pretty self-righteous and pleased with herself stepping into the meeting room. Aunt Melinda looked pretty good as well. Rose couldn't believe her; even despite everything she now knew, she still chatted with Ava as though nothing was amiss.

They had a mediator to make sure all behaved. And then the meeting started.

"I'm sorry I had to resort to this; however, I truly believe that all of you, good people, deserve to know the truth," Ava started, looking torn up, as though she struggled with a huge moral dilemma or something.

What a fake.

Rose couldn't stand to look at her, she couldn't wait to see that murderer behind bars.

"How dare you share intimate personal information about me with others?" Rose accused.

"Like I just said, I believe that all deserve to know the truth about you, how you've been deceiving everyone for years," Ava countered in the same manner.

"How did you get my DNA sample to begin with?" Rose challenged. "I never voluntarily gave it to you, so did Adrian steal it for you?" Rose accused; she couldn't help herself.

Adrian looked away, which made Rose believe she guessed it correctly. Gregory was right, and Adrian's behavior was the proof. That bastard was working for Ava, with Ava, all this time.

Ava scoffed, clearly not liking Rose mentioning that, but she recovered quickly. "Don't try to change the subject. The truth is out now, and that means you're no longer a Blaisdell," she informed, as though something like that was really up to her. "And I will be contesting your right my father's inheritance."

Your father, what a joke, Rose fumed. "My father will always be my father, no matter what you say. He claimed me, he raised me, his name is on my birth certificate. Some DNA test result changes nothing," Rose was adamant. Besides, it wasn't as though she couldn't take another DNA test and see if she really was Charles's daughter or not. Especially if, as she suspected, the one Ava had was fake.

"We shall see about that," Ava replied haughtily, and more than half the people gathered agreed with her, Aunt Melinda included.

"Besides, I'm pretty sure that test is fake, so, I'll be asking an independent laboratory to do the test again," Rose informed them all. "It's time to put this garbage about my heritage to rest for good."

"How dare you call me a liar?" Ava snapped, losing her temper.

Good, let them all see what a snake she truly is. Then again, with this crowd, that would probably be considered a good trait, not a bad one.

Rose's mother slammed her hands against the table, shushing everyone. "I've heard quite enough from you," she started. "You have no authority to dictate anything in this family," she said to Ava. "You will get your share, if you really are Charles's daughter, and nothing else. Rose will get hers, as Charles wanted, and that is final."

"I disagree," Ava said stubbornly.

"I don't care," Rose's mom snapped.

Rose gawked at her mother because she couldn't remember if she'd ever seen her this angry. The amber of her eyes was burning with a cold fury, not red hot, which usually made her break things around the house. Her mom looked scary, to be honest.

"And something else," her mom continued, "You will leave Rose alone if you want to be accepted into this home, into this family at all," she threatened without missing a beat.

Rose felt like hugging her mother. She couldn't remember the last time her mom had defended her in this manner.

The rest of the family simply looked at her mom in shock. Rose's heart swelled looking at her mother standing up for her, putting all those sycophants back in their place.

"Putting all sentiments to the side, facts and the law are something else entirely, and DNA evidence submitted can be considered while contesting the will," Adrian said coldly, speaking as Ava's attorney.

"If it's a legal fight you want, it's a legal fight you'll get," Rose's mother stood her ground. "And you can be damn sure that we will be having our own DNA testing done because I know Rose is Charles's daughter."

That enticed quite a few comments from the rest of the family, the peanut gallery.

"Are you sure about that, Thelma?" Aunt Melinda questioned, giving her a haughty look.

She rounded on Melinda right then and there. "I have put up with your threats to leak my affairs to the press since before I even got pregnant with Rose. What happened between me and

Charles was between me and Charles, and for his sake, I have held my tongue, but I won't do so any longer. You can say whatever you want to the press, but I know the truth, and Charles knew it too. We worked out our differences, and he was ecstatic when we got pregnant with Rose. Both of us recommitted to our marriage, and neither of us stepped foot outside of our marriage after that. Why do you think Charles treated you like the snake you are all these years, barely speaking to you and only inviting you over when the entire family was here? Because he knew what you were doing to me. He didn't want a scandal, so we both held our tongues and put up with your nonsense. Maybe we shouldn't have. Maybe he should have cut you out of our lives entirely."

Rose stared at her mom, impressed with how she was letting loose now. And she didn't miss what she'd said about her conception. If that was true, then Ava really had faked that DNA test.

Her mother continued, "I'd thought I would try once again to bury the hatchet with you and stay strong for the family because family was always so important to Charles, but then you had to go and try and steal from us. Well, I'm done, Melinda. Do you hear me? I'm done. I will not put up with any more from you."

Melinda looked pale and ready to run for a moment, but then she gathered herself and drew herself up, staring at them all. "I would never have actually done it. I just didn't care for the fact that you brought such shame on my brother and our family name. I was only looking out for the family."

There were murmurs from the rest of the family who were gathered, and they were all giving Melinda the side-eye. Rose decided it was time to get the conversation back on track, even though she was really interested to see where the rest of that would have gone. She had to resist; at the moment, she had more important things to do. Namely, outing Ava even more.

"Since we are all being honest today, revealing secrets, I have something to add as well," Rose said, standing up. "Since I'm being accused of deceiving this family when I've been a Blaisdell all my life, I want to show you that you are actually being deceived by someone else."

Aunt Melinda squirmed in her seat for a moment more, clearly thinking Rose was about to speak about their temporary alliance and making her look even more of a fool than her mother had. But Rose had no interest in doing that. Not right then, but maybe later.

"I think all of you should be aware that Ava has been black-mailing me into silence by threatening me with this supposed DNA evidence," she air-quoted that part, "but that's not all. She also threatened my life."

Both Adrian and Ava jumped up from their seats to call Rose a liar. Adrian went as far as to say he would definitely, in his client's name, sue Rose for slander.

"My private investigator has the video recording of the whole incident he's preparing to release; however, until he does, this will have to do," Rose said calmly, producing a small recorder Gregory had given her to use. He had extracted the audio recording of the altercation for her, which Rose was going to play for the entire room.

"This is a recording from my doorbell camera that I had installed after I began to suspect that Dad was murdered and Devon ended up in the hospital," she explained.

Gasps reverberated around the room.

"That will not be permitted in court," Adrian rebelled.

"We're not in court, Adrian, and this is a single-party state, so yes, it can be," Rose replied coldly, pressing play on the small, handheld recorder.

They all leaned forward, to make sure they would catch every word of the recording.

Rose held her head high while they all heard the audio of

Ava threatening her, and then smearing members of the Blaisdell family. Rose found that to be a nice touch.

In any other circumstances, it would be comical, hearing Ava rant about how everyone in the Blaisdell family was rotten and full of greedy, backstabbing people who were so stupid they would believe everything told by her. And how they definitely didn't deserve her loyalty.

The audio recording ended.

"Like I said, Ava, my family may be a lot of things, but they are still *my family*, and I am willing to risk my life to protect my family, especially from you," Rose concluded.

There was a moment of silence, as everyone was processing what just happened.

Adrian broke the silence first. "My client hasn't done anything wrong. This was all clearly taken out of context."

"And what would the context be then?" Joey gave Adrian a hard stare. "Enlighten us."

Adrian turned ghostly pale and gaped for a few moments.

And then Aunt Melinda turned to look at Ava. "I think you and that boy should leave," she told her sternly.

For a moment, Ava looked like she was about to rebel, to argue, and then thought better of it. She stood up, her eyes filled with fury. Adrian followed suit.

That went well.

Then again, it would be better if Rose could share with everyone everything she knew about the pair. Unfortunately, she still had no actual proof to back that up, just a few connections and theories.

Ava pointed a finger at Rose. "You think just because you suddenly grew a backbone that this is the end? You will pay for this," she hissed.

"Are you sure you want to threaten Rose in a room full of greedy backstabbers?" Joey deadpanned.

Without saying anything else, Ava stormed out of the room. Adrian followed her like the good, obedient dog that he was.

And as though the cherry on top was needed, one of her cousins was already on the phone reporting this newest threat to the police.

Sometimes good guys actually win. For the first time in weeks, Rose felt like her luck was turning.

THIRTY-ONE

Thanks to Aunt Melinda's anonymous call, Rose's audio recording, and other reports made by members of the Blaisdell family, and Gregory, the police finally decided to get involved and started properly investigating Ava.

And much to Rose's delight, Adrian as well.

He had been lying to her from the start, which meant he was equally to blame for everything. Even if he knew nothing about the poisoning, which Rose found quite unlikely, he was still an accomplice, to say the least.

Once again, the entire family was questioned by the police, but this time, the focus was on Ava and their dealings with the other woman. For a change, all the members of Rose's family spoke the truth, hiding nothing, simply making sure they wouldn't be implicated in these crimes in any way.

It was strange watching her entire family gather and actually be of one mind, united in their hate, as they gossiped about Ava. The whole sordid story came out, thanks to Gregory, who was helping Detective St. James put all the pieces together.

Once Detective St. James realized he'd been completely

wrong and stubborn about it, he was fully committed to getting to the bottom of things. Rose was glad about that.

That was how they learned that Dr. Ava Rothman's current and former places of work would be subpoenaed and screened for evidence, looking for her gaining access to the bee venom she used to poison Charles and Devon Blaisdell.

Dr. Michaelson had actually proven that the venom had to have come from a specific set of bees traced to two facilities, one of those being the Pinecrest Research Institute where Ava worked. To Rose, it was the best possible news because it meant something was finally happening, the case was moving forward. And she felt like they were one step closer to finding actual evidence against Ava and Adrian, landing them in prison for a very long time.

Rose was quite shocked, and utterly surprised, when things within her family started to change. Rose stopped being the laughingstock of the family thanks to her mother's outburst, where she stuck up for Rose and the airing of the supposed dirty laundry. Also, Aunt Melinda and Joey toned it down with their remarks and jibes since they were basically having to defend themselves from the entire family now.

Quite a few times, Rose had to pinch herself to make sure she wasn't dreaming. Then again, Rose had been the one who discovered the truth about Ava, unmasking her, exposing her for the fraud she was, and outing her as a potential murderer, which turned things around for the better. It probably helped that her mom had stood up and said she knew for a fact that Rose was Charles's daughter, and they'd get the test to prove it. Even Rose believed her in that moment.

Rose started receiving invitations to various events, coffee dates, and the like from cousins who really hadn't wanted to have anything to do with her over the last decade and a half. It felt strange to suddenly have them coming around, but good too. A few apologized for never reaching out before, saying they had never realized how much influence Aunt Melinda's petty gossip had over them and that they would try to do better in the future toward her. Rose was just happy to finally feel like part of the whole Blaisdell family, not just her immediate one.

And since the cat was out of the bag now, Rose decided it was time for the family to meet Gregory properly. After all, he was the one helping them, saving their asses from the start.

"I wish Rose had informed us of her plans beforehand and not kept us in the dark; however, welcome, Mr. Falcone, to my home, and thank you, for everything you have done so far. We much appreciate it," her mom said when Gregory arrived.

"Gregory is fine," he corrected.

The family had a million questions for Gregory regarding Ava, regarding Charles and his murder. But that wasn't all. Rose watched as several relatives asked to speak with Gregory privately. And she could guess what those conversations revolved around. They all wanted to know if Gregory had found some dirt about them while he was digging into everyone.

Gregory, being very professional, always had prepared diplomatic answers to ease all their worries. His focus, he told them at first, had been looking into Charles Blaisdell's associates, and now Ava and Adrian, nobody else. At least that's the answer he gave them. He didn't tell them that, yes, he had looked into each of them as well.

"Could you please tell us everything that you've discovered, from the beginning, so we can all be on the same page from now on," Rose's mom asked.

Gregory nodded. "Rose hired me several weeks ago to look into what actually happened to her father since she had some concerns regarding his sudden death, especially after Devon fell ill too. Since then, I discovered he was actually poisoned, and so I moved on to look into potential suspects of that crime. Over the last week or so, I've been looking into Ava, because all evidence gathered was starting to point her way, as well as Adrian's."

"And?" Joey asked impatiently.

"I made an interesting discovery yesterday evening, which I've already submitted to the police." He reached into his briefcase and pulled out a stack of papers.

"What is that?" Quite a few people wanted to know.

Rose had already known about it before he'd come to visit them. He'd informed her of the discovery shortly after making it. It was the reason Ava was doing all of this.

"I contacted Kenneth, and he allowed me access to Charles's email account and everything they had on Karin Rothman."

"Why would Kenneth allow that?" Melinda questioned.

"Who is Karin Rothman?" Rose's mother asked.

Gregory looked at Melinda. "He wants his brother's killer found. Don't you?"

Melinda was flustered, and it made Rose smile.

"Of course I do!"

His gaze moved to Rose's mom. "Karin Rothman is Ava's mother. It seems that Karin worked for Charles's company for about twelve years. She was young when she started working there, and from what I was able to discover, in and out of relationships, most of them abusive. She was seeing a man who was part of a gang, and he'd ended up in prison. It was about that time she started stealing from Blaisdell Elite Enterprises. When she was caught, Charles fired her and made her pay restitution."

"I didn't know that part," Rose murmured.

Gregory nodded. "She was pretty broke, trying to raise Ava, who was twelve when Karin was fired." He had the family's undivided attention now. They were hanging on his every word, it seemed. "Karin sent a series of emails begging for forgiveness and a chance to get her job back, but Charles denied her. After that, she resorted to threats. Threats that seemed empty at the time, but it seems that her daughter has taken over fulfilling them, considering what has happened."

"What kind of threats?" Rose's mom asked, her eyes teary.

"At first, she tried to guilt Charles into rehiring her, telling him that she was living on the streets and that she had only been stealing to keep the gang from coming after her. However, that quickly turned into her saying she would send the gang after him and his family."

"What!" Rose exclaimed. That, too, was new information to her.

"I looked into it, and none of that was true. She had no sway over the gang her former boyfriend was part of, and he's still locked up in prison for murder."

"I don't understand what all this has to do with Ava killing Charles and poisoning Devon. Why did she do that?"

Rose interjected, "She wants revenge. She told me that Dad ruined her family, so she was going to ruin ours. My guess is she blames Dad for firing her mom. She blames Dad for everything and, by extension, us."

"But how was she able to do all of this?" Joey asked. "How did she know Uncle Charles and Devon were allergic to bees?"

Gregory took over again. "Ava worked at the hospital and had access to medical records. She had access to blood samples and the like. She also worked for a DNA facility where she learned how to fake test results. And now she works for a research facility that works with bee venom. The exact venom that was used to kill Charles and put Devon in a coma."

"Will this be enough to prove her guilty, or could she say she's being framed? And is she really Charles's daughter? Her mom did work for the company," Joey played the devil's advocate.

"I don't think that she is. I think she faked those DNA results," Rose replied making a face.

"I agree, but if the evidence against her isn't bulletproof, a talented lawyer could find a way to get her out of any trouble," Joey pointed out.

It was obvious he was speaking from personal experience, Rose glared at him. Although to be honest, she had to admit that Joey had a point.

"She won't be able to slither her way out of this," Rose was adamant. "She tried to get me to agree to give her seven billion dollars. At the time she said she wanted to use it for the research institute she worked for, but I think that was a lie. She just wants what we have."

"She did what?" Rose's mother exclaimed, looking at her with narrow eyes.

Rose half-shrugged. To her that already felt like ancient history. "One day she came with this proposal, that we should simply give her seven billion dollars, more or less, without going to court," she explained.

"And you didn't even bother to tell me that?" her mother accused.

Rose glared at her mother. "I tried speaking with you about Ava many times, and each time I did, you would get all prickly and accuse me of being jealous," Rose pointed out. She had no problems publicly shaming her mother for choosing Ava over her.

Her mother remained silent.

"That's it, I'm convinced, Ava did it," Joey said, almost cheerfully.

Since this recent turn of events, he completely forgot that he should be angry that Rose and her mother tried to put him in jail. Bygones were bygones, and they were all united now against the common enemy. And Rose was completely fine with that. She didn't like fighting with Joey, at any rate. He was dangerous in a different way. Besides, he was still facing assault charges and would most likely be going to jail again. Maybe he was trying to keep them sweet so they could help him lawyer up.

"It is absolutely terrifying that we welcomed her into the family so easily and believed her lies," Aunt Melinda commented, and all agreed.

"Where is she now? Has she been arrested?" Joey asked.

"I believe the police are looking for her, and her accomplice Adrian," Gregory replied.

"I can't believe it," her mom murmured, putting a hand over her heart as she started to cry.

Rose wrapped her arms around her mother, in silent comfort.

Gregory's revelations were so huge and impactful that he gave everyone a lot to think about. Even Rose, who already knew most of this stuff, and suspected the rest, was pretty rattled by it all.

Rose thanked Gregory for coming as he was on his way out.

"Call me if you need anything, anything at all," he insisted.

She nodded.

That night, Rose decided to stay home, wanting to be close to her mother, to be there for her. Also, to watch over her, considering Ava's latest threats. Since they were all onto her now, there was no telling what that dangerous woman would try to do next, out of sheer desperation. That was worrisome, to say the least.

Rose was preparing for bed when there was a knock on her door.

"Are you asleep?" her mother inquired.

"No, come in," Rose replied.

Her mom sank down on Rose's bed and looked at her with remorse.

"Is everything all right?" Rose asked.

"I'm sorry, Rose. I'm sorry for everything, for not trusting you, for not supporting you, but most of all, I'm sorry for not being a proper mother to you," she said all in one breath as tears started to fall down her face. "I should have put a stop to those rumors about you not being your father's daughter a long time ago. I should have told you what Melinda was threatening me with, and maybe your life would have been a bit easier. I'm sorry. You know you are his, right?"

Rose started to cry as well. Those were the words she had wanted to hear from her mother for so long. She rushed into her mother's arms, and they embraced, holding each other tightly.

"I love you, Rose, with all my heart. Your father loved you too, you need to know that."

"I love you too, Mom. And I know he did."

As the two of them sobbed into the night, Rose knew she would do anything to keep her mother safe. No matter what.

THIRTY-TWO

Rose decided that until Ava was arrested, she needed to stay at the mansion, and now that her mom was finally on board with the truth, she needed to do more to protect them from Ava. She called Gregory and asked him what he'd suggest.

"I know a few retired cops who are skilled and trustworthy. You could hire them as bodyguards. Or, if it would make you feel better, I could look after you for the time being," he offered.

Rose didn't even have to think about that. "Actually, yes, I think that would make me feel better. Thank you."

It would be preferable to have him around than some stranger.

And that was how it was decided Gregory would be her bodyguard moving forward. At the same time, he found some suitable men who would watch over her brother and her mother as well.

Rose worried about Devon the most. He was all alone in the hospital bed, helpless and in a coma. She even spoke with his doctor to ask if it would be all right to move him back home, but the doctor recommended leaving him be, considering he was in such an uncertain state. So, she hoped that with some extra security and a lot of witnesses, Ava or Adrian wouldn't try anything foolish. Like trying to kill her brother anew.

Taking care of all the precautions, Rose hoped for the best as the search for Ava and Adrian continued. They were nowhere to be found, clearly on the run, knowing the police were onto them.

Rose suppressed a smile when Gregory arrived to watch over her. He was wearing a protective vest and was armed with a gun. It made her feel secure to know that he was prepared for whatever threat came her way.

He did a sweep with another security guard of the entire mansion before coming to join her.

"Is that truly necessary?" her mom asked him, waving in the general direction of the guards.

"Ma'am, this woman has already killed your husband and poisoned your son. It is necessary," he replied blatantly.

Rose approved. At times, it was the only way to handle her mother.

After Gregory familiarized them with a few security protocols he wanted to instill upon them, Rose's mother decided to retire to her room. She was the safest there, considering she had a panic room installed in her closet. Rose's father had gotten it built some twenty years ago.

Rose remained in the living room with Gregory. Pretty soon, she realized how bored she was. She couldn't stand all this waiting without actually doing anything. She felt like jumping out of her own skin.

Sensing she was on the verge of proposing something stupid, like going out for a walk to Ava's apartment to snoop around, Gregory said, "You know, we should definitely get you one of these, so you can be protected even when I'm not around."

That completely took her off guard, and she gawked at him.

"What exactly do you have in mind?" she asked for clarification, although she had an inkling where this was going.

He tapped his body armor.

Rose sighed with relief; for a moment there, she thought he suggested she should get herself a gun. Rose had never held a gun in her entire life, and they scared her.

"Ava's weapon of choice is bee venom," she pointed out. So, she really didn't see a point in having a bulletproof vest on her.

"That's true; however, don't forget she threatened you with a knife, which means adaptability," he pointed out in all seriousness.

Rose gave it some thought. He did have a point there. "Do you think she has a gun too?"

"She doesn't legally own one, I know that, but that doesn't mean she doesn't have one, so better safe than sorry."

Right.

"Do you have a spare?" she asked, pointing at his body armor. She promised herself before he arrived that she would listen to him no matter what. That she wouldn't be difficult. At least one of them should do what he said, knowing how her mother could get.

"I do, but it won't fit you. I know a place where we can get you one that will," he replied.

She wondered if she should get one for her mother as well. She cringed inwardly just picturing her mother's reaction to something like that. Thelma Blaisdell would rather die than put on body armor, Rose was sure.

Let's just hope it won't come to that.

"Do you want to go shopping?" Rose offered.

"Now?"

She shrugged. "It's not like we have anything better to do around here."

"Okay."

Gregory and Rose went shopping for all the protective gear

she and her mother would possibly need. She decided to equip her mother as well, just in case. As Gregory said, better safe than sorry.

Gregory treated this expedition as though it was an extremely dangerous mission, which meant he never allowed her to wander off too far away from him. All that was pretty surreal to Rose. Despite her upbringing, she'd always enjoyed a level of personal freedom. She couldn't believe this was her life now because some woman decided to target her.

Because of Ava, her whole life, and her family, were completely shattered. Rose had already lost too much because of this deranged scientist who wanted all of their money, but Rose wasn't backing down without a fight. She wasn't going to lose anyone else, and that was a promise.

Despite all her bravado, having Gregory by her side, and knowing the police were doing everything in their power to catch Ava and Adrian, it was beyond stressful being scared for her life twenty-four/seven. It almost felt like a full-time job. And she really didn't know how much more emotional pain, how many more blows she could take.

She was pretty quiet on their drive back, having too much on her mind.

"Are you all right?" Gregory asked, sensing her mood.

"Not really," she replied honestly.

"Want to tell me what's on your mind?"

"I'm a book editor, for crying out loud. I'm not equipped to deal with all of this. I should be meeting potential writers, not purchasing protective vests, dodging attacks from murderers."

Rose was very much aware of how much she sounded like her mother. She didn't care.

Gregory patted her arm. "I know this has been tough on you. However, you only have to be strong for a little bit longer. Ava and Adrian will be caught by the police soon, and everything will return to normal."

Nothing is ever going to be normal, she thought glumly.

Once they returned home, she still felt pretty restless. She couldn't stop thinking about Ava's last threat. *What did she mean by that?* And why was it so problematic for Rose to show she wasn't a pushover? Come to think of it, why had she singled out Rose from the start? Ava had tried to blackmail her with that DNA test result from the very beginning, and now she was once again threatening her for exposing her to the police.

What if Ava doesn't stop despite everyone knowing she is a killer? What if she continues targeting Rose's family? Perhaps, in her mind, it was worth doing time for all the money the Blaisdell family had at their disposal. That thought was so troubling that Rose had to stop thinking about it.

Ava is going to come at me, Rose was sure of that.

"Rose, are you all right?" her mother asked with concern later that day.

"I feel fine," Rose replied in a dismissive manner. But was she fine? Her heart was beating like crazy, she was feeling itchy, and she had problems swallowing, come to think of it. However, she presumed all those symptoms simply meant she was beyond freaked out.

Her mother thought otherwise. Dr. Moss was immediately called, despite her protests, and it was discovered that she was suffering from an allergic reaction.

That put them all on high alert. While she was administered some drugs, as they all waited breathlessly to see if she would have to be rushed to the hospital, Gregory called Detective St. James to explain to him what had happened.

Rose tried really hard not to think about the fact that she might have been poisoned, like her father, like her brother.

A forensic team was sent immediately to take samples of everything from the mansion. Rose tried to remember what she'd had to eat or drink in the last twenty-four hours, which was easy considering she couldn't eat that much, being a nervous wreck.

Nobody was that surprised when the results came back, and it was discovered that everything in the library was contaminated with bee venom powder. It wasn't only in the food and drink. That took Rose by surprise. Although it was true the pair from hell had plenty of opportunity to sprinkle everything with the bee venom powder, considering how many times they were invited to the mansion, Rose was afraid that they'd broken in, so she threw out all the food that could possibly be contaminated, and they had a professional cleaning service—making sure none of the workers were allergic to bees—come in and decontaminate the entire house. Of course, while that was done, they had to check into a hotel. Her mother was in hysterics over it.

Luckily, Rose started to feel better after Dr. Moss's treatment.

Unfortunately, she had been right, Ava was trying to get rid of them all.

She was unsuccessful, that is all that mattered.

THIRTY-THREE

The next day, although Rose felt fine, her mother wouldn't stop fussing around her, so Gregory took Rose to the hospital, for a check-up.

Despite Rose's protests, they decided that she needed a full examination to make sure the ingested venom wouldn't have any long-term consequences.

"I feel fine," she said for the hundredth time, on their drive to the hospital.

To be perfectly fair, she hadn't felt fine yesterday when she thought she was going to die like her father, because Ava managed to get to her. But after a boatload of medication, thorough cleaning of the house, and a good night's rest at the hotel, Rose felt like herself again.

"Better safe than sorry," Gregory replied stubbornly.

Rose wasn't the only one who was poisoned with the stuff. A couple of staff members had minor reactions to it from having it in their system as well, and Rose insisted the familycover all their medical expenses and give them the week off in compensation.

Thankfully, her mother was perfectly fine, there were no

traces of bee venom in her bloodstream, and as it turned out, she wasn't even allergic.

The powdered bee venom had been sprinkled all over the books, onto the furniture, and onto the blades of the ceiling fan. Rose imagined that she'd been breathing it in while she'd been in there reading, since she'd turned the fan on herself. Thankfully, she hadn't gotten as much of a dose as her dad or Devon.

Now, as they arrived at the hospital, Rose could see a group of photographers waiting. "How did they find out?" Rose fumed seeing them.

"Your brother's here too, they've probably been camped out waiting to catch a story," Gregory pointed out.

After spending God only knew how many hours in the hospital, doing all kinds of tests, the doctor gave her the all-clear, which meant she could go home. Before that, she went to see Devon. He looked like he'd lost a lot of weight, and she didn't like that.

I really need you to wake up soon, she prayed.

On the way back to the mansion, to join her mom and her guards, which was finally clean of all allergens, Rose was surprised to see Aunt Melinda was waiting for her in the yard.

What does she want now? Rose grumbled.

"Remember that you have a taser now, so if she starts to get on your nerves, just point and press," Gregory commented dryly.

Rose laughed.

"Do you want me to take care of this?" Gregory asked. His meaning was clear: one word from her, and he would kick Aunt Melinda out.

Rose indulged in that image for a moment before shaking her head. "No, no need," she reassured.

"Aunt Melinda," Rose greeted, stepping out of the car. "Why are you standing out here?"

Gregory got out of the car and came to stand beside her.

"I can't deal with your mother at the moment. Besides, I came to see you," Aunt Melinda replied in her usual manner.

I almost died, but let's see what I can do for you, Rose grumbled.

"Oh?"

"Since I did that favor for you, I need you to do one for me." Although it was phrased like a statement, it was more of a command.

Favor? Rose had no idea what kind of favor her aunt could want from her.

"What do you want me to do?" Rose asked, figuring it would be better simply to cut to the chase at this point.

"I need those false charges against me dropped," she said haughtily.

"I thought the police already dropped their investigation into you once they realized Ava and Adrian were the real culprits," Rose countered, perplexed by this request.

Aunt Melinda made a face. "Not *those* charges," she stressed the words. "The ones you and your mother made against me."

And then it clicked to Rose. She was talking about stealing.

"Aunt Melinda, you know there was nothing false about that, you did try to steal the Fabergé egg," Rose felt the need to point out.

Aunt Melinda looked like she was ready to explode. She definitely didn't like being reminded she did something wrong, something criminal even.

"I didn't try to steal anything," Aunt Melinda snapped, taking a step toward Rose menacingly

Gregory coughed as though to remind her he was there, and that he would not allow her to hurt Rose.

"You did, and you have only yourself to blame," Rose argued. "You tried to steal something important to my mother.

You only care about the money. The money you thought you were owed from my dad," she added, losing patience.

"How dare you speak to me in such a manner," Aunt Melinda exploded. "You are merely a bastard child, an affair baby my brother was stupid enough to bring into the family, yet that doesn't make you a Blaisdell, so know your place."

So, she was going to continue with her petty theories about Rose's conception. "I am my father's daughter, no matter how much that irritates you, no matter how much you wish it wasn't so," Rose yelled. She was done tolerating such insults.

"Your father is turning in his grave, you are such a disappointment to him, and to this family."

"I'm a disappointment?" Rose asked incredulously. She was so tired of her aunt saying things that weren't true about her dad. Rose knew he loved her and hadn't been disappointed in her at all. Well, maybe he had been a little disappointed in her choice of Adrian, but he had still loved her. It was Melinda he'd not wanted to see, Melinda and her thug of a son, Joey. He'd only tolerated them for the sake of the rest of the family.

"You are nothing like the rest of us," Melinda continued.

Rose knew Aunt Melinda considered that the biggest insult, but it wasn't, at least not to Rose.

"You're right, I am not, I'm honorable, like my father," Rose agreed. "Because if being a Blaisdell like you and some of the others means I need to steal, lie, cheat, and stab people in the back so I can advance in life and accumulate even more money that I don't need, then I don't want anything to do with it," Rose threw back in her face.

"What's all this ruckus? What is going on?" her mother demanded, joining them outside.

Rose and Aunt Melinda must have been yelling so loud that even her mother could hear them from deep inside the house. Not that Rose cared. Her aunt deserved another reality check.

"I came here to settle a score, and your daughter won't stop insulting me," Aunt Melinda complained.

Rose chuckled humorously. "Your perception of reality is astounding, Auntie."

Aunt Melinda pursed her lips, looking angrily at Rose's mom. "Are you really just going to stand there and allow your daughter to continue insulting me?"

"I see nothing of the sort happening. It's you who is the aggressor, Melinda, like always," her mom pointed out. "Luckily, I don't need to defend my daughter from the likes of you, she does an amazing job on her own."

Rose suppressed a smile and then realized she didn't have to, so she grinned like a Cheshire cat. It felt good to be on the same side as her mother.

Aunt Melinda started shaking her head, as though she couldn't believe Rose's mom had just said that to her, that she'd sided with Rose. "You've completely lost your mind."

"I'm simply done trying to make peace at the expense of my daughter. She has suffered for years and endured your abuse because I was trying to keep the family together. No more. I should have stood up to you all a long time ago. I'm putting my daughter first from now on."

"Do you really wish me as an enemy, Thelma?" Aunt Melinda warned.

"You were never a friend to begin with," her mom commented.

Aunt Melinda jerked as though Rose's mom had slapped her.

Rose had to admit that she was enjoying this moment immensely. She rarely got the opportunity to see this side of her mom, and it was amazing. The fact she was putting Aunt Melinda in her place again was simply priceless.

"I will remember this insult," Aunt Melinda was adamant.

"I will remember how I was treated the other day and today and act accordingly in the future."

"I really don't know why you came here today, Melinda, and I don't care. You're not welcome here anymore," her mom said firmly.

Gregory coughed again. "I believe that's my cue to escort you back to your car."

He discreetly lifted his jacket, showing he was armed. It was obvious that it wasn't up for discussion.

"I will leave," Aunt Melinda said, raising her chin ever so slightly. "And you will have to beg on your knees for me to return."

Rose suppressed an eye roll. "Instead of wasting your time here, go and speak with your lawyer. Try to prepare a good defense," Rose advised. "After all, you're still going to court," she said, unable to help herself.

To that, her mother started to laugh.

"That stupid case will never end up in court," Aunt Melinda said, undignified.

Yeah, right. That was why she came here begging for it to be withdrawn.

"I didn't steal anything," she insisted.

That's true, but only because I caught you in time.

"What do you mean it won't end up in court?" her mom asked, faking ignorance. "I will make sure that it does."

"Me too," Rose agreed with her mother.

"And I will also make sure that your money is useless. You won't be able to buy your way out of this, Melinda. You will be punished for your bad behavior," her mom added sternly.

Aunt Melinda looked frightened for the first time, and without saying anything else, she scurried away like a scared little rabbit, getting into her car and driving away.

Mother and daughter looked at one another and started to laugh.

"That was almost as gratifying as seeing her arrested in the first place," Rose admitted.

"I agree. What did she want anyway?" her mother added as an afterthought.

"Nothing important," Rose said dismissively.

"Right. We've wasted too much time on her as it is."

Rose couldn't agree more. She looked over her shoulder at Gregory and smiled, catching sight of her aunt driving through the front gate of the property, but she stopped short.

She thought she saw someone lingering just outside the estate. Gregory turned and followed her gaze. "What is it?"

Rose stared for another moment, then shook her head. "Nothing, I guess. I just thought I saw someone watching us. But it must have been a shadow."

Even as she said the words, she had to wonder if that was true. Had someone been there? *Was it Ava?* She couldn't be sure. A sliver of fear raced down her spine as Gregory escorted her back into the house.

THIRTY-FOUR

"Rose!" her mom called, her tone frantic.

"What's wrong? What's happened?" Rose asked, hurrying to her mom's side with Gregory following quickly behind her.

"That was the doctor. Devon is showing signs of waking up," she said, tears welling in her eyes.

"Mom, that's fantastic, we need to go over there," Rose suggested.

Within the hour, they were at the hospital, heading to Devon's private room. It was reassuring to see that a police officer and one of the bodyguards she hired were standing in front of his door.

Nobody is getting close to my brother.

To be perfectly honest, Devon looked exactly the same to her as he had the last time she came to visit him. He was still in a coma, as all kinds of machines helped him stay alive, but if the doctors said he was improving, then she was hopeful.

She started searching online, to see if there was something she could do for her brother, help him get out of the darkness he was stuck in. She was surprised to see how many useful tips she found and shared them with her mom and Gregory.

"Is there something he especially likes?" Gregory asked.

Her mom frowned, and Rose realized she didn't really have a clue what her son liked.

In a moment of inspiration, she knew exactly what she should try. "Video games," she said as she started playing music from his favorite video games over her phone, hoping the familiarity of it would help him, help his mind resurface.

They took turns talking to him, trying to catch him up to speed with all the current affairs, omitting everything bad, of course, reading to him about the successes of his favorite basketball team and so on.

That was Gregory's idea.

Her mom told him what was going on with the family, well, the ones they were still speaking to, and what was going on at the business.

Rose felt like that wasn't enough. She wanted him constantly stimulated so he would have a reason to wake up. She learned that was equally important as empowering his body, making it healthy again.

She decided to hire a couple of private care nurses to play music for her brother via headphones when no one from the family was around, knowing that was something he would enjoy and perhaps make him feel less alone – if he was even aware of something like that in the first place.

He was her baby brother, and even if he could be a pain, she loved him. She needed him to wake up, to hear his voice again.

Rose felt slightly better after their visits. She wanted her brother to improve, and if that meant bringing in more people to talk to him and play music for him, then she'd do it.

Gregory noted her change in mood over the next several days. "You seem to be feeling better, more in control," he commented.

She nodded. "That's because I'm finally hopeful Devon will wake up soon," she admitted.

"Did you doubt that he would?"

She hated to admit it out loud, but to him, she could. "I was afraid. Considering Dad…" she let her words trail off.

Gregory hugged her, holding her close. She wished she could stay in his arms, soaking in his strength.

The next morning, after a very pleasant dream, Rose found her mother and Gregory playing cards. They were playing for money, and by the looks of it, Rose's mother was actually cleaning the house. Rose found that adorable.

"Way to go, Mom," she complimented.

That led to some teasing between them all. It was good to just laugh for a change. They really hadn't done that in a while.

Considering how much time they started to spend with one another, it was no wonder they grew closer and got to know one another pretty well. It was obvious how much Rose's mother liked Gregory, and for some reason, Rose was happy about that, and not simply because life was much easier that way.

Her mom definitely treated Gregory better than she ever treated Adrian, Rose couldn't help comparing. Not that Rose was dating Gregory. *Is that the difference?* she wondered.

"Want to join in?" Gregory offered.

Rose shook her head. "Nah, I need coffee first."

While she was preparing some fresh coffee for herself, Gregory came to join her. "If I continue to play with her, I will go completely broke," he deadpanned. "Your mom is a card shark."

She laughed.

It was really good having him around; the house felt less cold.

"I'm sure I haven't said this enough, but I'm really grateful you're here with us," Rose said from the bottom of her heart.

"I'm glad to help, and I hope you know there's nothing I wouldn't do for you."

Rose knew she couldn't ignore the intensity in his eyes when he said that. She didn't want to.

"Gregory?" She said his name like a question.

Why am I so nervous? she wondered.

"Rose, I know this isn't the right time, still, I have to share my feelings with you. I really like you. You're smart, beautiful, kind, and devoted to your family, and I would very much like to take you out for dinner. I'm also aware that doing that isn't possible at the moment, but I have no problem waiting. Because you're worth it, and I wanted you to know that I'm interested."

Rose was utterly stunned for a moment. Not because she didn't want to hear it, but because it was exactly what she was going to say to him, well, not all of it, but some of it. She smiled and pushed up on her toes, pressing her lips to his cheek. Something inside her stomach fluttered as her lips met his skin.

"I will hold you to that," was all she said afterward, and he smiled.

Rose couldn't help smiling back.

Later that day, after word from Detective St. James that they'd found Ava's lab, Gregory reached for her. She allowed him to comfort her, and Rose reveled in his strength.

"I'm truly sorry that this is happening to you and your family," Gregory murmured into her hair as he held her.

Rose was done feeling sorry for herself though. She was going to stop that woman no matter what.

"It's not your fault Gregory; it's Ava's."

And she will pay for everything.

THIRTY-FIVE

"This is all my fault," Rose's mom said, coming into her room.

"What do you mean, Mom?" Rose frowned.

"I let that awful woman into our lives, I thought I was doing the noble thing, the right thing. What Charles would have done, but... look what she's done! She killed Charles, and my precious boy is in a coma. It's all my fault."

No, it's not your fault, it's mine. I didn't recognize Adrian's trap in time. If only I hadn't fallen for his act, fallen in love, then none of this would have happened.

At least not to her family, but perhaps to someone else, it would have. Because Ava didn't look like the quitting type. Rose knew it was true. Ava would have just chosen another wealthy target.

Instead of sharing what was actually on her mind, she said, "You can't think like that. This is not on you. Ava and Adrian did this to us," Rose insisted. "They are the only ones to blame for Dad's death and Devon being in the hospital."

"I won't let her win," her mom said with renewed strength, or at least huge determination.

"That's right, we won't let her get away with this. She will pay for killing Dad, for hurting Devon too."

Almost killing me. Twice.

Rose's mother nodded. "I spoke with Mr. Merser because I am resolved to update my will," she said.

Rose frowned. That felt like an abrupt change of subject. "Okay, why?"

"Because I've decided to leave everything to you."

Rose was startled by that. "Why would you do something like that?" she wondered. "Devon will be all right, he'll wake up soon, you'll see," she tried to reason.

Her mother shook her head as though Rose was missing the point. Her next words confirmed as much. "I'm not doing it because I don't have faith your brother will return to us."

"Then why?" Rose asked again, completely perplexed.

"I am doing it for one reason and one reason only. If Ava tries to kill me next, you will get my share of the inheritance no matter what," she said firmly. "You're my daughter, and I want to make sure you will be protected and secure, and I know you'll take care of Devon with whatever he needs. I've thought a lot about this, Rose. Devon is in no state to manage this money, and I'm afraid if Ava continues, she may go after him again. I really want to make sure you're okay."

Rose could only stare at her mother. She felt like her mind just exploded, at least a little bit. Was this really what her mother had been thinking about the last couple of days? Rose was as horrified as she was heartbroken. It pained her that her mother was actually thinking about her demise.

"Mom, nothing bad is going to happen to you, I promise," Rose managed to choke out, as tears started to fall down her face. That was partly because of the grief and partly because of all the anger she was feeling inside herself. She hated Ava so much; she wanted that woman not merely caught, but annihilated.

Her mom hugged her.

"You know, I never cared about the money. I only wanted you and Dad. I only wanted all of us to be a happy family," Rose said through sobs. "And, of course, I will always take care of Devon."

"I know you will. I'm sorry, dear, for not understanding how you felt sooner, but I promise, things will change in the future," her mother said.

"I love you, Mom."

"I love you too, dear."

Rose had no idea how much time passed while they held each other, and cried to one another, drawing comfort in the fact they still had each other.

Rose knew that nothing could be changed overnight, her mother was too set in her ways, but then so was Rose. However, she was hopeful that in the future they would be bigger parts of each other's lives.

Despite everything, despite all the horrors, there was a silver lining. Rose was relieved they would be able to put everything that happened behind them. Rose's urge to rub everyone's noses in the fact she was right was long gone. Her only wish now was for this nightmare to be over before anyone else got hurt.

"Oh, and just so you know, I think Gregory is a really nice man," Rose's mother said with a wink on her way out of Rose's bedroom sometime later.

Rose smiled at that. "Good to know."

The next day, Rose sat in her brother's hospital room, watching his chest rise and fall, keeping a sharp eye on his monitors. She almost didn't notice that a nurse had entered the room until she reached out and handed her a note.

"A woman stopped by and asked me to give this to you. She

said you'd know what it was about." The nurse smiled and left the room.

Rose stared at the envelope. Glancing at Devon, she decided to be safe. She'd leave his room before opening it. She feared that the allergen might have been put into it, and it would trigger Devon into going into cardiac arrest again, and she wouldn't have that. Carefully, she made her way downstairs and out of the hospital. She didn't want anyone around when she opened the thing.

Finally alone, she held the envelope away from her face and used the nail file in her purse to open it. She didn't want to touch what was inside, so she set it down on the ground and used the nail file to slide the paper out. Dread filled her as she read it.

Second floor, room 247. I know where your brother is. Don't be surprised when all the Blaisdells start dropping like flies.

Rose pulled her phone out and took a picture of the note, then stabbed the paper with the nail file and took it over to the trash along with the envelope. She wouldn't be responsible for anyone getting sick. Despite it being a bit gross, she picked up a couple of half-drunk soda bottles, and after dropping the nail file and papers into the garbage can, she opened the soda and poured it all over them. If that allergen was on them, it would hopefully be destroyed now, and nobody would get sick from it. She dropped the empty bottles into the garbage, then took the ends of the bag and tied it off so nobody would get into it.

The note had to be from Ava, and it was making her realize that they had been playing defense for far too long. And although she still hoped that the police would be able to do their freaking job and find where Ava was hiding, Rose was done waiting.

She looked at her phone and dialed her cousin. Part of her expected Joey wouldn't answer, considering everything that transpired between them.

"Hello?"

"Hi, Joey, it's Rose."

"I know. What do you want?"

Rose bit her lip before saying what was on her mind. "I'm done waiting, and I would really very much like to hire some of your friends," she didn't have to specify which ones, "for a very specific task."

That piqued his interest. "What did you have in mind?"

"I want Ava and Adrian found," Rose said simply.

Joey chuckled at that. "I didn't know you had it in you, Rose. Maybe you are a bastard after all," he added, as a compliment this time.

"Oh, Joey, you have no idea."

"I'm listening. Talk to me," he encouraged.

Rose laid down her plan to him.

Ava's and Adrian's days were numbered; they messed with the wrong family.

THIRTY-SIX

A couple of days after Rose and her mother had a heart-to-heart, Rose's phone started ringing.

Normally, that wouldn't be such a strange occurrence; however, the number calling was unknown. Rose decided to answer all the same because it might have been Joey with an update from one of his burner phones.

"Hello?"

"Thank God you answered," Adrian greeted in a strange voice. He genuinely sounded relieved she picked up.

"Adrian?" Rose stammered. He was the last person she expected would call her. He was on the run with that criminal for crying out loud.

"Rose, I need your help," he begged.

Now he comes begging... after everything he did. Bastard, she fumed.

"Please don't hang up," he added, right before she wanted to do just that.

"What do you want, Adrian?" she asked coldly.

"I'm so sorry, Rose, I had no choice," he cried.

Rose made a face. "You had no choice screwing with me?

Or you didn't have a choice killing my father and poisoning my brother?" Rose accused.

"That wasn't me. I had nothing to do with it, you have to believe me. It was all Ava," he was quick to defend and dump all the blame on his girlfriend.

Yeah, right.

"Ava is completely crazy, and I'm scared of her," he said in a rush.

Rose definitely believed that part. And not only because he sounded genuinely scared. It was obvious to everyone now that Ava was prepared to do anything. There was no telling what she could do next, so Adrian certainly should be afraid of her. Not that Rose had any sympathy left for him. He made his bed, now he should lie in it.

"If you're afraid of her, go to the police," Rose offered.

"No," he said, sounding on the verge of hysteria. "I can't do that. She will kill me. Please, Rose, you have to help me."

"How?" She heard herself ask, not actually sure why. She didn't want to have anything to do with the man. He helped that woman destroy her life and eliminate half of her family. If Rose had any sense, she would immediately report him to the police.

"Can we meet?" he asked, breaking her train of thought. "I'll be waiting for you at the place where we had our first date."

"Meet with you?" she parroted incredulously.

She had no intention of seeing him again, not after everything that was revealed. Before, she simply saw him as a spineless gold digger, and now she knew he was much more; he was a con artist and an accomplice in murder.

"Please, Rose," he begged. "You are my only hope. I know I hurt you, but you are the only one I can turn to. I'll try to get away from her, please come to meet me. Ava is genuinely crazy. Will you come? Please don't abandon me." His words came out in a huge jumble; it was hard to make sense of them.

Rose wanted to ask what triggered this but didn't, not wanting to appear too suspicious. Perhaps it would be better if he thought she was that gullible and naive.

Although a sane part of her knew she should merely flat-out refuse him, a truly crazy idea came to her mind. And that made her hesitate for a moment, as she tried to decide.

As she thought things through, Adrian continued to cry in her ear.

While she walked around the room, she turned, only to see Gregory standing by the door. She had no idea how much he'd heard; however, it was obvious he was trying to figure out what was going on based on her body language.

"Stop crying, Adrian," she snapped at some point, irritated.

"Please, Rose, tell me you will come to see me. I need you."

"I'll think about it," she hedged.

"You're my last hope. If you don't help me, she'll kill me."

And I am supposed to care about that, why? was on the tip of her tongue.

"I have to go. She'll notice if I don't join her soon."

"Where are you?" Rose tried.

Unfortunately, he had already disconnected.

Rose cursed.

Gregory whistled, stepping into the room. "So, Adrian decided to call and ask for help?"

Rose nodded. She was still baffled by it all. Insulted too. Adrian must have thought she was a complete idiot if he dared to call her and ask for a meeting. Did he really think he was God's gift to all women and that she would simply meet with him and do his bidding after everything he put her through?

Unbelievable.

Unfortunately, part of her really wanted to believe Adrian. Naturally, she silenced that goody-two-shoes part of herself. Adrian wasn't calling because he had a change of heart, but because he needed something. Whether he was genuinely afraid or this was simply a ruse to get Rose out of the house and separate her from all the security was beside the point. It didn't matter one way or the other because the end result was the same.

"He told me that he needs my help because he's afraid of Ava. Unsurprisingly, he denies any kind of involvement in all the crimes," she summed it up for him.

"You are aware Adrian is using your emotions, your good nature, to lure you into a trap, right?"

"Yep, I suspected that as well," she replied.

"The nerve on him. Does he truly think you're that gullible?" Gregory asked rhetorically, genuinely irked.

Sadly, in the past, she had been that trusting. A few months ago, she would most definitely have believed his every word, and rushed to help him no matter the dangers. Now she knew better.

That didn't mean she couldn't use that to her advantage. Perhaps it would be better if Adrian still believed Rose was that naive, and instead of letting him lure her into a trap, she could set one for him.

"Rose, I'm familiar with that look on your face. What do you have in mind?"

"To maybe accept his offer," she replied, feeling a bit devious at suggesting it. *Am I really doing this?*

"You want to meet with him?"

"It's an opportunity to lure him out in the open, finally catch him. Maybe we'll catch Ava too," she explained, with a small shrug.

"You know, I've been thinking the same thing. However, I don't like the idea of putting you in danger," Gregory said.

"We'll take precautions," Rose offered, hoping that would sway him. She really wanted to do this. Not because she was so keen to put herself in danger but because she truly believed this was their best option to catch the murderers.

Before she can hurt Devon again.

"We most definitely will. And we're calling the police, now," Gregory said sternly.

Once they had everything set, Rose rehearsed what she needed to say, then called Adrian. This time, Gregory was standing next to her, listening to the entire conversation.

"Rose, I'm so glad you called," Adrian greeted. The most daunting thing was that he sounded like he was actually telling the truth.

"I'll meet with you," Rose said, cutting short his unnecessary tirade. "Just tell me when."

"Tomorrow, at three p.m."

Rose looked at Gregory, who nodded. "Okay," she said to Adrian.

"And please, Rose, come alone. Don't call the police, they won't believe I'm innocent," Adrian continued. His tone begging.

"I'll see you tomorrow, Adrian," she said before hanging up.

"Good job," Gregory complimented afterward.

"Thanks."

Now we wait.

* * *

What followed was the longest twenty-four hours of Rose's life.

Rose didn't tell her mother about the plan. She wouldn't have allowed it, and Rose needed to do this. If their lives were ever to return to normal, they had to lure Ava out.

The police, wearing plain clothes so they'd blend in, were already in place all around the pier where Rose was supposed to meet Adrian before she even stepped foot on it. Gregory also accompanied her until she parked. After that, he remained at a safe distance, but close enough that he could intervene if necessary. Rose was also wearing the body armor she'd bought and had her taser ready.

Her heart was beating like crazy as she waited. For some reason, she couldn't stop thinking of her first date with Adrian. Looking at it from this fresh perspective made her want to slap herself. She had been so naive not to see it was all a lie from the start. Rose had been his mark from the very beginning, she was nothing but a job. A job Adrian did very well.

Rose checked her watch for the tenth time. She felt like time stood still.

Where is he? she wondered.

In a moment of panic, she worried he'd smelled a trap and decided not to show up.

Why is he late? He's never late. Did he change his mind? she stressed over and over.

While she debated if she should call him or not, she noted a dark van with tinted windows, parked by the pier. At first, she thought nothing of it, that perhaps the police had some backup there or something, so she stayed put.

And then she spotted Adrian pacing nervously beside it. Rose felt a hot flash of anger seeing him again but had to rein it all in. People were counting on her.

Rose took a deep breath, and then she started walking toward him, praying like hell that her backup, and Gregory, had spotted him too.

It's showtime, she thought, feeling utterly ridiculous in the process.

Just don't fuck this up, Rose.

THIRTY-SEVEN

Adrian physically sagged with relief as he saw her approach.

She couldn't help wondering why that was the case. "I'm here, as you asked," Rose said, feeling like a complete idiot all of a sudden.

This is going to turn badly for me, she had a moment of doubt.

"Thank you," he said looking around. "Did anyone follow you?"

"No. I mean, I don't think so," she corrected because anything other would sound too suspicious.

"Good."

Rose noted how he had a coffee cup in his hand. Usually, there would be nothing strange about it, Adrian was a coffee addict. Even while in hiding, he had to have his fix.

This particular cup was from a nearby cafe, her favorite. That made her wary, and fully prepared to refuse it if he offered it to her by any chance. She wasn't going to allow him to drug her, poison her.

He simply stared at her; it was obvious he had something to say and was hesitating.

"Why am I here, Adrian?" *After everything*, was implied. "Why did you ask me to come?" she asked impatiently.

He looked away like he was ashamed or something. "I know what you must think of me."

Oh, no, you don't.

"I need you to understand, I didn't have a choice," he defended.

He looked so weak, so unappealing on every level. *Did I really find him attractive once upon a time? Focus, Rose,* she snapped.

She frowned at his words. "What do you mean you didn't have a choice?" she questioned.

"Ava threatened me. She made me come and work for her, and now I know too much, I'm scared for my life," he said in a rush.

That sounded too vague for her. "What did you do, Adrian? How did she manage to threaten you?" she demanded.

He refused to reply and simply shook his head, as though what he would reveal was so horrible that it couldn't be uttered out loud. At least, she perceived it in that manner. This could all be just an act, after all.

She tried a different approach. "If you know something, Adrian, if you have proof against her, then you need to go to the police," she advised.

At her mention of the police, he started looking about, as though an officer would jump at him, arrest him, at any moment. He wasn't that far away from the truth.

"Perhaps if you testify against her, then you won't be charged as an accomplice," she pointed out since he remained silent.

"I can't do that," he replied stubbornly.

"Why not?" Rose question.

"Because I'm afraid, Rose. If I betray her, she'll send someone after me. She'll poison me in jail. I can't escape her.

She's completely mad. You don't know her like I do, she's a monster, and she won't stop until every Blaisdell is dead or in jail," he said in a rush, completely freaking out.

Rose's heart was pounding. He definitely sounded as though he knew a lot more about Ava than he should, than the rest of them. Meaning he sounded as though he had known her for years, not months, not weeks, or days. That was why she asked, "Adrian, how long have you known Ava?"

His eyes widened in shock, and a little bit of fear. *He's revealed too much,* she guessed.

"Did you know Ava before meeting me?" she pressed, eyes narrowing. She was aware she had a part to play. However, this was something she needed to know.

"Rose, I..."

It was obvious he was trying to find some kind of excuse; nevertheless, Rose was not about to let that happen.

"Were you involved with her from the start?" she demanded, taking a step toward him in anger. She already knew the answer, but she wanted to hear him admit it.

Rose really wanted to know if they had planned it all together from the beginning, as she suspected. What she wanted to know was if Adrian used her to get inside the house and learn all the family secrets. She was pretty sure he had, but she couldn't bring herself to utter those words. It was too painful.

Then again, perhaps she didn't even have to because Adrian went pale and hesitated with his reply. That right there told her everything she needed to know. All of her suspicions were correct.

"I see," she muttered.

Before either could say anything else, Adrian's phone started buzzing. He looked startled by it; he acted like he completely forgot he had it on him. Checking the screen, Adrian looked even more scared than before.

Rose didn't have to be a mind reader to know what that meant.

"Is that Ava calling you?" Rose demanded.

He remained silent. He appeared spellbound looking at the screen, looking at the phone that continued to ring.

What does she have on him? she wondered again because none of this made any sense to her.

"It's clearly a mistake I came here," Rose said next, hoping that would snap him from the stupor.

Just as Rose said that the door of the van slammed open. Ava emerged with a gun in her hand, looking crazed, her eyes bloodshot and her skin sallow. Rose made an involuntary step backward; however, Ava pointed the gun directly at her while tsking, firmly stopping her in her tracks.

She was in that van all this time, Rose thought, she realized Ava had been listening to their conversation. As Gregory said, as Rose suspected, this was nothing but a trap from the start.

"A final betrayal," Rose muttered.

Adrian definitely heard her.

Ava slapped Adrian with her free hand. "When exactly did you lose your balls?" she hissed at him.

"I had everything under control until you came," he defended. "And I didn't lose anything. This is just a bad plan," he tried to stand up to her.

While they fought, Rose tried to take another step backward. Unfortunately, Ava saw that as well.

"Don't move," she warned before she focused on her boyfriend. "We agreed on what you needed to do, and you completely chickened out," she accused.

He definitely didn't like she was questioning his manhood, twice in so many sentences. "Haven't I done enough already?" he protested.

Rose felt really strange having to witness this macabre

lover's quarrel. She would definitely excuse herself and leave if one of them didn't have a gun.

And then something occurred to her. What if the stupid van was blocking the view? What if Gregory had no idea what was going on? What if the police hadn't spotted Ava with a gun?

What if Rose was all alone with these two lunatics? All those thoughts made her panic, severely.

Keep it together, Rose.

"I'll say when it's enough," Ava practically yelled. "And if you'd only stuck to the plan, none of this would have happened."

Rose was dying to learn what the plan was exactly. She cringed at that thought for her poor choice of words. She was curious; however, she wasn't too keen on dying. She would very much like to survive this encounter with Ava.

Will I?

"I simply think we've done enough to Rose, we should leave her alone," Adrian said meekly, taking Rose by surprise, Ava too by the looks of it.

She looked ready to hit him again. "Have you grown a conscience somewhere along the way? Or did you actually start to have feelings for her?" she said, disgusted by either prospect.

"I'm only saying that this plan won't work anymore," Adrian tried to defend.

"If you had just killed her when I told you to early on in all of this, we wouldn't be in this mess now."

"So, is that your plan, to kill me?" Rose couldn't remain silent anymore. "Did you lure me here today to make that happen?" She was very proud of herself; of how calmly she spoke about her demise.

"Oh honey, the plan to murder you went south a long time ago. With you turning the family against me, I had to get creative, so we're going to kidnap you. I'm sure your darling mother would pay anything to get you back home, given one of her brats is already out of commission," Ava said, raising her chin, as though she was proud of herself. She seriously thought she'd won.

The joke was on her because Rose came prepared.

"Kidnap me?"

"Well, technically, my second plan was to drive you crazy and pin all the murders on you. However, someone grew a conscience." After saying that, Ava hit Adrian again.

Rose couldn't believe her ears. They had wanted her to take the fall for everything?

"It didn't seem right to me," he said. He also avoided looking at Rose directly. Was it possible he was actually sorry for everything?

Ava laughed at that. "You had no problems killing her father, poisoning her brother, and preparing to do the same to her mother, and killing Rose or getting her to take the fall was where you drew a line?" she mocked. "She's nothing! A minor inconvenience in the grand scheme of things! They don't deserve the Blaisdell wealth. I grew up with nothing while they had everything handed to them on a platter! I had to scrounge for scraps while they ate lobster and caviar! My mother could barely function after what Charles Blaisdell did to her. She was lucky to have finally gotten that job at the hotel. Do you know what she had to do just so I could have food and clothes? A place to sleep? She deserved better!"

"I can't believe it was you from the start," Rose yelled at Adrian, tears in her eyes.

The pair stopped fighting to look at her.

Ava clearly came up with the plan to destroy Rose's family; however, Adrian was the one who did the killing. There was blood on both their hands. Rose's eyes filled with tears knowing Adrian had been the one to kill her father and tried to kill Devon.

"I'm so sorry, Rose. When I learned how much you hated your family, I thought it would be good for you too," he tried to defend.

Rose was scandalized. "What? I don't hate my family! Did you really think I wanted my parents dead? My brother? Are you crazy?"

"It didn't have to come to this," he said, taking a step toward her. "How about we split the money?"

"Don't come near me," Rose warned.

"Adrian, stop messing around," Ava ordered, clearly losing patience. "Rose, get into the van," she said waving her gun.

Rose knew she was as good as dead if she got into that vehicle. Sadly, if she made a run for it, there was a chance Ava would shoot her in the back. She was wearing body armor, but if she shot her in the head, she'd be dead, and she just couldn't take that risk.

"Get in the van now," Ava repeated since Rose simply stood in place.

"No," Rose rebelled.

All of a sudden, Adrian grabbed Ava.

"Run, Rose," he yelled as he pushed Ava against the van.

"You bastard," Ava screamed.

Without actually thinking what she was doing, Rose started running. At some point, she looked behind her, to make sure nobody was following her.

She was horrified to see Ava manage to push Adrian away. She aimed the gun at him and then pulled the trigger.

She shot him straight in the head, and he fell instantly dead to the ground.

She shot him!
She killed him!
Oh my God.

THIRTY-EIGHT

To say Rose was horrified by this turn of events would be a freaking understatement. Ava had actually killed Adrian. She shot him without a second thought, as though he was nothing to her. Rose didn't have time to try and wrap her mind around that because she was running for her life, quite literally.

The moment Ava shot Adrian, she started shooting toward Rose.

Since they were in such a public place, in the middle of the day, the shots alarmed everyone. People started running, kids started crying and screaming. In a matter of seconds, the pier turned into a madhouse.

Rose spotted Gregory running toward her. He had a grim expression on his face, his gun drawn. Unfortunately, her relief was short-lived and replaced by severe pain in her left arm. Ava had managed to wound her.

She's going to kill me, Rose panicked.

In an act of utter desperation, Rose changed direction and, at the last second, jumped off the pier into the murky water. She could hear both Ava and Gregory screaming after her. Ava, out of frustration; Gregory, out of desperation. Rose hoped that by getting into the water, she would manage to escape Ava.

She was wrong. Not even that stopped the other woman from trying to shoot her. Taking a deep breath, Rose dove deep into the water, starting to swim beneath the docks. Everything was dim, muffled, for what appeared like an eternity, although she knew not more than thirty seconds had passed.

Once she resurfaced safely beneath the dock, she heard screams, shouts, and sirens from the police. She also heard Gregory calling out to her. Her first instinct was to yell back to him, to let him know she was all right. However, the fear of Ava discovering where she was made her remain silent, forcing her to stay hidden.

Oh my God, oh my God, oh my God. The image of Adrian falling, dying in front of her, ran through her mind. That was all she could see in front of her eyes. Ava had killed him. His last act on this earth was to try and save Rose. Then again, he'd also killed Rose's father and tried to kill her brother. One good deed couldn't erase all the bad he did.

"Rose? Where are you?"

Oh my God, oh my God, oh my God, what a freaking mess. More shots were fired.

And this mess was far from over. Ava was armed, deranged, and trigger-happy, as it turned out. Rose hoped this didn't end with a suicide-by-cop scenario. No matter what, she really didn't want anyone else dying. She wanted Ava behind bars. She had wanted that for Adrian as well. Sadly, he was dead now. Because Ava killed him.

Rose started shaking from head to toe, swimming in that cold water. Any longer and hypothermia might get to her before Ava did, and she realized she would have to get back to shore.

She figured it was safe to do so by now, considering how many cops were milling about the pier. It could mean that Ava was in custody or gone. Who in their right mind would linger, after all?

Reaching the beach, while Rose was in the shallow waters, Ava jumped in front of her from the pier, landing in the sand, with the gun facing her.

Oh, no. Where the hell is everyone? Why haven't they stopped her yet?

Ava laughed as Rose jumped, startled. Very quickly, Rose assessed the situation. She couldn't return to the water; Ava would definitely kill her since she was standing so close to her. There was nowhere to run this time around, she was trapped.

"I'll kill you, you little bitch," Ava spat. She'd lost all reason, it was in her eyes.

Seeing how those were the last moments of her life, Rose decided to make them count. "What did I ever do to make you hate me so much?" Rose demanded.

Ava was startled by her question. She clearly expected Rose would start begging for her life.

"You have everything in this world, and you don't deserve it," Ava screamed, before completely calming. "My mother was a saint. She didn't deserve what your father did to her. If he had only paid her a higher wage, she wouldn't have resorted to stealing. And then to make her pay him back for everything she took, just so she could feed me?" Ava's entire body shook with outrage. "Do you know, I purposely transferred to the same college as you so I could learn everything about you? The perfect daughter. So loved and cherished. What a crock. I promised my mother I would destroy everything Charles Blaisdell held dear, starting with you."

Rose narrowed her eyes at Ava, trying to figure out how to keep her talking until help arrived. "You're not a Blaisdell, are you."

Ava smirked. "No, but you'll be taking that secret to your

grave. You know, I was prepared to let you live, but you got in my way."

Yeah, she was prepared to let me live, in jail, Rose thought.

"But not anymore," Rose guessed.

"Not anymore," Ava agreed.

"What will you accomplish by killing me?" Rose stalled. "The cops know everything. Hell, the family knows everything. You aren't going to get away with this."

"In killing you, I'll get everything I've always wanted," Ava replied with an evil grin.

"You won't get the money. Our lawyers will prove you're not related to my father. And you know you'll be arrested for killing my dad, me, and Adrian," Rose pointed out.

"Let me worry about that." Ava smiled smugly. "Do you want to know what I remember about you from college? You were always the poor little rich girl, always looking to be loved for herself and not for her daddy's wealth. Getting my revenge plan was so easy once I realized exactly what type of man you'd fall for."

Rose hadn't realized how much her insecurities had been visible to everyone around her. If she lived through this, she was going to need some intense therapy.

"I've been planning the Blaisdells' demise for years. You made it very easy, and now I need you out of the way so I can make the rest of my plans come to fruition."

Since Ava was aiming at her, Rose realized the chitchat was over, and she closed her eyes, not wanting to see her end approaching.

The gun went off, and Rose tensed, preparing for the impact.

Nothing happened.

Rose opened her eyes, only to see Ava falling to the ground. Gregory was standing nearby with his gun pointing at her.

Once Ava went down, he rushed to her, to remove the weapon from her.

He got here just in time, Rose thought, relieved. *He saved me.*

He shot Ava, but he didn't kill her, as far as Rose could tell.

"Are you all right?" he asked, keeping his weapon trained on Ava.

"I am now," Rose replied simply.

Rose forced herself to move. Gregory met her halfway, to help her get out of the water. She practically fell into his arms, and he had to carry her the rest of the way.

"You shot her," she stated the obvious, as she shook from the cold, her teeth chattering.

"Yes, I did," Gregory replied calmly.

"Thank you."

"You're bleeding," he noted then, horrified.

"I think she just grazed me," she tried to brush it off. "To be perfectly honest, it didn't hurt that bad. It was probably the adrenaline."

Since a few officers came to take care of Ava, Gregory put his gun away and took Rose to the ambulance. The EMTs immediately put a warm blanket over her as they checked her vitals and looked at her injured arm.

She could see Detective St. James in the distance barking orders, walking about, making sure all the threats were eliminated. They were. Ava took care of Adrian, and Gregory took care of Ava. *Some twisted happy ending.*

Rose really thought this was it, that Ava would kill her.

After a quick examination, it was determined that Rose should be taken to the hospital.

There was another ambulance at the ready, and Ava was taken to that one and then rushed to the emergency room. Gregory had shot her in the stomach, which meant she needed immediate medical attention, or she would die.

Rose realized, at least in her current state, that she wouldn't be too broken up about it if it came to that. After all that woman did terrible things, she killed Adrian and tried to kill Rose as well. So, it wouldn't be such a big loss if she succumbed to her injuries, but she actually hoped Ava lived to pay for her crimes.

Speaking of injuries, Rose's were minimal. However, her arm still needed to be stitched up. Gregory remained by her side the whole time.

"Do you want me to call your mother?" he asked on their drive to the hospital.

"Please don't, I don't want to worry her."

He gave her a look. "She needs to know what happened."

"And she will, I'll call her, I promise. But please, I don't want her to see me like this."

Gregory nodded, reluctantly. "I'm afraid she may already have. The press have been here filming."

Rose cringed at that. She hoped her mother hadn't turned on the news. "Let's hope she sees me before she sees that news broadcast."

Rose only needed a couple of stitches, and thanks to the shot she got to numb her arm, she didn't feel a thing.

"You'll have a nice little battle scar," Gregory complimented, and she had to laugh.

"Thank you for saving my life, by the way," she smiled at him.

"You already thanked me," Gregory replied.

"I did? I don't remember, so thank you again."

"Don't mention it," he said sternly before cracking a smile. "I will put it on your tab," he joked.

Rose snickered again. "Is the bill going to be huge? Am I going to go bankrupt?" she asked, continuing the joke.

"You might. However, I'm open for negotiation."

"What do you mean? Like paying in installments or in favors?"

"Preferably in favors," he said, wiggling his eyebrows at her.

She laughed. For the first time in months, she felt free to relax and just enjoy the moment. She hoped it lasted.

THIRTY-NINE

Rose was discharged from the hospital the same day since she didn't have any major injuries. On their way out, Gregory asked about Ava, but nobody would tell him what condition she was in.

"I'll call St. James later," he told Rose, getting into the car.

Unfortunately, the bandage around her arm was so big that there was no way she could avoid telling her mother what happened at the pier that day. She had hoped to leave out the part where she'd been shot, at any rate, but now that wasn't going to be possible. Besides, she might have already seen it all on the news. Though if she had, she probably would have been blowing up Rose's phone, so maybe she'd get lucky.

Rose was still trying to wrap her head around what had happened herself, considering Adrian had died in front of her eyes, and Ava had once again tried to kill her and almost succeeded right before being shot herself.

It was a crazy day.

"Oh my God, Rose, what happened to you?" her mother demanded, eyeing Gregory, as though secretly accusing him of not doing his job properly.

"I'm all right," Rose assured her mom, before proceeding to tell her everything.

Rose was prepared for a lot of yelling and screaming. However, that didn't happen. Surprisingly, her mom took it pretty well that Rose almost died after being used as bait to catch a couple of murderers. Maybe she was simply out of reactions to give after so many weeks of upheaval.

Then again, it definitely helped knowing both Ava and Adrian got what they deserved. Those were her exact words, although it was obvious that her mother was slightly disappointed that Ava was still alive. Rose's mother could be pretty ruthless when she wanted to be, Rose noted, not that she disagreed.

Rose wished she could be more like that, but she wasn't. She continued to stress about every single thing that happened that day at the pier. Rose wondered if she should have acted differently. If there was a chance she could have saved Adrian. Not out of the goodness of her heart but because she wanted him to pay for the crimes he committed. For killing her dad. For poisoning Devon. Death seemed like an easy way out.

Rose remained home with her mother. Although the danger was now gone, her mother wanted to take care of her, and Rose decided to let her. It felt nice, after all.

Gregory stayed as well, though she wasn't sure why, and that felt nice too.

A couple of days later, once Rose felt better, her mother asked if she would pack up her dad's office and forward any legal documents to Mr. Merser. The family lawyer would be the one sifting through them so all relevant business-related documents could be sent to Rose's Uncle Kenneth, while the rest would be filed away. Considering Rose had nothing better to do, she agreed.

"Do you need my help, dear?" Mom asked, although her

face was telling a different story. This was her least favorite room in the entire mansion.

Rose decided to end her suffering. "That's okay, Mom, I can do it on my own," she assured her.

"Call Gregory to help you."

Rose made a face. "He's a PI, Mom, not a personal valet."

Rose's mother waved dismissively on her way out of the study like Rose was acting foolishly. Deciding to listen to her mother, Rose called Gregory to see if he would come to help.

He agreed immediately.

About an hour later, they dug into the work at hand. Rose's father had a lot of papers in his office, and pretty quickly, Rose realized that they would be there for quite a while. Not that she minded. Gregory was good company.

"How will I know the difference between personal documents and business?" Gregory asked her, as they started to gather everything.

Before beginning with all that, they had gone out to get some boxes first. On the way back home, Rose realized she was starving, so they stopped to grab some takeout as well.

"That's easy. Everything is business related with my father," she replied in all seriousness, although it sounded like a joke.

They worked in silence for a bit, which was quite a treat. Without her extended family members milling about, without all the dangers pressing against them, it was nice to simply be, and enjoy the silence, enjoy the calmness that returned to the Blaisdell home. She liked how her relationship with Gregory was so easy and uncomplicated. Not that they were in a relationship. *Yet.*

The downside was that it made her sense her father's absence that much more. Rose had to admit, if only to herself, that going through her father's things, all his files, basically his life, wasn't easy. Stopping to read some of his notes she stumbled upon, seeing what he was working on before he died, only made her miss him more.

And it was her fault he died. She brought that danger into their lives. She was the reason Adrian had access to poison them all.

I should have listened to you, Dad.

Although her mother forbade her from thinking like that, how could she not? It was true Rose had caused all this pain and suffering to her family by being so gullible. That was actually the hardest pill to swallow, that she was played for a fool. That lapse in judgment cost her father his life, and she was sure she would need a lot of time and a lot of therapy to recover from all she had been through. From all she put her entire family through.

Will I ever be able to forgive myself?

It wasn't all bleak though. Rose had managed to save her mother. Thanks to Gregory, Rose's life was saved as well. And there was no doubt in Rose's mind that they managed to save quite a few more lives because that crazy woman was on a killing spree before they stopped her.

Rose tried really hard not to think about the fact Ava could have done a lot more damage if she ever managed to get a hold of all the money and put her project in motion. That was quite a daunting, scary thought. Luckily, all that was prevented now. With her behind bars, Rose calmed herself.

All the same, that didn't prevent Rose from tormenting herself with thoughts that there was a chance she could have saved her father too if she'd recognized what Adrian was doing from the start.

Don't go there, she warned herself, for the hundredth time.

Still, she went there, over and over.

Rose's feelings were all over the place, chaotic, regarding the 'mole' of her ex-fiancé. Although it seemed as though he had a change of heart in the end and stood up to Ava, which cost him his life, Rose would never be able to forgive him for coming into her life with the sole purpose of killing members of her family for money. He couldn't atone for killing her father by saving her life. That wasn't how things worked.

Adrian used to say all people were greedy, but now Rose knew he was talking about himself. Although she was grateful to Adrian, in a way, for saving her life and for coming through in the end, she was also horrified by how easily and completely he deceived her.

Though it became apparent he had some second thoughts, that he wavered, he had still done despicable things alongside Ava. He was a monster, just like Ava.

They really were a perfect couple...

"Hey, Rose, look at this," Gregory said, snapping her from her glum thoughts.

Although she knew she should be happy she was still alive, and that everything was over, she couldn't help brooding as well.

"What?" she asked, raising her head to look at Gregory.

He handed her a piece of paper.

"What's this?" she asked before she started to read.

"It looks like a DNA test result," Gregory explained.

It was a DNA test analysis that was twenty-five years old.

What? she thought, her eyes scanning the document. Her hands trembled, and she let out a gasping sigh of relief.

Rose couldn't believe it. Her father had ordered a DNA test when she was just a little kid. All this time, he'd known the truth. He'd been there for her, cared for her, been proud of her, and always wanted the best for her. He'd even stood up to his little sister and her nastiness for her.

I am his daughter, Rose thought as her eyes filled with tears. Sure, her mom had told her that she was, had sworn she was, but this was actual proof.

Melinda's threats had all been lies.

Then another thought struck her.
Ava lied.
Ava had lied about everything.

FORTY

Six months after the final confrontation with Ava, Rose's life had completely transformed.

For one thing, it was peaceful nowadays, and she appreciated that more than anything.

She definitely needed a fresh start from the person who killed her father, and that was why she decided to let go of the lease on her apartment and move somewhere else, as there were too many bad memories attached to it. There was no way she could remain there after Adrian tarnished every nook and cranny of it.

So Rose found a modest, three-bedroom, two-bath home with a fireplace in the living room in a quiet neighborhood on the edge of the city.

It had a lovely yard, where she envisioned herself spending summer nights listening to crickets and reading on the patio. And in the spring, she would definitely plant a nice garden. Overall, it was her version of heaven.

Her mother complained that she had moved too far away from her, but Rose believed it was just perfect in every way. It was what she needed, after all. Despite all the nagging, her mother helped her remodel and furnish the entire house. The end result was breathtaking.

Deciding it was time to take that leap of faith, Rose invested a large sum of her money to start up her own publishing house. She called it Charles's Gift, in honor of her father.

In the aftermath of Ava's capture, Devon finally woke up as though on some level he had become aware the danger was gone. They all knew he would have to stay in the hospital for a bit longer and go through physical therapy, which Rose knew he'd hate, but he was on his way to a full recovery, which was all that mattered.

They rushed to the hospital the moment he woke up and opened his eyes, though sadly, it took him a while to start talking again. A few days later, he called Rose from his hospital room.

"How are you feeling today?"

"Like shit," he replied in his usual manner.

"Do you need something? Do you want me to bring you some food?" she offered.

"You don't have to fuss about me, I'm fine. I'm just bored in this hospital," he said.

That was her brother, all right. He had her worried for a moment, but he was fine.

"You'll be home soon," she tried to comfort him.

"Yeah, I know. Look, I just wanted to say thank you," he told her, taking her by surprise.

"No need to thank me, Devon. You know I will always be here for you." At the end of the day, he was still her baby brother, and she loved him.

"Yeah, I have to, because I know I have been a shitty brother to you. I believed Aunt Melinda's lies, and I treated that piranha like she was the sister I wanted you to be. It was an awful thing to do. So, thank you for coming to see me, for caring enough to try and help me."

"I love you, Devon, the fact you're an asshole will never change that," she said, trying to lighten the mood.

He chuckled. "Good to know, that's not what I meant. I heard it, Rose."

"You heard what?" she asked, confused.

"I heard music playing, and I knew I had to follow it. It was hard, but that's what woke me up. You saved me, Rose."

She wiped her teary eyes with the edge of her shirt, unable to say anything.

"Anyway," he continued, "I love you too. And I'll see you tomorrow, right?"

"Right," she managed to choke out before they said their goodbyes.

Rose had never lost faith, and her brother woke up, that was all that mattered. He had a life ahead of him.

Her mom wanted to throw Devon the biggest welcome home party of the century once he got out of the hospital. Surprisingly, he said no to such an idea.

Devon then shocked them all by saying that his days of debauchery were completely over. He had learned his lesson and was turning over a new leaf. He was going to go back to school. He had decided to get his business degree and be a better brother and son.

He had changed. Although Rose was sorry that he had to go through all of that, she was happy for him as well. Devon deserved to be happy like the rest of them.

Rose would never have believed it could happen, but now she had a much better relationship with both him and her mother. Not to mention, her relatives were very apologetic about their part in tormenting her and were trying to make amends and atone for a change.

Not all, mind you. Joey and Aunt Melinda hadn't changed their stripes, but the others had. Rose was aware that her mother's outburst and the DNA test her father ordered years ago were what persuaded her relatives to fully accept her as his legitimate daughter. However, Rose didn't care, deciding to simply forgive and forget. Life was too short to be bitter.

Speaking of bitterness, Rose's mother made good on her promise, and Aunt Melinda and Joey were forever banished from the Blaisdell mansion. They were not invited to any family gatherings, and Rose certainly appreciated that. Nobody needed such toxic people in their lives.

As for Ava, she fully recovered from her injuries and was arrested. She was charged with two counts of murder, attempted murder, fraud, extortion, and a lot of other offenses. The district attorney was thorough and demanded a maximum penalty for everything.

Rose and her family also decided to file a civil suit against her. Rose wasn't ashamed to admit how vindictive they all felt, so they sued Ava into oblivion. They could definitely afford it.

Suffice to say, Ava lost in that regard as well.

Her lawyer tried to play the insanity card; however, it didn't work, and she was forced to pay for all her crimes in full. Every single one of them, even some Rose hadn't been aware of prior to her trial.

In the end, Ava was left as alone and penniless as she'd tried to make Rose.

Karma is a bitch.

It had come out during that trial that Ava had changed her surname from Ross—her actual father's last name—to her mother's maiden name, Rothman, because she didn't want anyone knowing she'd killed her mother's boyfriend when she was a teenager for trying to assault her. It had also been revealed that she'd met Adrian in her twenties and helped him kill his uncle, for the inheritance.

Ava and Adrian had gotten exactly what they deserved. Rose called that divine justice.

In the end, to make herself feel better and be able to move

on with her life without anyone or anything holding her back, Rose decided to write a book about her experiences. She knew her editors would be more than happy to help her shape her work into something worth reading.

Who could say? Perhaps what happened to her could help someone else cope with their experiences. That was the power stories had. She even had plans to put all the proceeds from the book sales, as well as a healthy portion of her inheritance, toward her new charitable venture: The Blaisdell Arts Foundation. She wanted to offer scholarships and funding to talented artists, writers, and the like, and provide help to those just getting their start. It was something she knew her father would be proud of as well. He'd always had a love of art.

"If the book ever turns into a movie, who will play me?" Gregory joked as they walked through the park, which had become their tradition.

"I don't know, maybe they'll find someone hot to attract the female viewers," she teased.

She'd thought she would never be able to trust another man after Adrian's deceit, but then she reminded herself how she already did. She had trusted Gregory with her life, which made it quite easy to trust him with her heart as well.

Rose had never felt happier in her entire life. She only wished Dad could see her. He would approve of Gregory; she was sure of that.

I love you, Dad. I miss you. She sent prayers to the heavens, knowing he was watching over her, finally at peace.

She had found her peace as well.

A LETTER FROM COLE

Dear reader,

I want to say a huge thank you for choosing to read *His Secret Child*. If you did enjoy it, and want to keep up to date with all my latest releases, just sign up at the following link. Your email address will never be shared and you can unsubscribe at any time.

www.bookouture.com/cole-baxter

I hope you loved *His Secret Child* and if you did I would be very grateful if you could write a review. I'd love to hear what you think, and it makes such a difference helping new readers to discover one of my books for the first time.

I love hearing from my readers – you can get in touch with me through social media.

Thanks,

Cole Baxter

facebook.com/ColeBaxterAuthor

tiktok.com/@colebaxterauthor

PUBLISHING TEAM

Turning a manuscript into a book requires the efforts of many people. The publishing team at Bookouture would like to acknowledge everyone who contributed to this publication.

Audio
Alba Proko
Melissa Tran
Sinead O'Connor

Commercial
Lauren Morrissette
Hannah Richmond
Imogen Allport

Cover design
Jo Thomson

Data and analysis
Mark Alder
Mohamed Bussuri

Editorial
Ruth Jones
Melissa Tran

Printed in Great Britain
by Amazon

46989526R00179